DIVINE DEFEAT

The marquess's touch sent rays of warmth radiating from Adriana's shoulder through the rest of her body, and when he moved his hand beneath her hair, the warmth changed to tiny shivers.

"Please, I am very tired," she said.

"You are not tired," he said. "Merely nervous."

"Very well, then, I am nervous," she said. "We have been married only a few hours. You must allow me time to grow accustomed both to marriage and to . . . to this." She spread her hands and opened her eyes wide, certain that she could win him over. Surely he would leave her to sleep alone if she but managed the matter adroitly.

But Adriana was about to learn how little she knew about the Marquess of Chalford—and about herself. . . .

AMANDA SCOTT, a fourth-generation Californian, was born and raised in Salinas and graduated with a degree in history from Mills College in Oakland. She did graduate work at the University of North Carolina at Chapel Hill, specializing in British history, before obtaining her MA from San Jose State University. She lives with her husband and young son in Sacramento. In 1987 she won the Romance Writers of America's Golden Medallion Award for Best Regency Romance for *Lord Abberley's Nemesis*.

THE MADCAP
MARCHIONESS

AMANDA SCOTT

A SIGNET BOOK

NEW AMERICAN LIBRARY

NAL BOOKS ARE AVAILABLE AT QUANTITY DISCOUNTS
WHEN USED TO PROMOTE PRODUCTS OR SERVICES. FOR
INFORMATION PLEASE WRITE TO PREMIUM MARKETING
DIVISION, NEW AMERICAN LIBRARY, 1633 BROADWAY,
NEW YORK, NEW YORK 10019.

SIGNET TRADEMARK REG. U.S. PAT. OFF. AND FOREIGN COUNTRIES
REGISTERED TRADEMARK—MARCA REGISTRADA
HECHO EN DRESDEN, TN, U.S.A.

SIGNET, SIGNET CLASSIC, MENTOR, ONYX, PLUME,
MERIDIAN and NAL BOOKS are published by
NAL PENGUIN INC., 1633 Broadway, New York, New York 10019

First Printing, May, 1989

1 2 3 4 5 6 7 8

PRINTED IN THE UNITED STATES OF AMERICA

1

The new Marchioness of Chalford slammed the door of her bedchamber behind her, dropped the silver-fringed white train of her wedding gown, and glared at the two young women who waited within to assist her in changing to her traveling dress. "It quite passes my understanding," she said, her golden eyes flashing, "how men in general can be such delightful creatures when brothers are the greatest beasts in nature."

The elder of her two listeners, a plump and cheerful minx of twenty-three summers whose best feature was the thick auburn hair piled artistically atop her head, chuckled with delight. "And husbands, Adriana? What think you of husbands?"

Grinning suddenly in response to her friend's sally, Adriana Barrington Blackburn pulled the silver-lace-trimmed hat free of her tawny hair and tossed it onto the tall green-muslin-draped bed before she replied with an attempt to sound casual, "Oh, husbands are delightful, too, Sarah, as you must know very well." Then, with a twist of her mouth, she added, "At the very least, living with Chalford must be an improvement over living with Alston and his stupid Sophie, or living with Papa. Randy"—she turned toward the younger girl—"will you ring for Nancy? Chalford wishes to leave as soon as we can, so that we might reach Maidstone before dark, and I've got to change down to my skin. Sophie's detestable brother insisted upon breaking a piece of cake over my head, though anyone but that skipbrain would know the tradition's gone quite out of fashion. He sent a shower of crumbs and sugar icing down the back of my gown."

With a chuckle, Lady Miranda Barrington rose from the chair near the bed, from which vantage point she had been watching her elder sister with open amusement. She was eighteen years of age, three years younger than Adriana, and was enjoying the end of her second successful Season in London. As she stepped lightly to pull the bell cord near the bed, she said, "I rang several minutes ago, but I daresay the servants are all at sixes and sevens with so many people in the house, so it will do no harm to ring again. What has that wretch Orson done now to put you in such a pet? You don't usually pay heed to his nonsense."

Adriana sat down on her dressing chair, pulling pins from her long, thick hair as she did so and throwing them onto the table. "It is not enough that he insisted we be married by special license so as not to have to call the banns and so we might be married from this house instead of from Saint George's, but now he is downstairs telling Chalford what a distressing lot of money such a license costs, just as though he had paid for it rather than my lord. Everyone knows Alston would skin a flint if he could." She peered into the looking glass, licked her right index finger, and smoothed her eyebrows as she continued, "And there stood dearest Sophie, right beside him, nattering about the cost of bride cake and food for everyone, and then describing in tedious detail how she had insisted that this and that be done so as to have everything in the first style of elegance, merely because I have married a marquess. I tell you, Sarah," she added, meeting her friend's gaze in the mirror, "Sophie has a common mind, and that's all there is about it."

"Well," said Sarah Clifford with her slow smile, "no one ever accused Alston of marrying her for her looks, her social position, or her good sense."

" 'Twasn't sense but pence," said Miranda with another laugh, "and we two ought to be the last to criticize Orson for marrying her, since he is using either his own money or Sophie's to provide dowries that neither of us should otherwise possess."

Adriana frowned at her sister. "Really, Randy, you ought not to call him Orson when others are about or speak so freely about private matters of finance."

"Pooh, little mother, who is to hear me save Sarah, who knows everything there is to know about us, through having known the pair of us all of our lives?"

"Very true," Sarah said, "though I expect there are few people in London whh do not guess the source of your portions."

Adriana sighed. "How lowering to reflect that one's father is famous only for having gambled away a fortune."

"Oh, you malign him, Dree," said Miranda, leaning over her to pick up the silver-backed hairbrush from the dressing table and beginning to brush Adriana's hair. "I am persuaded that he is equally well-known for his temper, his pride, and his enormous capacity for port. 'Tis his gout, after all, that keeps him tied by the heels in Wiltshire on your wedding day."

"He misses Mama," said Adriana on a languishing note. She shot a twinkling look at Miranda in the mirror.

"Then he began missing her at least eight years before she died, for he has overindulged himself in port for as long as I can remember," Miranda said with a laugh as she attempted to untangle a snarl. "Stop twisting about, Dree. You make my task more difficult."

"I'd prefer that you help me out of this gown first," said Adriana, getting to her feet. "The crumbs tickle." She was the shorter of the two by an inch, but the sisters looked very much alike, except that Miranda's eyes were brown with green flecks, while Adriana's were the exact color of golden topazes. And, too, Miranda's stylishly cropped and crimped hair was a shade lighter and not so thick or long as her sister's.

As Miranda obediently put the hairbrush back on the table and began to unfasten the tiny hooks down the back of the silver-and-white gown, Sarah rose at last from her place upon the settee near the window and moved to help. Minutes later, as Adriana stood in her creamy silk shift, trying to dislodge the last of the cake crumbs, the door opened and her abigail entered, a small, brisk, dark-haired woman who took one look at the three, threw up her hands, and clicked her tongue in disapproval.

"I'll just take that gown, Miss Sarah, before you get greasy fingermarks all over it, and you there, Miss Randy, look out you don't step on Miss Adrie's good half-boots."

"Really, Nancy," Adriana protested, laughing, "you should address Lady Clifford properly, and me, too, now I think of it."

"Well, and so I shall when I see proper ladies to address," said Nancy, undaunted. "A marchioness wriggling barefoot in her shift don't look like much to me, and if Miss Sarah ain't been licking icing from her fingers, then she's changed a deal more than I shall believe. Just the same cheeky pair o' lasses you was yesterday and no more. Oh, Miss Adrie," she wailed suddenly, "to think ye've gone and got yourself married, 'n' all."

"Oh, Nancy," retorted Adriana mockingly, "do stop weeping and fetch out my traveling dress. You behave as though I were going off alone, as though you'll never see me again, when in point of fact you're going with me, for goodness' sake."

"And what am I to do in a great castle, may I ask?"

"Why, look after me as you have done these many years past, you peagoose. Only consider, there will be no one shouting at either of us over trivialities, and a marchioness's abigail is a person of great distinction. You will take precedence over nearly every other servant in the place."

"I sympathize with Nancy," Sarah said. "The thought of either of you living in a castle is difficult to contemplate."

"Well," Miranda said, skipping quickly out of Nancy's path as the abigail made her brisk way to the wardrobe, then moving toward the window, "I shouldn't mind it in the least. I do wish I could live with you instead of with Orson, Dree."

Adriana smiled. "You are only worried because I shan't be here to protect you from Alston's wrath when you fall into mischief, as you will the moment I am gone." When Miranda turned away to look out the window, she added more seriously, "I told you that I don't know Chalford well enough to ask him yet, but no doubt we will all meet in Brighton, for Alston and Sophie mean to travel down next week like everyone else, in time for the races. We can discuss the matter then, I believe, though to be sure Chalford has said nothing yet about when he means for us to go."

"Then how do you know he means to go at all?" Sarah asked.

"Well, because everyone does, of course. Are not you and Mortimer going?"

"Of course. He has purchased the same house we hired last year, in the Steyne. You remember." Sarah blushed. "He said he was forced to do so because of its having such fond memories that we must always spend the month of August there. But not everyone goes to Brighton with the prince, Dree," she added quickly. "Some still fear a French invasion of the south coast, you know."

"A fine thing to talk about, I must say," said Nancy, glaring at Sarah, "when Miss Adrie herself is going to the south coast to live."

"And to the exact place where the invasion is most likely to begin," said Adriana with a grin, "though I confess to a much greater fascination for the smugglers who supposedly practice their trade there. I know little about them now, but I can tell you I mean to learn a great deal more while I am on the spot."

Nancy shot her a sour look, but Miranda, turning, promptly demanded to know exactly where Thunderhill was located. "When you said before that it overlooked the Straits, I envisioned it perched atop the white cliffs of Dover," she said.

"More like atop the brown bluffs of Hythe," retorted her sister. "I don't know much more about it than that, only that Chalford called it an ancient pile of stones that will most likely put me off being a marchioness altogether. He said it rather proudly, though," she added thoughtfully. "At all events, it is located right on the coast betwixt the town of Hythe and Romney Marsh, so I expect it will be damp, but I daresay we shan't stay there long in any case, only when there is nothing else to do. What with house parties and hunting in the fall and winter, Brighton in the summer, and the spring Season in London—well, how much time can one have to spend at home?"

Sarah, who had been thinking, looked puzzled now. "You know, Dree, Chalford invited us to stop at Thunderhill on our way to Brighton, and although Mortimer agreed to it to please me, he did complain that it would double our time on the road. If we are all going to meet in Brighton, why would Chalford expect people to extend their journey by so much just to pay a bride visit? I believe Mortimer said he expects to see Alston and Sophie and Sally and George there, too."

"Well, as to Sally and George, they invited us to spend tonight at Prospect Park, but Chalford prefers to take the Maidstone Road, so I believe he did bid them come to us next week instead. Alston has said nothing to the purpose, and you know what your husband is like. He does not like to travel, only to get from where he is to where he wishes to be as quickly as possible. Both Brighton and Thunderhill are on the south coast, for goodness' sake. How far apart can they be? You make it sound as though it is as far from one to the other as it is from London to Brighton, and that surely cannot be the case."

"Miss Sarah and Miss Randy," said Nancy sharply just then, "this be no time for geography lessons. Miss Adrie must get dressed. 'Twouldn't be no good atall to begin her married life by keeping 'is lordship a-waitin'." Then, as suddenly as before, she began to weep as she hurried to help Adriana dress.

Sarah shook her head with a fond smile. "Nancy is behaving more properly than you are, Dree. Do you not know that it is the fashion to be overcome by virgin sensibility and overawed by the solemnity of this occasion? Why, I daresay that if Chalford encourages his tenants to celebrate your wedding, you will even find the strength to attend their party."

Her friends both laughed and Miranda said, "You had that from Mr. Richardson's last book, Sarah. Sir Charles Grandison's bride stayed home a-weeping on just that very occasion." She grinned at her sister. "Do you feel like a milk-white heifer led to sacrifice, Dree, as did that poor lady?"

"No, of course not, though I do wish people wouldn't smirk so when they look at us, or make such teasing remarks as they do. But in spite of it all, I feel more as though I have been rescued from the dragon Alston by 'a verray parfit gentil knight.' " She laughed then at her own words. "Not that I can imagine Chalford in armor on a white horse, waving a lance about."

"It would be shining armor," Sarah pointed out, "and a well-made lance."

"I think he would make an imposing sight," Miranda said with a mischievous twinkle. "Any dragon would be routed in a trice."

Smiling, Adriana considered their words while she allowed Nancy to help her into her moss-green, russet-trimmed traveling dress. Then, sitting again so that her dresser might arrange her hair and help her pull on her tan kid half-boots, she said, "You know, I daresay you are both wrong, and the dragon would merely sit back upon its long tail and laugh. Somehow, one simply cannot imagine Chalford behaving violently. He is far too self-possessed and mild of manner."

"I like him," Miranda said simply.

"Well, so do I like him," retorted her sister, shooting her a sharp look in the mirror. "He is my husband, after all."

"Like?" Sarah raised her slim, arched brows. "I had

hoped you would feel stronger sentiment than mere liking, Dree."

"Well," retorted Adriana, "I for one am very glad I have not made such a fool over Chalford as you made of yourself over Mortimer two years ago. I remember, Sarah, and I am very thankful that I have not set the whole town in a buzz over my behavior. I certainly never was guilty of creating a scene that very nearly got me barred from Almack's."

"Mortimer told me that night that I was too good for him, that he dared not ask Papa to consider a suit from a mere baron, so of course I did not behave sensibly. And Almack's becomes increasingly and foolishly rigid, I believe. Had I not begged Mama to speak to Lady Sefton, Mortimer would not even have been allowed to cross the threshold that night. Was anything ever so ridiculous? I am more glad than I can tell you that I fought to marry him, Dree. I love him, and I had hoped that by now you would feel some of those same tender feelings for Chalford."

"Have I not just said that I like the man very well? Goodness, what a piece of work you make over so small a thing. His behavior has been utterly correct, and you surely don't think Alston allowed us to be private with each other for more than fifteen minutes when he made his offer. I scarcely know him."

"Then I am surprised that you agreed to marry him, Adriana," her friend said quietly.

"Well, I am not surprised in the least," said Miranda, turning from the window where she had been watching the view of Berkeley Square. "I would marry the boot-boy if it would get me out of this house, and Chalford is *not* the bootboy."

"But surely you have had other offers," Sarah said, looking at Adriana. "Why, I know you have."

Adriana grimaced. "I am an earl's daughter, Sarah, as you are yourself, but neither my father nor my brother is as conciliating as your papa was about your love for Clifford. No one less than a viscount would do for me, and then only a viscount who, like Alston or

George Villiers, will one day become an earl. The men in my family keep themselves on a very high form, my dear. The fact that no viscount or earl of our acquaintance was interested in a young woman with a mere five thousand pounds as her portion did not deter them from rejecting out of hand any other offer I received. And just consider my competition on the Marriage Mart if you will. Why, Sally Fane's inheritance is said to be over one hundred thousand pounds, which is much more even than Sophie has. Sally and I came out together, as you know, but George never even looked at me. Nor did the handsome Earl Cowper, once he had met Emily Lamb. No one of consequence did, though I am said to be prettier than Emily and I'm not nearly as silly as Sally can be. You were satisfied with Clifford, Sarah, but a mere baron would never do for Viscount Alston's sister or the Earl of Wryde's daughter. They quickly sent what suitors I had to the rightabout.''

"Goodness," said Sarah, "you never confided this to me before. How does Alston dare to insist that you look so high for a husband when he married a tradesman's daughter himself?''

"Not at all the same, my dear." She tilted her chin high in the air in imitation of her brother's haughty public demeanor. "He sacrificed himself to save the family's groats." Grimacing expressively, she continued in a more natural tone. "There wasn't much left by the time he came of age, you know, and though he very sensibly refused Papa's ingenuous suggestion that they break the entail and sell some land, he needed a great deal of money to keep himself in the sort of comfort Papa has taught him to demand. And once he realized the extent of Papa's debts and knew the responsibility for paying them would one day fall to him, he looked about him for an heiress willing to sell herself for a title. Hence his marriage to the delightful Sophie Ringwell. It was her money that finally gave him the power to force Papa to give the reins of Wryde into his hands. Imagine an ironmonger with money enough to dower his daughter with nearly sixty thousand while retaining so much that his son feels sufficiently puffed up in his own conceit to make improper suggestions to ladies living under his sister's roof.''

"Claude doesn't!" Sarah bit her lip to keep from laughing. "Dear me, he's so—so—''

"Wet is a good word," Adriana said. "I could not explain it all to you before without sounding old-cattish, Sarah, or so I believed." She wrinkled her nose in a self-deprecating way. "In truth, my pride would not allow it. I had thought to remain a spinster all my days, you see, so anything I gave as a reason must sound self-pitying at best, and that I could not bear."

"And then a marquess offered for you." Miranda sighed. "It is just like one of Mrs. Radcliffe's tales. Dear Chalford."

"It was with the greatest astonishment that I learned of his offer," Adriana said. "Alston informed me of it after I had met the man but four times, danced with him perhaps as many times, and talked to him for not more than half an hour altogether. And for the most part, I daresay I merely flirted as I always do, not making any effort to attach his affections, you know, for it never entered my head that a man of such rank and wealth would consider matrimony with a woman in my financial position. I said whatever it entered my head to say. He is a most comfortable man to talk to, that I will say for him. He listens with such a flattering air of attention, and though he rarely talks about himself, I remember once actually asking him what it was like to have enough money to do as one pleased."

"Adriana!" Sarah made no effort to conceal her amusement. "What did he say?"

"That he didn't suppose anyone ever had that much money because the more money one has, the more responsibilities one incurs and thus the less likely it is that one may do as one pleases." Adriana sighed. "I hope he doesn't prove to be as great a nickpenny as Alston has become. One expects wealthy men to live wealthily."

"But you must know how he means to go on," Sarah said. "Surely, he has made arrangements for you."

"Oh, yes, the settlements." She smiled tolerantly. "I had nothing to say to them, of course, and I am sure he has made me a most generous allowance to be getting along on at Thunderhill—well, Alston certainly thinks it generous, and he was impressed when Chalford refused to quibble over details and agreed to whatever he suggested—but Alston believes I ought to get along on pennies, and Chalford cannot realize how expensive London is, or Brighton. A marchioness has an image to present to the *beau monde*, after all, and I don't intend to be remiss in my duty."

"Well, you will bring Chalford 'round your thumb in no time," Miranda said. "You are very good at that sort of thing, Dree, having practiced so long with Orson and Papa, neither of whom is conciliating in the least, which Chalford appears to be. Moreover, if he did not quibble, it is because he desires you to have what you wish. I have seen the way your husband looks at you, my dear. If he is not besotted, he is very close to it. In any event, he will give you whatever you ask for."

Sarah frowned, and Adriana, catching her look in the mirror, said quickly, "I sound like a spoilt child, do I not?"

Sarah shook her head. "Never that, my dear. To speak frankly, I think you are a little frightened of what lies ahead and trying hard to pretend that you are not. No, no, do not poker up. Remember, this is Sarah, who knows you well. Though I was in love with my husband, I was frightened about what lay ahead—and confused, too. You scarcely know Chalford, so your apprehension can only be greater than mine was. And your mother is not here to tell you how you should go on. Not," she added with a laugh, "that mine was of any assistance to me. She only blushed and mumbled until I hugged her and told her I would learn what I must from dearest Mortimer."

"Here be your bonnet, m'lady," said Nancy before Adriana could speak. Silently, she let the abigail settle the russet bonnet over her intricately twisted coiffure. The bow, however, she tied herself, under her right ear. Then, pulling on her tan gloves, she stood, shook out her skirts, let Nancy arrange her demitrain, and declared herself ready to go down to her husband.

Miranda and Sarah both moved forward quickly to hug her, and Adriana found that she was blinking back as many tears as her abigail before she managed to get herself out the door. Once she reached the wide staircase leading down to the hall, however, she had herself well in hand again and nodded and smiled to the guests milling below, waiting to bid her farewell. Her gaze swept the crowd, then came to rest upon one particular gentleman standing at the very foot of the stairs.

Joshua Blackburn, eleventh Marquess of Chalford, seemed somehow aloof from the excited group surrounding him. There was a coolness, a calmness that separated him from the others. He too had changed to clothing more suitable for travel, but he was precise to a pin in his buff breeches, black boots, and the snugly fitting dark-blue coat that seemed only to emphasize the powerful breadth of his shoulders and the narrowness of his waist and hips. One lock of dark hair had escaped the brush's control to fall over his left temple, and his dark-gray eyes glinted with unmistakable approval when his gaze met Adriana's. She smiled at him, then her gaze shifted quickly, scanning the group again, darting from one person to another as she smiled and nodded and continued to make her graceful descent.

When she was close enough, Chalford held out his hand to her and she placed hers within it, grateful for the warmth of his grasp and the strength of his presence. The first time she had seen him, at Lady Sefton's rout after the opening sessions of Parliament, she had assumed from the way he carried himself and the way he unconsciously drew the attention of everyone else in the room that he must be a man of wealth and power, and she had been surprised to learn that few of the women knew him at all. The men who knew him said only how much they liked him and what a pity it was that such a bruising rider to hounds passed so much of his life in such humbug country. Once she had made his acquaintance, she had learned quickly that he rarely talked about himself, which made the initial impact of his personality all the more incomprehensible to her.

Now he smiled at her, and she smiled back, but before either of them could speak, Viscount Alston, beside the marquess, said in a sharp undertone, "What can have kept you so long, Adriana? We have all been waiting this half-hour and more."

She turned, automatically assuming a look of contrition. Then, suddenly, awareness struck her that she no longer had to answer to him, and she smiled. "Dearest Orson," she said, gently emphasizing his name, delighted when the irritation in his expression sharpened to anger, "I wished to be certain nothing was amiss with my appearance on so important an occasion."

At Alston's side, his plump, pink-satin-draped viscountess had been examining Adriana's attire and now shook her head in disapproval, making the three purple ostrich plumes adorning her elaborate coiffure bob wildly. "I am surprised at you, Adriana," she said. "Such a plain dress to choose, and no jewelry at all. Your mama left her personal jewels betwixt you and dear Miranda, did she not?" Without waiting for a reply, she added, "The pearls at least, I should have thought, and a ring or two more to deck your fingers. Not that the ring Chalford gave you is not exquisite, for of course it is." She fluttered her sandy lashes at the marquess, then returned her gaze to Adriana, saying more brusquely, "You have a position to uphold, after all."

"Ah, Sophie, I can never glitter so well as you do," Adriana replied gently. "I am but a drab moth beside a butterfly, and I know better than to attempt imitation." She shot a mocking glance at her brother, enjoying herself but thinking, too, that it was as well she would not have to answer to him for that little barb. He was visibly fuming, but she knew he would never reprove her with Chalford at her side. Indeed, he would not wish

Sophie to realize that what Adriana had said to her was
not a compliment. His wife was very nearly preening
herself.

Behind her, Adriana heard a familiar chuckle, and
though it was all but drowned out by the noise of the
others in the hall, she knew she must divert her brother's
attention before he noted Miranda's amusement.
Accordingly, she smiled at Alston again and said
sweetly, "Thank you for a lovely wedding, Orson
dear." Then, raising her voice above the din, she said,
"Do, everyone, stay as long as you like. Alston and
Sophie will be distressed if you do not, for there is food
and drink to last all the day."

Cheers greeted her words, and she found her hand
clasped more firmly than ever in her husband's as he
urged her toward the tall front doors, which swung wide
at their approach. With more cheers and whistling, their
friends and relatives made a path for them, then
followed them out to the awaiting carriage.

Chalford, grasping Adriana by the waist, easily lifted
her into the chaise, then leapt in behind her and signaled
the postboys to horse. With a surge, the light, well-
sprung vehicle leapt forward as he was latching the
door, and Adriana's last view of the merrymakers made
her chuckle. Miranda and Sarah were waving and
laughing, but Alston and his lady stood on the topmost
step, both looking anxious and rather grim.

Satisfied, the new marchioness leaned back against
the squabs. "I hope everyone stays until dawn."

"You practically ordered them to do so, did you
not?" was the calm response.

She looked at him but she could read nothing in his
expression that suggested disapproval. Nonetheless, she
was moved to say apologetically, "It was not well done
of me, I suppose, but Sophie has driven me wild with all
her complaints about the expense. One moment she
talks about candles at seven shillings the dozen, and the
next she is insisting that there must be ten linkboys hired
whether the guests stay on after dark or not—just on the
chance that they will—or it will not look right. And how

they can call it a wedding breakfast and serve six varieties of ices from Gunter's, I cannot tell you, but Sophie insisted that it was the thing to do and Orson, for all his nipfarthing notions, never tells her she mustn't do what she has set her heart upon doing."

"You called him Orson when you took leave of him," said Chalford, "or I should not have realized you speak now of your brother. I've never heard him called anything but Alston."

Adriana grinned. "He detests being called Orson. Miranda and I have been forced to call him only by his title ever since the day I shouted at him that he ought to have been eaten by a bear." Chalford looked puzzled, so she explained, "We are all named after characters in Shakespeare's plays. I am from *The Comedy of Errors*, which my friend Sarah says is appropriate, and Miranda is the admired heroine of *The Tempest*, of course, while Orson is from *Twelfth Night*."

"I do not recall a scene in the play where Orsino is eaten by bears, however," Chalford said, amused.

"No, of course not, but years and years ago, I discovered on the shelf in our nursery an old child's tale about a boy named Orson who was carried off by a bear and raised with her cubs. Because the character was actually called Orson, not Orsino in the Italian way, I said Mama must have got the name from the bear story, not the play. Then came the day when I said the mama bear ought to have eaten him, that I hoped one would someday. Miranda was scarcely more than a baby at the time, but she was like an echo, saying everything I said, and the two of us kept repeating that last refrain until he soundly boxed my ears and ordered us never again to call him anything but Alston. I have—in his presence, at any rate—obeyed him until today."

"Your farewell was a declaration of independence?"

She glanced at him uncertainly. "In a way, I suppose it was. Have you any brothers or sisters, sir?"

"One of each," he replied, "and I must confess to you that my sympathies lie entirely with Alston."

"Were they there today? Although I know your

parents to be deceased, I know little else about your family."

"Barring a few cousins, none of my family was there," he said quietly. "My brother, Ned, is married to a Scottish lady and lives thirty miles north of Edinburgh. I think he would have come, had Molly not been expecting at any moment to be confined. My sister, Lydia, is also married. She wrote that she would have come to London had it not seemed foolish to do so when she had only just got home to Sussex, not knowing before she left that I intended to commit matrimony. She trusts you will forgive her and looks forward to meeting you once we are settled at home."

"If she lives in Sussex, perhaps we might visit her when we go to Brighton," Adriana suggested.

"Perhaps, but since we will not go to Brighton before Lydia comes to Thunderhill, as she generally does each September with all her offspring, you will meet her first at home."

"Not go to Brighton!" Adriana stared at him. "But of course we will go. Everyone is going to Brighton, if not for the races then certainly for the prince's birthday celebration."

"Not everyone, my dear, for I do not, and nor will you. Your duties at Thunderhill will keep you entirely too busy."

2

Adriana, having sense enough not to debate the matter at once, turned to look out the window, for experience had taught her that when a gentleman took a notion into his head that ran contrary to her own wishes, she was generally wiser to approach the matter obliquely, rather than to confront it straight on. To argue with either her father or her brother was useless, served only, in fact, to set them to bellowing at her, but since she was accustomed to getting her own way in the end, even against such stiff opposition as theirs, she did not despair. Having spent too many years buried at Wryde before Alston could be coaxed into sponsoring her come-out, she had no intention of simply giving up the parties and amusements she had grown to love. She would do her duty gracefully as mistress of Thunderhill Castle, but its master must learn to cater a little to her wishes, too.

The horses made little speed while wending their way out of Mayfair via Piccadilly, the Haymarket, and Whitehall, and even after the chaise crossed Westminster Bridge, there was still a great deal of traffic and four turnpikes to be negotiated before they turned onto the Maidstone Road. All the hustle and bustle was fascinating, however, so when Chalford announced quietly, as the chaise rattled across the Croydon Canal, that although they were but three and a half miles out of London, they were now in Kent, Adriana started a little at the sound of his voice.

As they had passed through the Newcross tollgate but moments before, the tollkeeper had tipped his hat to her and winked, and she had grinned at him. Remembering this incident, she turned to face her new husband warily, suddenly conscious of the way he filled the chaise, aware that for the first time in her life she was shut into a small space with a man, other than her brother or father, to whom she was answerable for her every action. Looking at him now, it seemed impossible that she could have ignored him for seconds, let alone for half an hour. But surely that much time had elapsed since she had turned away in order not to shout her displeasure at his calm rejection of a sojourn in Brighton.

Searching for a safe topic of conversation, she said, "I have not driven on this road before, sir, but I am given to understand that the Kent countryside is very beautiful."

"We think so," he said.

Reassured by his tone, she smiled. " 'We' being the men of Kent, I daresay. I doubt you are a Kentish man."

He regarded her with a touch of sleepy amusement in his dark-gray eyes. "Do you actually know the difference between men of Kent and Kentish men, Adriana?"

She bit her lower lip, gazing at him from beneath her thick, sable lashes, then answered carefully, "I believe it is merely a question of which side of the River Medway one claims as home. Men from the east are men and those from the west are Kentish."

He chuckled. "And maids from the east are maids, while those from the west are Kentish. Do you know the reason?"

She shook her head, confessing, "I was not even certain I had the sides of the river correctly."

"The most generally accepted tale is that when William, Duke of Normandy, was marching on Dover after his victory at Hastings, some men came to welcome him, and in consequence, obtained from him a confirmation of certain ancient privileges. They called themselves 'invicti,' the unconquered, and they became known as the men of Kent. The others, who opposed the

Conqueror, were pushed west of the Medway and came
to be known as Kentish men."

Her eyes twinkled. " 'Tis not nearly so old a tradition
as I had thought, then. Only from those upstart
Normans. I must tell you that Barrington roots are
buried deep in the days of the Angles and Saxons, or so
my father frequently boasts."

Chalford nodded. "Then you will prefer the legend
that when Britain was divided into kingdoms, about the
year 450, King Vortigern of Kent called upon the Saxon
leaders Hengist and Horsa to help him in his fight
against the Picts and the Scots, which they did, but in
the process a lot of Saxons who accompanied them
remained in the area. Many of the Britons didn't like the
Saxons and retreated west, beyond the Medway, calling
themselves Kentish men. Those remaining became
known as men of Kent. Since Thunderhill is not so old
as that, I prefer the first tale."

"Goodness," exclaimed Adriana, "do you mean to
say that Thunderhill dates from the days of the
Conqueror? I hope there are carpets, and glass in the
windows."

He smiled. "You will be comfortable, I believe,
although part of the castle does indeed date from the
eleventh century, when the Conqueror conferred the
earldom of Côte de Tonnere on my ancestor, the
Norman knight Simon de Tonnere. Simon was expected
to help defend the south coast, of course, for the chalk
spur on which the castle stands overlooks the Channel at
a point where, in time of war, one must always
anticipate possible attack from France. After Earl
Simon built his castle, he and his descendants lived there
uninterrupted for four hundred years."

Chalford's attention was diverted just then, and he
said, "Look to your right. We are passing through
Eltham, and those are the ruins of an old palace
belonging to Henry the Seventh. The great hall's
magnificently carved roof is in a particularly fine state
of preservation even now."

Adriana eyed him with suspicion. "See here,

Chalford, I hope you aren't thinking of dragging me about to look at old ruins. We shall never reach Maidstone before dark if you do.''

"Perhaps another day," he said. "I've no wish to stop before Foot's Cray. I've arranged for changes at every stage, but even so it will take the best part of four hours to reach Maidstone even if we don't dally along the way."

"I heard that the Prince of Wales once drove all the way from London to Brighton in under four hours," she said demurely.

"His highness actually took ten hours to accomplish a journey from Carlton House to Brighton and back again. That was in '84," he told her, "and he rode; he didn't drive. Three years later his record was broken by a certain Mr. Webster, who traveled from Westminster Bridge to Brighton on one of his own phaeton horses in three hours and twenty minutes. No one knows the fate of either horse, but if they survived, you may take my word for it that they must have suffered lasting injury. As I've no wish to kill any of my horses, we will travel more sedately."

She sighed, wondering if Chalford realized she had been baiting him. He wasn't looking at her now, so she couldn't see his eyes, but his voice was even and calm, as indeed it always was. At other times when she had made some quip or other, she thought she had seen a gleam of warm amusement in his eyes, but now she could tell nothing about his mood. She would, she decided, have to learn more about him before she would know the best way to go about convincing him that he would enjoy a visit to Brighton. Turning in her seat, she said, "What happened in the fifteenth century?"

He looked puzzled for a moment, then his brow cleared and he said, "You mean with the de Tonneres?" When she nodded, he smiled. "The line died. One of the daughters married into the Blackburn family, who anglicized the castle's name. We have held it ever since, with the brief exception of a time when Cromwell's forces took over. That Blackburn very sensibly left the country, returning only when Charles the Second restored the family's ranks and properties. It was necessary for the family to restore a good part of the castle as well, since the Parliamentary forces did not behave as one generally hopes one's guests will behave.''

Adriana nodded understandingly. "The Duke of Norfolk is one of Papa's friends,'' she said, "and he has said much the same thing about Arundel Castle. Only no one did anything to repair Arundel until he began to work on it twenty years ago. The Fitzalan-Howards simply lived elsewhere in the meantime.''

"I know Norfolk,'' Chalford said amiably. "He sponsored me when I took my seat in the House. But his example aside, we Blackburns live at home. And home is Thunderhill.''

With an effort Adriana refrained from grinding her teeth. The conversation was not encouraging, and belatedly she remembered how little her friends in London had known about the marquess. Clearly he had not, in the past at least, spent much time there, a state of affairs that ought now to change.

"When did you take your seat, sir? I do not recall seeing you in London for the Season before.''

"I took my seat when I came of age, just as might be expected,'' he said, adding with a rueful smile, "I am not very politically or socially inclined, so I fear I have not been assiduous in performing my duties in Parliament. Indeed, until last month, I do not believe I had set foot in the place these past eight years. But it has been very strongly suggested for some time now that I look about me for a wife.'' He smiled tenderly at her. "Since the Season in London is the most sensible time to look, I accepted an invitation from one of my many aunts, bowed to the pressure exerted by two others, and agreed with my sister when she insisted that this year was as good as another. I didn't realize, however, how easy a task it would prove to be.'' He took her hand in his and gave it a gentle squeeze. "I am glad I listened to all my advisers.''

Blushing, she smiled back at him, for once incapable of a flirtatious response. His hand felt warm, and its warmth spread to her body, radiating through her in a pleasant but most unsettling manner. She was grateful when they drew into the yard of the Ship Inn in Foot's Cray and she could withdraw her hand from his. The change was accomplished with speed, and he did not suggest refreshment, so they were away again within ten minutes. Still conscious of that odd radiance within and feeling at a loss for words, Adriana turned her attention rather firmly to the road, and Chalford made no effort to reclaim it. Instead, with a self-deprecating grimace, he leaned back to doze in his corner.

The scenery was splendid. The chaise passed fields of waving flax and wildflowers spreading like Persian carpets to the right and left of the road. It rolled through deep shady woods, where oak, beech, hornbeam, and elm trees towered above them, making tunnels, then out again into the bright sunlight. As they approached the North Downs, hazel coppices, colonies of flowering dogwood, and sprawling banks of honeysuckle dotted the grassy, rolling hillsides. Though Adriana enjoyed it all, she found herself glancing with increasing regularity at her companion, at first to reassure herself that he still dozed, but as time passed, with growing exasperation at being ignored.

He was certainly a handsome man, she thought, regarding him closely for a few moments. More handsome, actually, in repose than when he was awake. He looked more boyish now, less guarded in his expression, more vulnerable. Odd to think of a man being vulnerable. Men had everything their own way, unless one knew how to use their absurd vanities to one's own advantage.

Chalford stirred when they stopped for the change in Farningham and again in West Malling, but although she dropped her reticule once, noisily, and opened and shut her window twice, he slept soundly through Larkfield and Ditton and came awake only when the chaise rattled over the stone bridge across the Medway. They were entering Maidstone, a town situated on a pleasant slope above the river and surrounded by beautiful gardens, fruit orchards, and vast, towering hop plantations.

Chalford sat upright, looking out his window before turning to smile at Adriana. " 'Twas a rapid journey," he said.

"You slept, sir, so of course it seemed rapid."

His look was a steady one. "I thought you preferred to look at the scenery rather than to converse with me. If I've neglected you, I apologize."

She shook her head, adding mendaciously, "There is no need. I enjoyed the scenery. Are we truly in Maidstone now?"

"Yes, and we stay at the Mitre in High Street. I thought you would prefer the privacy of an inn. I hope I was not wrong. There would be more amusement, perhaps, at Prospect Lodge."

She grinned at him, in charity with him again at once, for though Sally Villiers was one of her dearest friends and she liked the viscount, too, she felt nothing but gratitude to Chalford for having refused their invitation to spend several days with them at their home near Tunbridge Wells.

"I daresay I shall miss neither the amusement nor the certainty of hearing Sally giggle every ten minutes," she assured him. "Only think, sir, she will be a countess one day. Why, she is no more like Lady Jersey than buttermilk is like Scotch whiskey." Wrinkling her nose, she added thoughtfully, "Not that one would wish her to be like her ladyship."

"It is to be hoped, in any event, that Sally will be more discreet," Chalford said dryly. "She is nearly as great a flirt as the countess was used to be in her youth, after all."

"Oh, everyone flirts," Adriana said casually, glancing out her window again when he did not immediately reply. "What is that great Gothic structure

towering above us, sir?'' she demanded suddenly as they
passed beneath the walls of a stone palace that loomed
above the cobbled street.

"The Archbishop's Palace," he told her. "Maidstone
is the county town of Kent, and thus the archbishop
thought it behooved him to have a residence here as well
as in Canterbury. We are nearing the inn now, I believe.
Are you hungry?"

Nodding, she realized she was famished, although it
was only five o'clock and she was accustomed to dining
much later in town. "I didn't eat very much of Sophie's
feast, I'm afraid."

His dark brows lifted. "I hope you have not been
sitting there starving while I slept."

"No, of course not. I am not so meek as that, sir."

"You are very free with your sirs, Adriana. My name
is Joshua, and my closest friends call me Josh. I hope
you will number among them."

She looked down into her lap, suddenly and
unaccountably shy. "My friends call me Dree," she
said.

"I prefer Adriana."

She looked up indignantly. "Well, perhaps I shall
prefer to call you 'sir' then."

"As you like," he replied equably.

For no good reason that she could call to mind,
Adriana suddenly experienced a nearly overpowering
desire to box his ears. Fortunately, the chaise drew up in
the innyard just then, and her attention was safely
diverted. She was able, a few moments later, to accept
Chalford's assistance in alighting with her dignity
unimpaired.

The Mitre was an elderly U-shaped inn, built of Kent
rag stone, with ancient, massive gates of oak still
hanging on their original hinges at the entrance to the
yard. Opposite the stables, just past the snug coffee
room, there were stairs of solid oak blocks leading up to
the inn proper. Chalford had bespoken a private parlor
and had sent a courier ahead to see all in readiness, so
Adriana soon found herself seated at a white-linen-

draped table before a cheerful fire, attended in style by a dignified footman and a beaming, rosy-cheeked maidservant.

"I daresay Miskin and your Nancy will be along shortly with the rest of our baggage," Chalford said as he took his seat opposite her, signed to the footman to begin serving them, and asked the maidservant to draw the curtains. Smiling at Adriana, he added, "I know it is still light outside, but I prefer to dine by candlelight. My aunts keep country hours."

"You said you had any number of aunts," she replied. "I suppose they visit you often."

"Two of them live at the castle."

"Live there? But they were not at the wedding."

"No, for Aunt Hetta fears the French invasion will come if she is not there to prevent it, and Aunt Adelaide believes that she must be home if I am not, to run things." A frown fluttered across his brow as he tasted the wine then nodded permission for the footman to fill Adriana's glass. "You may find it difficult at first to assert your authority, I'm afraid. Aunt Adelaide is accustomed to being mistress of the castle."

"Well, she may continue to act so, with my goodwill," said Adriana. "I spent ten thankless years after my mother's death trying to play mistress of Wryde and to keep my sister out of the mischief she delights in without irritating my father or coming too often to cuffs with my brother. Wryde House is a rabbit warren of rooms, and I was far too young for the task, even with our housekeeper and dearest Nancy to assist me."

"But surely, since your brother's marriage—"

"Oh, to be sure, Alston has done much to bring the estate into order since he married Sophie and convinced Papa to turn over management to him, but though Sophie has no turn for household management, she issues orders right and left, so we were constantly at odds, even at the London house. I promise you, sir, I shan't repine if your aunt wishes to continue to manage things for a time."

He nodded, his expression enigmatic. At first she thought she had displeased him, but then he smiled at her and she decided she was wrong. The meal was excellent, and Miskin and Nancy arrived before they had done, their carriage having made nearly as good time as the chaise, due, Nancy told her mistress, to Miskin's having insisted that the horses be sprung whenever the condition of the road would allow it.

"In a proper hurry he was," she said when they were alone in Adriana's bedchamber an hour later. "Not but what I wanted to get here in good time, too. 'Tis a lovely, cozy room, this, Miss Adrie, though the paneling ain't so fine as that in the parlor. All them lovely carved shields."

"Those are heraldic devices, Nancy. No doubt the coats of arms of famous guests at the inn, though I'm afraid I don't know one from another." She glanced about her in approval. A small fire crackled in the hooded fireplace, throwing a warm glow onto the carpeted hardwood floor, and candles burned in polished silver holders upon dark wood tables on either side of the wide, curtained bed. "I love velvet," she said, stroking the cloth.

"Like a dark night sky, they look, same as them at the window," Nancy observed. There was a knock at the door. "I ordered a bath, m'lady. That'll be the lads with it now."

Adriana nodded, moving to the window to be out of the way while the tub was dragged in and placed before the fire. Servants carrying buckets came next, and when the bath was ready, Nancy helped her remove her clothes, then stood ready with cloth and soap. "Will you do your hair?"

"Goodness, not tonight. It wouldn't dry for an hour or more, and I wish to sleep."

Nancy chuckled. "I doubt you'll be let to sleep yet a while, Miss Adrie. His lordship be like to have other notions."

Adriana, on the point of entering the tub, stiffened, then forced herself to relax. Chalford had been casual over their meal, and their conversation had been desultory. Indeed, they had behaved like long acquaintances, and she had been so comfortable that she had scarcely given a thought to the fact that this was her wedding night. Now the thought overwhelmed her, making it an effort to force her muscles to relax again, but she managed it and sank down into the warm water. Looking directly at her abigail, she said with casual aplomb, "I daresay his lordship will not wish to assert his rights in such a place as this inn. No doubt he will wait until we reach Thunderhill."

Nancy's eyes widened and she seemed about to speak, but when Adriana's gaze caught hers and held it, she kept her tongue behind her teeth and busied herself with the soap, lathering her mistress, being careful not to get her hair wet. The tub was large and the soapsuds soon made white mountains atop the water. Adriana, feeling at ease again and playful, scooped up a handful and turned toward Nancy, her eyes alight, her intent clear.

"Now, Miss Adrie, none o' your fooling about," warned the maidservant, watching her with grim wariness.

Adriana leaned forward and blew just as a small door, hitherto unnoticed in the corner of the room, opened to reveal his lordship standing calmly upon the threshold.

"A provocative scene," he said with a smile.

"Chalford, how dare you!" Adriana demanded, sinking back into the tub and noting with dismay that the soapsuds were collapsing all around her. She crossed her arms protectively.

"Dare?" the marquess said, raising his brows. "I am your husband, my dear."

"And I am in my bath, sir. You promised me privacy."

"So I did, though I didn't really mean total privacy, you know. I'll leave you now if you insist, but only for fifteen minutes. I trust you will then be prepared to receive me."

She had said the first thing that entered her mind

when she had seen him standing there. Though she knew
perfectly well that he had meant privacy away from the
knowing looks of their friends, and nothing more, one
used what little one had. "Your bedchamber is next to
this," she pointed out, carefully calm. "I did not even
know that that door connected the two."

"The chamber yonder is naught, I fear, but a dressing
room," he said quietly.

"Then you must beg a cot or bespeak another bedchamber, for surely you will not wish to linger here after
so tiring a day."

His eyes twinkled. "I slept in the chaise, my dear."

"Well, I did not."

His gaze held hers. "Fifteen minutes, Adriana."

When the door had shut behind him, Adriana looked
at Nancy, only to discover that her handmaiden had
turned away to fetch her a towel. "I daresay you wish to
say you told me so," she said tartly. "Well, I have no
intention of—of— Oh, hand me that towel, Nancy, and
fetch my robe."

Her features carefully controlled, Nancy obeyed the
order with alacrity, and moments later Adriana was
wrapped in a forest-green velvet dressing gown, her feet
snugly encased in matching mules. She sat down upon a
stool and began taking pins from her hair. In the pier
glass she could see damp tendrils curling about her face
and neck. Leaning forward, she pinched color into her
cheeks, wondering why she should look so pale after her
warm bath. Nancy began to brush her hair.

"How much time has passed?" Adriana demanded.

"I do not know, m'lady. Perhaps I ought to leave you
now."

"No! That is, I prefer that you stay," Adriana said
with an unsuccessful attempt to sound dignified. Her
heart was pounding, and despite the pinching, her
cheeks looked pale again. Her gaze met Nancy's in the
mirror. The abigail shook her head. "Please, Nancy. I
wish it."

"He would only send me away, Miss Adrie. You
needn't fear him. He is a kind man."

"I don't fear him," Adriana said indignantly. "How silly to think I might. 'Tis only that I am tired and wish to sleep."

A tap on the corner door, followed immediately by the opening of that door, ended their discussion. Again Chalford stood upon the threshold. He had taken off his jacket, waistcoat, boots, and neckcloth, and seemed somehow even bigger in his shirt sleeves than he had looked before.

Adriana's breath caught in her throat. Swallowing carefully, she said, "I have not yet donned my nightdress, sir."

"You have no need for a nightdress," he replied, signing to the abigail to leave them. A moment later Adriana was alone with her husband.

They looked at each other for a long moment before Chalford closed the door gently behind him and moved toward her. Adriana stiffened on her stool, her lips parted, her breath coming quickly, her breasts rising and falling beneath the soft green velvet of her robe. As he came closer, her right hand moved of its own accord to the deep vee of her neckline. She clutched the two halves of the robe closer together. When he touched her shoulder, she started nervously.

"Steady, sweetheart, I won't hurt you." The endearment surprised her, for he had never called her that before. His voice came from deep in his throat, sounding even lower than usual, and the sound of it set her nerves atingle. His touch sent rays of warmth radiating from her shoulder through the rest of her body, and when he moved his hand beneath her hair, grasping a handful and twining it around his fingers, the warmth changed to tiny shivers wherever his fingers touched her neck.

Drawing a long, steadying breath, she forced herself to look directly up at him. "Please, sir, you must see that I am not at all ready for this. I am very tired."

"You're not tired," he said, smiling down at her in a way that made her look away again. "You are merely nervous, Adriana, as you were this afternoon in the

chaise. I regretted the impulse that startled you then and
did what I could to make you comfortable by sleeping,
but there is nothing at all out of the way about being
nervous at a time like this. Indeed, some would consider
it unbecoming in a young bride to behave otherwise."
His hand moved again under her hair to stroke her neck.

Taking another, quicker breath, she said, "Very well,
then, I am nervous. You are right. I have no experience
with this sort of thing, Chalford, and we have been
married only a few hours. Surely, you will not force me.
You must allow me some time to grow accustomed both
to marriage and to—to this." She spread her hands and
opened her eyes wide to look at him, certain that her
vulnerability would stir him as argument had not. He
was a gentle man, a kind man, a man who had always
before seemed anxious to please her. Surely, he would
leave her to sleep alone if she but managed the matter
adroitly.

His smile became warmer. There was amusement in
his dark eyes, but she could not accuse him of laughing
at her, for his voice when he spoke was even gentler than
it had been. "Waiting would be wrong, sweetheart.
Your imagination would only blow the business bigger
in your mind than it is now. Now you are only nervous,
but time and anticipation would turn nervousness to
fear. We don't want that." His hand tightened against
the back of her neck, and when he bent to kiss her, she
did not try to pull away, knowing her strength would be
as nothing against his.

His breath was sweet, his lips soft. At first he seemed
only to taste her, his kisses like the whisper of a summer
breeze, just brushing her lips, teasing her. Then his
touch became firmer and she found herself responding,
tasting for herself, wanting more. She scarcely noticed
when his free hand moved beneath her right arm and he
urged her to her feet. She obeyed him as though she
were in a dream. But when his hand moved against the
side of her breast, she gasped.

"You are so soft, sweetheart," he murmured against
her lips, "so very soft and lovely. Touch me."

Her hands had been in her lap until she stood. Now they were at her sides, just hanging there, as though she had forgotten she had hands. She lifted them to his waist, and at first they felt heavy, as though they were under some sort of spell over which she had little control. She felt the fine material of his shirt beneath her fingertips. She felt, too, his body beneath the shirt. He was not soft. Not in the least.

His arms went around her, drawing her closer as his lips claimed hers more possessively than before, encouraging her response, demanding it. And she responded, not merely with her lips but with her body, melting against him, feeling suddenly as though she were someone else altogether, no longer Adriana but someone softer, more pliant, someone whom Chalford gently bent to his will while Adriana watched from a vantage point high above.

His right hand moved between them to the opening of her robe, pushing the velvet aside, caressing her skin, moving slowly, tantalizingly, over the soft silken mounds of her breasts. When his fingertips brushed across the tip of the right one, Adriana gasped again at the sensations thrilling through her body. No longer in any way detached from what was happening, she gave herself up to passions that threatened to overcome her.

She felt Chalford's hand move downward, then felt his fingers briefly on the lacing at the waist of her robe. The robe fell open. Both his hands moved to her shoulders now, beneath the velvet. He held her a little away from him. Slowly, he eased the material off her shoulders. It caught at her elbows.

"Put your hands down now, Adriana," he said quietly.

She obeyed without a word. The robe slid to the floor with a whisper, and she stood naked before him. Gently, Chalford lifted her into his arms and carried her to the bed. When she felt the chill of the sheet beneath her body, she shivered and reached for the coverlet.

"No, sweetheart, I want to look at you."

Her hand paused in its motion as her gaze shifted to

meet his. The candlelight made her skin glow like the inside of a ripe peach, and as Chalford began to remove his clothing, his gaze explored her body with shameless hunger.

She stirred languorously. Her lips parted. She murmured, "Joshua," the single word a verbal caress.

Without taking his gaze from her body, Chalford flung the last article of his clothing to the floor and moved to claim his bride.

3

The next morning Adriana awoke to a feeling of disorientation. The bedchamber was dark except for a vertical slit of light in the center of the near wall, but she was facing the wrong way to be looking toward her window in her brother's house. She began to roll onto her back before she sensed the bulk of his body behind her. Memory flooded her senses then, setting warm rivers aflow in her veins.

"Good morning, Adriana."

She held her breath, hoping he would think she still slept, that he would say no more until she brought some order to the chaos of her emotions.

"Look at me, sweetheart. I know you are awake."

Slowly, she turned, conscious of her nakedness beneath the coverlet, and his, remembering all she had learned of his body the night before, all that she had let him take from hers. Heavy warmth crept into her cheeks, and she was grateful for the dimness. He would not see her confusion.

He was lying on his back, his arms folded back so that his hands cradled his head upon the pillow. She remembered how big his hands were, how gentle they could be, how strong and demanding, and her confusion grew. When first she felt and then saw through the shadows that the arm nearest her had begun to move purposefully toward her, she pulled a little away from him without thinking why she did so, but he didn't seem to notice. He merely reached for her and, with apparently no effort at all, slipped his arm beneath her shoulders and drew her to his side.

Her head fitted into the hollow of his shoulders as

though the one had been created for the other, and with his arm around her and the warm length of his body touching hers, she relaxed again, her cheek against his bare chest. She could hear his heart beat and feel her own, and as time passed with comfortable silence between them, hers slowed until its pace matched the steadiness of his.

As though he, too, had been aware of her changing pulse, Chalford moved then, turning toward her, pushing the coverlet away from her with his free hand, then caressing her as though he would test his memory of her body. Without haste, clearly knowing exactly what he was doing, he stirred her senses again, making slow, sensuous love to her until she squirmed with delight beneath him, gasping his name, begging him for release.

Afterward, she lay quietly in his arms again. He had not said a word throughout and she began to think he had fallen asleep. She stirred.

"What is it, sweetheart?"

"Nancy will come."

"So she will."

She could hear the smile in his voice, and awareness of it kindled her temper. "What will you do, sir? Lie here and watch while she dresses me, or leap out of bed to astonish her with your brawny nakedness?"

"The first plan sounds best," he replied.

"Joshua!"

He chuckled. "Very well, I'll go. But 'tis under protest, sweetheart, and only because I am not yet fully acquainted with your Nancy."

"And when you are better acquainted with her?"

"She will know better than to come in when you are in my bed," he responded. There was silence while Adriana digested his words. Then, as he swung his feet to the floor and reached for his breeches, he said over his shoulder, "Miskin might come in then, but your Nancy will not."

Coming swiftly to her knees, Adriana flung her pillow

at him, but it missed because he moved just then to draw the curtains. Gray dawn light flooded the room.

His breeches slung over his shoulder, he turned, grinning. Then, with a chuckle, he said, "Very pretty, my lady, but if Nancy comes in now, she will no doubt suggest that you cover yourself. You needn't do so on my account of course."

Horrified by her wanton posture, Adriana snatched at the covers, pulling them up to her chin, then wished she had something harder than a pillow to throw at him when, still chuckling, he turned away toward the corner door.

When they were both dressed, Miskin served their breakfast in the private parlor, taking the dishes from the inn servants at the door and carrying them to the table before the fire. His attitude was perfectly respectful and correct, but Adriana was embarrassed by his presence, certain that he must be aware of what his master had done the night before, and wondering if he could tell about their morning activities merely by looking at them. She found it hard, too, to look at Chalford, to respond to his remarks in a tone anywhere near as casual as his own.

"Still glad we did not go to Prospect Lodge?" he asked suddenly after a long period of silence.

Her eyes widened and she looked directly at him for the first time since entering the parlor. His words had brought a sudden vision of Sally Villiers to her mind's eye, and it was as though Sally stood there, in that very parlor, one slim hand covering her mouth as she tittered and teased.

"Merciful heavens, yes," Adriana said. "I can just imagine the things Sally would say."

"My goodness me," Chalford said in a mocking falsetto, "what have we been doing all morning, my dear ones?"

Stifling laughter, Adriana shot a glance at the man-servant, but Miskin was at a side table ladling equal portions of sliced fruit in syrup into two compotes and

seemed unaware of their conversation. When she looked
again at her husband to find him smiling warmly at her,
her embarrassment melted away, and she smiled back,
thinking marriage might be rather pleasant. That he had
proved to be not so easily managed as she had hoped
meant only that she would have to exert herself a trifle.

By the time they finished breakfast, their chaise was
ready and they were off. Chalford showed no
inclination to doze this morning and willingly answered
Adriana's questions about the countryside through
which they passed. For the first five miles there were no
villages, only trim hedges, rolling downland, and
occasional cozy-looking white weatherboarded cottages
with neat brown- or yellow-tiled roofs. Chalford
explained that over most of this rolling, grassy land, two
thousand years before, had lain the dense forest known
to the Romans as Silva Anderida. "Even as late as the
fourteenth century," he told her, "it was nearly
roadless and unmapped, impenetrable enough for
Edward the Third to require twenty-two guides to get
him from London to Rye."

"And now it is all gone?"

"Oh, there are woods still, lots of them. You'll see.
But the only thickly forested part nowadays is in the
Weald, to the west of us. The downs are excellent for
growing the world's largest sheep. The rest is fertile,
productive farmland."

"Do you own a lot of tenant farms?" she asked,
recalling the way it had been at Wryde and
remembering, too, Sarah's teasing remarks about a
possible wedding celebration for their tenants.

He shook his head. "Not so many as you might think.
One of the privileges confirmed by the Conqueror was
the 'gavelkind,' whereby land is divided equally among
all a man's sons, instead of going automatically to the
eldest. Thus, we have many small yeoman farms here
instead of a few huge estates. That isn't to say, though,
that I don't help when I can or that local loyalty to
Thunderhill isn't as great as it might be somewhere
else."

Their conversation continued in this desultory fashion, punctuated from time to time by long periods of comfortable silence. They changed horses at Lenham and again at Ashford, the little town at the confluence of two branches of the River Stour.

As the postboys climbed back into their saddles, Chalford said, "Less than ten miles now."

Eagerly, Adriana turned her face to the window again, to watch the passing countryside. Ten miles was nothing. She was certain she could smell the sea in the air already. The road ran along the base of the North Downs, the hills rising to their left, the East Stour on their right, meandering gently alongside the road, narrowing as they left Ashford behind. Large black clouds appeared beyond the river, moving toward them, and the sun was sinking lower in the sky directly behind them. She realized with a start that they were traveling almost due east.

"I thought 'twas the south coast," she said without thinking how cryptic her words might sound.

Chalford smiled. "The coastline from Hythe to Dungeness Point runs north to south," he said. "We are twenty-seven miles west of Calais, thirty northwest of Boulogne. None of that makes it any less the south coast, however, and there will be times, during storms particularly, when you will feel surrounded by the sea at Thunderhill. Our sunrises are spectacular, however, for the sun appears to rise straight out of the sea. And the sunsets over Romney Marsh are no less beautiful."

She gave a little shiver. "A castle on the edge of a marsh sounds like the setting for one of those gothic tales Miranda delights in, Joshua, something about which Monk Lewis would write—damp and dreary, eerie and mysterious."

He chuckled, watching her, delight lighting his eyes. "The marsh holds its mysteries, all right, but it isn't really a marsh at all, you know, only a vast land of water, grass, wind, and solitude, a maze of hedges, dykes, ditches, and roads. Tiny hamlets dot the landscape, sometimes no more than a stone's throw apart, but each one an entity with secrets of its own. Look ahead to that arched stone bridge," he added suddenly.

The bridge was no more than a single ancient arch with sparkling water racing over rounded stones beneath. Adriana could see that the road forked on the far side, the right fork winding steeply up a ridge of the North Downs that looked as though it had somehow shot away from the others.

"The left fork leads to Hythe," Chalford said. There was silence until they reached the midway point on the bridge, Then he said, "Now look up there, on the hill."

Adriana looked and gasped. Thunderhill Castle looked like a child's notion of what King Arthur's castle might have been, like Windsor looked from Eton on a clear day. Built of gray stone, its turreted enclosure walls, curtain walls, and tall, round, pointed towers dominated the crest of the escarpment upon which it sat, looking solid, mighty, impenetrable. The black clouds rising behind it gave the castle an ominous look.

"I didn't know," she whispered. "It's so big."

"Big enough," he agreed. "Once there were a number of these fortresses all along the coast, built to hold England for her Conqueror and his successors. Not many remain, and fewer still are habitable. Only Thunderhill, Arundel, and one or two others. Dover Castle has been turned into a martello tower with a gun battery to defend Dover against Bonaparte's invasion fleet. Other such towers, new ones, are being erected in Hythe and on Dungeness Point. The sea has receded, you see, so although we can see the Channel clearly from the castle, we're too far back from the water for a successful gun emplacement."

"Are we really in danger here?" she asked.

He smiled at her. "In the entire history of England since the late eleventh century, there has been no invasion to speak of. Usurping kings have landed, to be sure, but their armies were here already, so they don't count."

"But one reads in the papers daily that Bonaparte is preparing a huge fleet at Boulogne and means to invade the south coast." She had scoffed at such rumors in the safety of London, but here they did not seem so laughable.

"Well, if he does," Joshua said comfortably, "we shall surely be the first to know. The coastline from the beach below Thunderhill to the mouth of the Rother at Rye provides the best landfall for his ships. There are no steep cliffs to hinder him, and until they get the Military Canal dug, the road across the South Downs remains clear all the way to London."

"You don't sound concerned."

"I'm not, and you needn't be. Aunt Hetta will insist that you stand to be murdered in your bed, but you needn't heed her. She likes to be occupied, and preparing for the invasion is her present object in life."

"What is she like?"

"You'll see." He said no more, and though the castle had disappeared from sight behind a grove of hornbeam and oak as they began the uphill climb, it soon appeared again, its enclosure wall looming above them. The north-lodge gates were open, and it was not long before the chaise rattled across an ancient wooden drawbridge spanning a grassy moat, passed through an equally ancient but well-kept barbican, and emerged in the grassy quadrangle around which the castle was built.

Chalford explained that Thunderhill, like Windsor and Arundel, consisted of two wards or enclosures that were separated by a central mound, dominated by its huge stone keep. West of the quadrangle and its oval gravel drive was the old tilting yard, now a peaceful rose garden. As he finished speaking, the chaise drew up before the main entrance and the sun disappeared behind roiling black clouds.

"Looks like we're here none too soon," he said, eyeing the sky. "By the look of those clouds, it's going to come down pretty heavily."

"It's summer," Adriana protested.

"Only July," he said. "Our best weather comes in August. We'll have some more good thunderstorms before then." Leaning forward to push open the chaise door, he glanced at her searchingly. "I hope you aren't afraid of thunder or lightning."

"Oh, no, of course not," she replied airily. Then, to forestall other such questions, she turned her attention pointedly to the entrance, a tall portico flanked by long colonnades, where a footman could be seen hurrying to meet them. In the shadows behind him, she could see the shapes of other persons moving in his wake.

Chalford ordered the footman to see to the trunks strapped to the chaise, then held out his hands to assist Adriana. By the time she stood firmly upon the ground, they were surrounded by people, but only a moment's glance was necessary to inform her that there were but five persons, three females and two males. One of the men was the second footman, who hastened to help with the trunks. The other was an imposing personage whom she knew must be the butler, Benstead. No nobleman stood with such dignity or bowed with so stately an air.

Before she met Benstead, however, or the house-keeper, Mrs. Motley, she was presented to Lady Adelaide Corbett, a majestic, gray-haired dame of sixty, who was nearly as stately in manner as the butler, and to Lady Adelaide's sister, the Lady Henrietta Blackburn. This lady—smaller, much thinner, and fifteen years younger than Lady Adelaide—had dancing blue eyes and soft brown hair lightly sprinkled with gray. Her unfashionably full skirts arustle, she bubbled up to greet them, smiling and chattering like a child.

"Oh, Joshua, how pretty she is! Lady Chalford, you simply must not stand upon ceremony with us, for we are family, don't you know, and have lived here all our lives, except for my sister's living in Yorkshire when Corbett was alive, of course, and I just expect we are going to get on famously. Will we not, Adelaide?" The last was added with a quick look over her shoulder at the woman standing so erectly behind her.

"Indeed," was the gracious reply.

"Oh, I just know we shall," Lady Henrietta rattled on, "and you will be the greatest help to us, my dear, for there is so much to be done and so little time and so few hands to do it. Do you know, Joshua," she added, turning quickly to confront her nephew, "that absolutely nothing has been done about storage for all the grain and potatoes, let alone for the meat? Goodness knows the free traders can always find storage spaces. You must look into the matter at once."

Adriana pricked up her ears at the casual mention of free traders, but Chalford said only, "Surely I may first step inside, Aunt Hetta. It is beginning to rain."

A flash of lightning lit the quadrangle as though to underscore his statement, and Adriana braced herself, but the thunder did not come immediately, and when it did, it came in muted, distant rolls.

Chalford smiled down at her. "We'd best get you inside, sweetheart, before you get soaked."

They hurried up the steps, across the deep porch, and into the entry hall. This chamber, with its black-and-white-checkered floor and arras-draped walls, was modest compared to what Adriana had expected, its only magnificence provided by the two central columns that appeared to hold up the high, painted ceiling.

"Come in here," Chalford said, taking her elbow and guiding her through a pair of tall, heavily carved doors in the center of the right-hand wall. "I don't know that it will be a great deal warmer, but there will be a fire."

Adriana looked about her wide-eyed, for they had entered the great hall, a huge room with a fan-vaulted ceiling rising two stories above them. There were two fireplaces, set at right angles to each other, one in the north wall, opposite the entrance, and the other in the center of the west wall. Both were large enough for her to stand upright in, had she wished to do so, and both contained huge, roaring fires; however, she quickly discovered that it was necessary to move right into the northwest corner before the heat from either could be felt. Even then she shivered, rubbing her arms through her woolen sleeves.

"Benstead, fetch her ladyship a pot of hot tea," Lady Adelaide ordered, settling her wide skirts as she took her place in a high-backed chair near the north fire.

"Indeed, we should all be grateful for some refreshment. Won't you sit on that green brocade sofa, Lady Chalford?" she added with graceful hauteur. "It is quite the most comfortable seat of the lot."

"Please, call me Adriana, ma'am," Adriana said, striving to sound as sure of herself as Lady Adelaide did and convinced that she had failed miserably. Remembering suddenly that Chalford had expected her to wrest the reins of management from this woman, she felt goose bumps dancing upon her arms.

Lady Adelaide's only response was a regal nod, but Lady Henrietta exclaimed, "How delightful your name is, my dear. *The Comedy of Errors* is quite my favorite of Mr. Shakespeare's plays. So humorous, is it not? But now, Joshua, you simply must attend to me. We shall soon have a crisis if you do not. Adelaide says the matter is not urgent, but pray tell me, if you will, just what we are to do with all that food if we have no proper place in which to store it when the time comes to do so?"

"Let the man sit down, Hetta," commanded Lady Adelaide sternly, signing to a footman to move the fire screen so that it shielded her somewhat from the heat of the leaping flames. Once she was satisfied as to its placement, she looked at Adriana and said, "I am persuaded you must be wondering what all the fuss is about. My sister is deeply concerned lest that Bonaparte fellow send his little ships to land upon our beaches. He won't, of course," she added, as though to do such a thing would be a social solecism. "The French never have done so, and I daresay they never will. A disorganized people, the lot of them."

"Well, I must say," protested Lady Hetta. "And what about the Conqueror, if one might ask?"

"I daresay one need not consider a deed that took place over seven hundred years ago," replied Lady Adelaide placidly. "Now, pray, do not interrupt again, Hetta. Such a habit is unbecoming. As I was explaining, Adriana, there are some who believe that if the French do land here, the way to confound them is to remove all the foodstuffs from their path. The first plan was to burn everything, but of course few people would tolerate such foolish waste, so now the plan is to harvest every seed and grain stalk, kill every sheep and cow, and to store the food in secret places. Only, of course, no one thought about where those secret places might be. So they are at a standstill, which, of course, was to be expected," she added with a basilisk eye upon her sister.

"You may scoff, Adelaide," said Lady Henrietta bravely, "but you cannot deny that French ships have been seen nearly every day off their coast. Dozens of them," she added dramatically.

"Not off our coast, however," retorted Lady Adelaide, "and they certainly dare not land here. Where is your home, Adriana?"

This diversionary tactic proved successful, and both ladies listened with interest as Adriana told them about Wryde and the Wiltshire countryside in which it lay. She did not mention such crass topics as gaming debts or incapacity due to port, of course, and the conversation went smoothly. Lady Adelaide acknowledged previous awareness of Lord Wryde's title, but admitted that she did not know the Barrington family. "That you come from Wiltshire accounts for it," she said grandly. "From some odd cause or other, I know very few persons in Wiltshire."

They finished their tea, and Lady Adelaide offered to show Adriana to her rooms, but Chalford shook his head, saying, "I reserve that privilege unto myself, ma'am, if you please."

He took Adriana's hand as she arose from the little sofa, and led her across the entry hall, through the lavender-and-white dining room with its long, highly polished table, and into the principal stair hall. At the top of the wide, winding stairs he turned right, into a comfortably appointed drawing room, its tall, arched, leaded windows facing east to the Channel.

"This is the marchioness's sitting room," he said as

Adriana hurried to look out the nearest window. "Your bedchamber is through that door yonder, and your dressing room, too. There is no door to the bedchamber from the long gallery, but there is one to the dressing room, so you have access to the rest of this floor without always having to pass through the stair hall."

She had just realized that, thanks to the curve of the hill atop which the castle sat, she could now see over the enclosure walls. Jagged flashes of lightning lit the dark-gray sky above the Channel, and she could see that the tide was running high, that whitecaps glistened on the waves. Still, she heard every word Chalford said to her, and when he was silent, she turned.

"Where is your bedchamber, sir?"

He smiled. "Across the stair hall, the door opposite this one. Would you like to see it?"

She nodded, then easily interpreting the gleam that leapt to his eyes, she repressed her own stirring desire and added firmly, "I would also like to see the rest of this place, if you please."

His sigh was melancholy. "Very well, but you won't see it all today, I'm afraid. There are over a hundred rooms, including chambers and halls that are little more than ancient ruins, particularly those nearest the keep."

"Is the keep habitable?"

"A portion of the lower section could be, I suppose, but for the most part, it's inhabited by owls. My sister suggested turning the whole place into quarters for guests, but we couldn't think of what to do with Sir Francis and his friends."

"Sir Francis?"

"Sir Francis Drake, Sir Walter Raleigh, Lady Jersey, Lord North, Norfolk, and other such notables live there —in fact, the owls. My grandfather and grandmother named the first of them after famous and infamous Englishmen, and the tradition has continued. The latest is his highness the Prince of Wales."

She chuckled. "I want to see them one day."

"Of course, but for now, I suggest you satisfy

yourself by exploring the hall block. Most of the rooms we use are here and on the ground floor. There is a central block and two flanking wings. My aunts' chambers are on this floor in the south wing, above the state apartments. My bedchamber is in the northeast tower, and the library is in the north wing on this floor with an outside stairway. Once you get those landmarks firmly fixed in your memory, you will have no difficulty finding your way about.''

''Where are the kitchens and the housekeeper's rooms?''

''Below my bedchamber and the library. Actually, the kitchen proper is in the basement, but there is an upper chamber, which includes the butler's pantry just north of the dining room, by the stair hall.'' He laughed at her look of bewilderment. ''Never mind, you'll learn. For now, let us look at the long gallery.''

They passed out of the drawing room, back into the stair hall, and turned left, emerging through a pair of carved doors upon a gallery fully two hundred feet long, its length punctuated on the west side by a series of tall, narrow windows that overlooked the quadrangle. Adriana realized then that the long gallery was directly above the colonnade. The east wall was hung with portraits of the Blackburn and de Tonnere families dating, Chalford told her, to the thirteenth century. He pointed out portraits of his parents, but when she asked him to tell her about them, he said only that, since they had both died when he was young, he scarcely remembered them.

When their tour was done, Adriana was more confused than ever. Out of a wealth of information, she remembered little more than that the southeast-tower room off the long gallery, which had served the ladies of the family as a morning room for many years, had recently been turned into a breakfast parlor. Chalford had laughingly explained to her that, although the change meant the servants, at great inconvenience to themselves, had to carry the breakfast dishes the full

length of the hall block and up the second stair, the
change provided a more convenient location for the
aunts to break their fast.

"And that, I need not tell you, is what counts with
Aunt Adelaide," he added, his eyes atwinkle.

"But you are master here, are you not?"

"I am." He smiled at her. "Do you think I allow my
aunt to rule to roast?"

She was sure, having seen Aunt Adelaide, that he
must, but she knew it would be impolite to say so.
Instead, she said, "If the inconvenience to the servants
is so great, then—"

"The castle is not run for the convenience of the
servants," he retorted lightly. "If the food were to come
cold to the table, certainly other arrangements would be
necessary, but there are warming dishes on the sideboard, and one cannot deny that the southeast room is
more pleasant in the morning than the dining room.
Before, the dining room must have seemed a day's
march on an empty stomach for the aunts. And," he
added with another chuckle, "Aunt Adelaide
complained that the scenes carved in the plaster there
discouraged her matutinal appetite."

Adriana was able to examine the dining room and
judge these scenes for herself at the supper table. The
lavender walls set off the white plasterwork carvings
nicely, displaying a veritable paean to Bacchus. The
overmantel depicted a sacrifice to the god with fat
garlands of vines tumbling over the sides of a basket
supported by two snarling panthers. The same vines
decorated the fireplace surround as well as the many
empty rococo frames carved into the walls at points
equally spaced about the room.

"I see you are looking at the frames, Adriana," said
Lady Adelaide when she had been served from a platter
of sliced beef. "I had the pictures removed after my
brother's death."

"Removed, ma'am?"

"My father, the ninth marquess, had a penchant for
hunting scenes and still lifes of dead game. Not suitable

for a dining room, I believe. The hunting horns, foxes' masks, and bows and arrows entwined with the vine leaves in the frames, though engagingly symmetrical, do not please me either, but Chalford has a liking for them, as he does for that dreadful eagle hovering over us. Thus, they remain. I do not choose to look upon them."

Unable to help herself, Adriana looked up to see that at the center of the ceiling there was indeed a great plaster eagle, its wings outspread, its long, sharp, gilded talons curling around the chain that suspended the giant chandelier above the table. Light from the many candles made the eagle's eyes glitter and gave its golden beak a threatening prominence. She looked away, only to encounter her husband's gaze instead. Chalford's eyes were lit with amusement.

"Tell us more about your family, Adriana dear," Lady Henrietta said then. "You mentioned earlier that you have a brother and a sister—just as Chalford does —but you did not tell us very much about them. Are they both married?"

Adriana smiled at her and willingly described her siblings, Miranda in warm tones and Alston as diplomatically as she could, adding, "Since my father is in poor health and dislikes going into company, I was married from my brother's house. My sister and my best friend, Sarah, Lady Clifford, stood up with me."

The discussion passed to the wedding guests, and Adriana discovered that the Lady Henrietta had a passion for gossip, particularly gossip having to do with members of the *beau monde*. She wanted to hear about Emily Lamb's recent marriage to the Earl Cowper and was willing to discuss the royal family at length.

"With whom did you pass the night, Adriana?" asked Lady Adelaide suddenly in the midst of an exchange of information regarding the latest reports of the king's health.

"We stayed in Maidstone," Chalford put in quickly, thus sparing Adriana's blushes. Then, without taking so much as a breath, he turned to Lady Henrietta and asked her to tell him more about her recent activities on behalf of the neighborhood. "For I am persuaded you have done a great deal more than organize the potential devastation of the countryside," he said.

"Indeed, yes," she assured him. "Everyone is making inventories of their possessions, there are plans to flood the marsh if necessary, and men have boomed the entrance to Thunderhill Bay. If you bring the *Sea Dragon* into the harbor, you must have one of the lads show you how you must go, though your captain might already know, I suppose."

"Goodness," Adriana said, "how does one boom a harbor?"

"Logs are chained across most of the entrance," Chalford explained with a grin. "They float beneath the surface and wreak havoc with ships trying to make landfall, particularly at night."

"An unnecessary obstruction to shipping," pronounced Lady Adelaide, signing for the servants to clear the first course.

Adriana looked around, wondering who would see the signal, for there was no servant in the room. Then she noticed an arched sideboard on the north wall that had small jib doors on each side leading to the butler's pantry. Mirrored panels on the reveals of the arch allowed the butler and footmen to survey the table even though they were outside the room, out of hearing. The niche also gave added prominence to the display of gold and silver plate massed on the sideboard in the French manner, flanking a formal pyramid of apricots, peaches, and grapes.

Her attention was drawn back almost immediately to her companions, particularly to Lady Henrietta, who was once again defending her project to her sister. "Really, Adelaide, you must not underestimate the danger. You have said yourself, any number of times, that the French are not to be trusted. We might all be murdered in our beds if proper precautions are not taken."

Although Chalford shot Adriana a look that sorely

tried her equanimity, reminding her as it did of his prediction earlier in the day, Lady Adelaide did not so far forget her dignity as to enter into argument upon the subject. Her opinion was clear nonetheless, and Adriana had no difficulty under these circumstances in believing that Lady Henrietta exaggerated the danger. Thus it was that when she was awakened late that very same night by Lady Henrietta's shrieks that the French had landed at last, she sat bolt upright in Chalford's bed, stiff with terror.

4

The bedchamber door had been flung wide, and Lady Henrietta stood upon the threshold, her thin figure outlined by light from the stair-hall window behind her. The sound of her sobbing breaths carried easily to the bed, and the echo of her shrieks seemed to linger in the air.

Chalford's arm was around Adriana now, and her own breathing, in consequence, was calmer. At the sound of his deep voice, she felt calmer still. "What exactly leads you to believe the French have landed, Aunt Hetta?" he asked.

"I've seen them, that's what," she gasped. She was holding herself upright by clinging to the door frame.

Adriana slipped quickly from the shelter of Chalford's arm and, heedless despite her thin nightdress of the damp chill in the air, hurried to Lady Hetta's side, saying anxiously, "Come, ma'am, sit down. So much excitement cannot be good for you."

"We've no time to rest, child. The castle must be aroused. The men must take up arms."

Chalford was also up now, shouting for his man-servant as he slipped into a pair of breeches and moved to light a candle from the banked embers in the fireplace. "Where did you see these Frenchmen?" he asked as he got to his feet again.

"On the beach below my window, of course. Do you think it wise to show a light, Joshua?"

He chuckled. "If the Frenchies can see this candle from a beach on the other side of the castle, they've got mighty fine eyesight, Aunt Hetta. Now what, precisely, did you see?"

"Lights on the beach where there oughtn't to be any," she replied testily. "Oh, if only Adelaide had listened when I begged her to help us. With her directing the others, so much more might have been accomplished."

"How many lights?"

"Three or four. There is no moon, but I saw shadows. The clouds have broken and the reflection of the stars in the water gives light to the beach. I daresay they expected the storm clouds to give them more cover. Oh, do hurry, Joshua. We must waken everyone. I sent my maid to rouse the other maidservants and I tried to waken Adelaide, but of course she would only say she meant to sleep, regardless, and that dreadful woman of hers would not let me enter the room to try to make her listen to me."

"Take heart, ma'am, it would take an intrepid Frenchman to breach those defenses. Ah, here you are, Miskin," he added, turning toward the dressing-room door, upon the threshold of which stood his manservant in hastily donned breeches and shirt, awaiting his instructions. "Her ladyship believes the French have landed on the beach below the castle. Rouse a few of the men and see what there is to see, will you?"

"Yes, my lord, at once," replied his man without batting an eyelash. It was, Adriana thought, watching him, as though his master issued such orders daily.

Chalford turned his attention to his aunt. "There, you see, ma'am, all is in train now. Miskin will rout them in a trice."

"A manservant and a few footmen to stand against the French navy, Joshua? You cannot be serious. Fortunately, Martha and the other maids will have begun to rouse the menservants by now."

"Well, I cannot help but think you will wish later that you had not acted in so precipitate a manner, ma'am, for I must own that I see little likelihood of your intruders proving to be members of the French navy. I daresay that if they were, you would have noticed more than three or four lights, and I'm quite sure that you would have seen the bulk of more than one ship on the water. You did not mention seeing even one."

"Well, no," she confessed, "though to be sure one cannot see all of the bay from my window. I am persuaded there must be a ship down there somewhere."

"Yes, very likely, but not more than one, I'll wager. Can you not realize what it is you must have seen, ma'am?"

While she thought the matter over, he took the opportunity to light several more candles, and this time she made no protest. Adriana looked from one to the other in bewilderment.

When Lady Henrietta spoke at last, her voice was smaller. "Do you truly think that is all it is, Joshua?"

He nodded. " 'Tis a dark night, and whoever landed made it past your entrance booms, which argues an excellent spotsman. The French would not have been so fortunate, or so skillful."

"Who would?" Adriana demanded. "What's a spotsman?"

Chalford grinned at her, and Lady Henrietta said with a sigh of resignation, "Free traders."

"Smugglers!" Adriana's eyes widened with excitement, and she stared from one to the other. "Right here on your beach?"

"Our beach," Chalford said, smiling at her. "I'm nearly certain of it, and 'spotsman' is smuggler's slang for one who can bring a boat in on the darkest night to a precise landfall."

His calm manner reminded her of what she had heard about the attitude in Kent toward the "Gentlemen," as they were called, and she nodded wisely. "I see. Nothing to fear, then."

"Nothing at all," he agreed. "Aunt Henrietta will suffer some joking when it becomes known that she mistook the Gentlemen for Frenchies, but that is all."

"All!" Lady Henrietta regarded him with an air of reproach. "That is very easy for you to say. Can you not imagine what odious observations Adelaide will make when she hears of this?''

Laughing at her, Chalford pulled the bell cord. "Since the servants are up and about, you might as well have a cup of tea to soothe your nerves, ma'am. I mean to have something stronger, myself. Miskin will bring word to us soon enough."

They had their refreshment before the fire, which Chalford had poked into flames again, and Miskin entered the room soon after the tea had been served.

"As you expected, m'lord, no more than a small run in progress. The lads and me thought it best to allow the Gentlemen to get on with their business undisturbed."

"Wise of you," Chalford said. "How many were there?"

"Thirty or thereabouts. We observed them from the cliff path. The tub lines were still attached to the cutter when we turned back to the castle, but I believe most of the tubs had been hauled ashore. The goods were disappearing into the marsh as quick as the men could carry them, so I doubt there'll be a sign of life in half an hour."

"There, you see, Aunt Hetta, you can go back to bed without fearing further disturbance."

She glared at him. "It would serve them right to have the riding officer descend upon them, scaring me as they did."

"I'll wager Mr. Petticrow's nearer Dymchurch than Hythe tonight," Chalford said, turning with a smile to add for Adriana's benefit, "No one knows the riding officer's habits better than the men he's trying to catch."

"There's only one officer?"

"One for each five miles of coastline. Even if the Gentlemen didn't make it their business to know his schedule, keeping him under observation would be easy enough."

"But how can they know before they land where he will be?"

"Bless you, sweetheart, our local smugglers aren't seamen. They keep their feet firmly on dry earth. The ships come in from France or Holland, and they don't sail into harbor without a signal from shore telling them it's safe to do so."

"There are no English ships involved in the smuggling?"

"Oh, no, a good many of them are English. I just meant the sailors generally stay aboard ship and the landsmen deal with the goods that come ashore. Once they disappear into Romney Marsh, I'd defy any man, alone, to follow them. I told you what a maze it is of roads, dykes, ditches, and hedges, and since it's impossible to find anyone in Kent or Sussex who will agree to act as riding officer, the men in that position are at a great disadvantage from the outset in knowing so little of the countryside. Our present man is from Berkshire. Even if he did know Kent well, one man would stand no chance against so many."

"They would kill him?" Her eyes were rounder yet.

He shrugged. "That has certainly been known to happen, but it is unlikely nowadays, since the Gentlemen have only to intercept the officer and render him helpless long enough to get the goods to safety. There is no need to kill him."

Lady Henrietta said firmly, "I am persuaded that no one could be so degraded as to wish harm to Mr. Petticrow, who has always been all that is kind. Why, when the Payton child in Lydd was injured falling from the roof of his cottage—where he'd no business to be in the first place—it was Mr. Petticrow who rode his horse all the way to Hythe to fetch Dr. Simmons, who knows more than Dr. Bailey in—"

"Yes, Aunt Hetta, to be sure," Chalford cut in gently. "Mr. Petticrow is a kind man, as anyone will agree, but if he has made any significant progress against the local Gentlemen, I for one will be surprised to learn of it."

Lady Hetta frowned, then said with dignity, " 'Tis a

very difficult job, Joshua, and he is not, perhaps, a very clever thinker, but he is a vast improvement over that dreadful Mr. Hensby, who preceded him here. Remember how shocked we all were when he ordered a patrol to search the church during Sunday service? The very idea! Marching right up the center aisle, even into our private chapel. Desecration!"

"The church," exclaimed Adriana, looking from one to the other. "Surely not!"

Chalford looked at her, dark eyes atwinkle. "Not very wise of him, certainly. That was Hensby's last official act, over six months ago. We have had Mr. Petticrow since then. I rather think Hensby was a young man more to be pitied than otherwise."

"Joshua, how can you say so?" Lady Henrietta demanded indignantly. "Our very own church!"

"And the first time within memory, I daresay, that there was nothing in its cellars or belfry that did not belong there," retorted her nephew. "Really, Aunt Hetta, can you doubt for one moment that someone slipped the information to poor Hensby with the intention of causing just such an incident as that raid? There was nothing his superiors could do once the members of the congregation were roused to fury, as they were, other than to send Hensby packing." He smiled at Adriana. "Hensby, I might add, was a zealous young officer with a persistent curiosity, who annoyed the Gentlemen much more than does Mr. Petticrow." He glanced at Lady Henrietta, surprising her in the act of covering a large yawn. "Back to bed for you, ma'am. I daresay there will be no more alarms tonight."

"I shall sleep all day tomorrow," declared Lady Henrietta, getting obediently to her feet and setting her teacup on the side table. "I do not wish to hear what Adelaide will have to say about this uproar." She left them, adjusting her nightcap and clutching her dressing gown tightly around her thin form.

Adriana looked up at her husband with a smile. "Will she really?" she asked. "Stay in bed, that is?"

He chuckled. "She is neither wise enough nor lazy enough to do so. I'll wager she breaks her fast in the morning room."

Morning dawned grimly gray, with large black clouds looming threateningly over the Channel, the waters of which were just as cheerless. Adriana, upon rising, gazed out the bedchamber window in dismay. Her hopes having been raised by starry skies in the middle of the night, she found it annoying to be faced by storm clouds at dawn and informed her husband that Thunderhill's weather did little to detract from its gothic atmosphere.

"Content yourself with the knowledge that the weather must be just as bad at Brighton," he replied lightly.

"Yes, but all our friends would be there," she reminded him. "There would be amusements, things to do, and people to talk to."

"You will have plenty to do here," he said. "There are, after all, people and amusements at Thunderhill, too."

Surprised by a sudden, sharp surge of anger that threatened to overcome her, Adriana dared not trust her tongue, so without another word she turned her back upon him and hurried to her dressing room, where she found Nancy waiting for her. Before she had finished dressing, however, the door from the long gallery opened without ceremony, and Chalford stood there, his temper apparently unruffled, his attitude seemingly no more than that of a gentleman wishing to escort his wife to breakfast.

It occurred to Adriana, accustomed as she was to certain nuances of masculine temper, that perhaps he was restraining his annoyance with her out of regard for Nancy's presence, so once they were alone in the long gallery with the door to the dressing room firmly shut again, she looked at him uncertainly.

He smiled at her. "Hungry?"

Her impulsive tongue threatened to betray her again, but she held back the sharp words, aware that she would sound childish if she snapped at him now, particularly when she was not certain why she was angry but had an uncomfortable, gnawing suspicion that it was because her walking out like she had had failed to annoy him. Telling herself firmly that to be married to a man who did not indulge in flights of temper was a vast improvement over what she had known before, she nodded in dignified response to his question, and allowed him to tuck her hand in the crook of his elbow. Thus, they entered the cheerful yellow-and-white breakfast parlor, looking the very picture of connubial content.

As Chalford had predicted, both aunts were present, sitting opposite each other at the round mahogany table. The silence in the room was nearly palpable, the only sound being the whisper of the middle-aged second footman's movements as he lifted covers and stirred the contents of one dish after another. At their entrance, he turned from his task to hold Adriana's chair.

"Good morning, Lady Adelaide," she said, sitting.

"Good morning," replied that lady with a regal nod. "I trust that Hetta's nonsense did not undo your rest."

"Not at all, ma'am." She turned to Lady Hetta, who had not looked away from her plate, and said gently, "Good morning. I hope you were also able to get back to sleep."

"Oh, yes," murmured her ladyship, bobbing her head. "Good morning, Joshua dear."

"For goodness' sake, Hetta," said Lady Adelaide, "stop sulking and sit properly. You've made a fool of yourself and been scolded for it, but it is scarcely the first time and I daresay it will not be the last. This cowed attitude of yours is most unbecoming, and I cannot think why you cultivate it. Sit up at once and behave yourself like a proper gentlewoman."

"Yes, Adelaide, I beg your pardon," said Lady Hetta, straightening obediently. "I fear I have the headache a little."

"And no wonder, up at all hours as you were, rousing the household to no purpose whatever. You deserve to have the headache. I am sure it is no wonder that we do not all have the headache. It is surely no fault of yours that we do not.''

''Oh, pray, ma'am, do not scold her anymore,'' Adriana begged impulsively. ''I am sure a great many people are worried that the French will invade England, and only think if it should really come to pass and Lady Henrietta should chance to be the first to give the alarm. 'Twould be most exciting and heroic.''

'' 'Twould be entirely apocryphal,'' said Lady Adelaide. ''Even the French are not so foolhardy as to attempt to invade England's shores. Nor are they skillful enough to do the thing properly if they were to attempt it. There is nothing whatever to fear.''

Lady Henrietta stiffened and her little pointed chin rose determinedly. ''We are half again as close to Boulogne, Adelaide, as we are to London, and the harbor at Boulogne, as everyone knows, is where Bonaparte's flotilla gathers and daily grows larger and more menacing. We watch from our own windows while the Military Canal is being dug at the bottom of our hill, but it is no more than laid out now, across Romney Marsh to Rye. Its length—the dug-out part—can be measured in yards. Pray, what protection do you suppose it will offer us when it cannot possibly be finished for months, even years, to come?''

'' 'Twas a foolish notion at best,'' replied her sister. ''I daresay that children will one day fish in it, and that it will therefore then serve some useful purpose, but as a defense it is laughable, so 'tis fortunate it is not necessary. England still rules the seas, and our coasts are defended perfectly well.''

''Oh, dear, how can you say so when we have fifty miles of beaches that are well nigh defenseless?''

Lady Adelaide sniffed. ''I do not propose to dignify that foolish question with a response, Hetta. Furthermore, it is not a suitable topic for the breakfast table.'' She turned to the footman. ''His lordship will wish to have fresh coffee, Amos, and Lady Chalford will have a pot of tea. See to it as soon as you have served them, if you please.''

"Aye, m'lady." The footman, who had been serving Chalford, bowed and moved on to attend to Adriana, who had been looking, wide-eyed, from one aunt to the other.

She recollected herself swiftly and, being very hungry, paid little heed to the conversation between the others until such time as Lady Adelaide said imperiously, "You say, Joshua, that you have invited houseguests to stay. May one ask how many are to be expected and when they may be expected to arrive?"

"And how long will they stay with us?" asked Lady Henrietta, brightening at this agreeable change of subject. "I think it will be most stimulating to have houseguests."

Chalford smiled at her, then turned toward Lady Adelaide. "I cannot answer your questions, ma'am, for I do not know all the answers. The weather must play some part, you know, for it is likely that some of our guests will elect to remain in town until it clears. Otherwise, we may expect guests daily, for I told everyone to stand on no ceremony, merely to come if and when they like and to stay as long as they like."

"Well, I am sure you have every right to issue such broad invitations, Joshua," said Lady Adelaide in a tone that belied her words, "but you might have considered how much easier it will be for your servants to prepare for guests if they can be told how many to prepare for and when to expect them."

"It cannot matter," said Chalford. "There is plenty of room, and we have never yet run out of food." The words were said lightly, but he continued to look steadily at Lady Adelaide, and to Adriana's surprise she nodded and looked away first.

"As you say, Joshua."

Lady Hetta said suddenly, "You must have been very sorry, my dear Adriana, to have been married without your father by you to give you into Joshua's keeping, but I daresay that with everything happening so quickly, there was no alternative."

"Such haste," Lady Adelaide interjected before

Adriana could reply to this abrupt statement, "as well as the fact that you were married from your brother's house, Adriana, indicates that you must have been married without banns."

Adriana smiled at her. "For that, you must blame my brother, Alston, ma'am. He insisted upon a special license, you see. I daresay," she added with a smile, "he wished to be rid of me quickly, once he had found someone willing to marry me."

"It was I who suggested the special license, sweetheart," Chalford said. "I am an impatient man, so once I discovered there was no thought of your father's attending the ceremony, I'm afraid the notion of waiting three whole weeks before being allowed to claim you for my own became intolerable."

"Waiting three weeks to get back to Thunderhill is more the case," Lady Hetta said, chuckling. "We know, for Lydia wrote in her last letter, ages ago, that you had had your fill of London."

Adriana, who had glowed at her husband's words, experienced deflation at Lady Hetta's. She looked at Chalford now, keenly. "I am sure Alston said he'd decided upon a special license in order that we might be married from the house instead of at the church. 'Twas too public at Saint George's, he said."

"Yes, he said that," Chalford agreed, "but we both wanted the matter finished quickly, and banns do take three weeks."

"Banns are common," declared Lady Adelaide. "To have one's name shouted out in church three weeks running . . . Well, no person of gentle breeding could wish for such a thing. Much better, too, to have had the ceremony in a private house where one is not subjected to the stares of strangers. You did right, Chalford. I am pleased with you."

Adriana looked searchingly at her husband. "Did you truly wish only to get home quickly, sir?"

He returned her look. "I always wish to get home, sweetheart, and this time more than ever. After all, I was bringing you with me, was I not? To kick our heels in London once the business was agreed upon seemed absurd when to avoid such a course would take no more than the greasing of a fist or two."

"You make the special license sound like a bribe."

"Well, is it anything less? One pays handsomely for the privilege of being married in one's own good time, outside the church. I agree with Aunt Adelaide, in that I should not have liked hearing my name or yours shouted out in public, nor would I have liked our being gawked at by the common mob, which is what would have happened had we been married at Saint George's. A special license was more sensible, all 'round."

Adriana was silent, scarcely listening as Lady Henrietta hastened to assure her that Chalford spoke the truth, that she would not have liked the publicness of banns or a church wedding either. Adriana didn't believe for a moment that such factors had anything to do with anything. Lady Hetta had been right before in saying that he had merely wished to get home.

Though Miranda had insisted that Chalford had fallen head over ears in love, and though Adriana had been given more than one reason to hope that might be the case, it was not. He had simply found a wife, a suitable mistress for Thunderhill. The fact of the matter was, she decided, that she had married a man who was already married to his home. Prying him out of a castle that came first in importance with him was going to prove a major undertaking and no mistake, but prying him out was becoming hourly more important if she was not to be buried alive there.

"May one ask how many we are to expect?" asked Lady Adelaide when, the wedding having been fully discussed, the subject of the visitors had come up again.

"Of course," Chalford replied, smiling at her. "I invited a good many, because I thought it would help Adriana adjust to her new home if she had lots of her friends around her. I daresay we shan't have more than ten or a dozen at a time, though, so there is no need for any extraordinary preparation."

Adriana blinked at him. She remembered with a

shudder the sort of upheaval that had occurred at
Wryde whenever guests of any number were
anticipated. How could Chalford be so casual about ten
or a dozen arrivals?

Lady Adelaide nodded, however, and over the next
few days, Adriana learned that, just as he had said,
there had been no need for alarm. Guests arrived and
were dispatched to bedchambers without the least
upheaval or rearrangement of their routine.

Viscount and Lady Villiers were the first to arrive,
late Monday afternoon. Sunday had continued stormy,
with heavy rain into the night, but by midmorning
Monday the skies began to clear, and when the stately
barouche lumbered into the quadrangle and up to the
entrance of the castle, it could be seen that the
coachman, though bundled in yellow oilskins, was perfectly dry.

Adriana saw them from the long gallery and hurried
downstairs, grateful that she had decided to dress in one
of her most becoming gowns in order to offset the
gloom of the day. Her rounded bodice and puffed
sleeves were in the latest fashion, as were the high waist
and slim skirt of the green gauze gown. If the dress did
little to protect her from the chilly drafts in the castle,
she ignored that detail, particularly now with Sally just
stepping down from her carriage. Not for worlds would
Adriana trade fashion for comfort. Feeling with one
hand to be certain that her tawny hair, dressed by Nancy
in a riot of curls atop her head, was still neatly confined
there by her pale-green bandeau, she hurried down to
greet her first houseguests. Only when she reached the
entry hall did it occur to her that a marchioness ought
properly to receive visitors in her drawing room.

Lady Henrietta, however, was already in the entry
hall. "Who is it? Do you know? Oh, isn't this exciting?
I cannot think when it was that we last had real houseguests—other than Lydia and the children, of course, or
Ned and Molly, or one of Chalford's schoolfriends, you
know. Oh, who is this, my dear?"

Adriana had a sudden sense of being carried back in

time. Many times in the days before her mother's death had she perched in the curve of the grand stairway at Wryde to peer through the banister at newly arriving guests, wondering who they were and how long they would stay. Lady Hetta made her feel like one of a pair of conspiring children. She smiled at her. " 'Tis Viscount and Lady Villiers,'' she said in a low voice. "He is Lord Jersey's son and she—"

"Oh, yes, of course, I know all about Sally Fane," said Lady Hetta, her cheeks reddening slightly. "Or all about her poor mother, that is. I think it was dreadfully unkind of Sarah Child's father to leave all his money away from her and her husband to her daughter, don't you know. A wicked thing."

"Well, it made Sally Fane the greatest heiress of our time," said Adriana with a small sigh. "She took London by storm. Left the rest of us standing entirely in the shade."

"Oh, I do hope Adelaide will be civil to her."

"Why on earth would she not be?"

"Well, my dear," Lady Hetta confided, "banking is all very well in its way. Indeed, I do not know how we should go on without them—bankers, I mean. But it is still trade, don't you know? At least, so Adelaide regards it, and though dear Sally Fane's papa is the Earl of Westmorland—not that I've heard much good of that man, I can tell you—her money derives from Robert Child, who was only a banker when all is said and done."

Adriana choked on laughter. "But, my dear ma'am—" She could say no more, for the front doors were open wide, their guests on the point of entering the hall. Adriana hurried forward, her hands held out in welcome. " Sally . . . my lord, how very kind of you to visit us so soon."

"Well, my goodness me, what else could we do?" demanded the slender, brown-haired young lady who swept forward to fling her arms about Adriana. "You were so rude and ungracious as to refuse our invitation to spend your wedding n—"

"Now, Sally," interrupted Chalford calmly, having come from the great hall, behind Adriana, "you know better than that. May I present my aunt, Lady Henrietta Blackburn. Aunt Hetta, this is Lady Villiers." He stepped past them then and clapped the viscount on the shoulder, adding, "And her husband. Villiers, well met. Welcome to Thunderhill."

"Passable little cottage you've got here, Chalford," said the viscount gravely. "A touch of paint and a new shingle here and about, and it ought to be snug enough for the pair of you. Humbug country, though, man. Can't expect guests during the hunting season, any more than we expect them at Prospect Lodge. You'll have to come to us at Osterley Park, or better yet, spend a month with me at Middleton Stony. I'll show you sport."

"And show me a clean pair of heels," retorted Chalford, laughing. He looked at the others. "No finer seat in the hunting field than Villiers'. He shows them all the way."

"Oh, goodness me, yes," chirped Sally. "George looks simply like a god or something when he's on a horse. You never saw his equal for sport. Why, everyone says so, don't they, George?"

The viscount beamed at her, then looked at the others as though he were inviting them to beam at her, too. "It would scarcely become me to agree with you, my dear, particularly when Chalford is like to know, if his lady does not, that I overturned us in my curricle, most ignominiously, not two weeks ago."

"Gracious," exclaimed Lady Hetta, "I hope you weren't hurt."

"Bruised but not broken," Villiers assured her.

" 'Tis nearer three weeks ago," Sally said, "and you did not overturn us." She glanced from one to another of her audience. "It was the most awful thing, for we were thrown out. The pole broke, and if George had not been quick to turn us against a post when the horses bolted, we might have been killed."

"As it was," Villiers said dryly, "the force of our

meeting with the post caused us to fly out of the curricle like a pair of damned birds. Do you mean to entertain us right here, Chalford, or does this hovel of yours have another room?''

Adriana's amused gaze collided with that of the young third footman, who looked scandalized. Chuckling, she glanced at Sally, whose dark-brown eyes were alight with laughter, and said, "I think we had better repair to the great hall, don't you?''

"Goodness me, does this place actually boast a great hall?''

"Now, Sally," Chalford said, "you know it must. It's got a keep, too, like any decent castle ought to have.''

"Oh!" exclaimed Lady Hetta, suddenly looking from Lord to Lady Villiers in dismay. "Joshua, what if—?'' She broke off, staring at her nephew helplessly.

He looked back, bewildered, and Adriana, not knowing what to make of the pair of them, leapt into the breach. "There are owls living in the keep," she said. "Some of them have the most amusing names.''

Chalford choked, looked again at his aunt, and then burst into laughter. "You must come and meet them after supper," he said. "One of them"—he grinned at Villiers—"is named after your illustrious mama.''

"My goodness me," said Sally with an appreciative chuckle.

5

Lord and Lady Villiers planned to stay only three nights at Thunderhill, because, as Sally confided to Adriana, his lordship's parents expected to descend upon them at Prospect Lodge the week following the Prince of Wales's birthday. "For George's birthday is that Monday, you see," she explained early that evening as they descended the stairs in the keep after a brief, chilly, and disappointingly dimly lit expedition to visit the owls in their noisesome abode. "It gives us barely the month in Brighton. You are so fortunate that Chalford's mama is deceased, Adriana."

"Sally, what a dreadful thing to say!"

"Yes, isn't it," Sally agreed complacently as she lifted the skirt of her pale-blue crepe gown a bit higher, "but my goodness me, only think if you had my mama-in-law looking down her nose at you all the time. I daresay no one ever thought to name a fat, haughty owl after the tenth Marchioness of Chalford."

Adriana's amber gauze dinner gown covered less of her than the green dress she had worn earlier, and she paused on a step to rub her bare arms in an attempt to warm them. Though she had never known the tenth marchioness, she had had the experience of meeting Lady Jersey on more than one memorable occasion and might well have expressed agreement with Sally's feelings had it been within the realm of propriety to do so. She said instead, "Though I do not have a mama-in-law, I do have Lady Adelaide, and I certainly have no wish for her demise."

Sally waved Lady Adelaide away with an airy gesture. " 'Tis not by any means the same thing, I promise you.

Why, my goodness me, Adriana, can you imagine Lady Adelaide carrying on a practically public love affair with the Prince of Wales or putting evil-smelling stuff in his wife's hair on their wedding night just to put the prince off bedding her?''

Choking with suppressed laughter, Adriana looked quickly over her shoulder to see if the men were near enough to overhear them, hissing as she did so, ''Sally, you mustn't.''

''They cannot hear us,'' Sally said, ''and, goodness me, even if they could, do you not think George knows how I feel about his mama? He is not overfond of her himself.''

''Still, you must sometimes make life difficult for him,'' Adriana said quietly, glancing back again. The men were well behind them on the torchlit staircase that wound down the inner wall of the keep, and although she could hear only murmuring sounds from above, she feared that her voice and Sally's might carry better up the stairway than the men's voices carried down. ''Why, only the week before Chalford and I were married I heard you telling everyone at Lady Prentice's rout how charming the Princess of Wales is and lamenting the way she is treated.''

''I spoke no more than the truth,'' Sally said firmly.

''But, my dear, only think how Lady Jersey must react when such tales are carried to her, as surely they must be. I cannot think she does not express her displeasure to her son.''

Even in the gloom between torches she could see Sally's careless shrug. ''He knows I cannot like her, Adriana. Nor will I attend to her strictures. I mean to be my own person, one day to lead fashion and to be a great political hostess, too, for George will make a stir when he takes his seat in the House of Lords. I'll see to it. I have neither the intention nor the desire, now or ever, to bow and scrape to a royal har—''

''Sally!''

''My goodness me, Adriana, 'tis only a word—and the correct word at that—but if it offends you, I shall refrain from its use. I shall say merely that I do not cater to my mama-in-law's sensibilities. I choose my own road."

It had begun to rain before they emerged from the keep and they were forced now to run for shelter. By the time they reached the porch, the heavens had unleashed their full fury. Jagged shafts of lightning with cracks of thunder crashing at their heels cut through roiling black clouds directly overhead. Adriana was shaking when she entered the hall.

Chalford looked at her as Sally and George hastened toward the warmth of the fires in the great hall, and when Adriana moved to follow them, he stopped her with a gentle hand upon her upper arm, saying in a worried tone, "You are cold, sweetheart."

Another flash of lightning above the open quadrangle lit the colonnade outside, and the great crash of thunder that came but a second later made Adriana wince. "I am all right, sir, or I will be when we reach the warmth of the fire."

"That gown is ridiculously ill-chosen, and damp besides," he said more firmly, letting his hand move up and down her bare arm in a way that sent shivers of a different sort through her. "You go up and put on something warmer. I ought never to have let you go out to the keep without a thick cloak to wrap about you."

"I do not even own such a cloak," she told him, speaking quickly. "Really, Chalford, I am perfectly—"

The crash this time was so loud the walls vibrated with it, and with a startled, frightened cry, Adriana flung herself at her husband and buried her face in his shoulder. When his arms wrapped securely around her, she shuddered with relief but clung even tighter.

Several moments of silence passed before she began to relax. Indeed, not until a muted roll of thunder could be heard in the distance did she draw a long, sobbing breath and move to free herself from his embrace.

"This storm is moving fast," he said quietly.

"Good. Then it will soon be over."

"With another, more than likely, on its heels."

She bit her lower lip.

"Why didn't you tell me, Adriana?"

"Tell you what?"

He looked at her but did not speak.

Finally, she shrugged and turned away, striving to make the movement look casual. "It is childish to fear thunderstorms."

"The fear is no less real," he said, gently taking her by the shoulders and turning her to face him again. "I nearly sent you upstairs alone to change your dress. You must tell me when you are afraid, sweetheart, so that I can help, so that I don't make matters worse." The third footman approached just then from the south end of the hall. "See to our guests' needs, Jacob, and tell them that we will be with them again directly."

"Really, Joshua," Adriana protested when the footman had gone and she found herself being urged, gently but no less adamantly, toward the stair hall, "there is no need to change my dress. 'Tis scarcely damp at all, and I will be quite warm enough in the hearth corner of the great hall. Why, Sally is wearing no more than I am."

"Sally is not my wife," he pointed out. "If Villiers chooses to allow her to freeze herself to death, that's his lookout, not mine."

"I don't know that what George chooses counts for a great deal with Sally," Adriana said before thinking.

"He is her husband." Chalford said no more. Indeed, he seemed to think he had said enough, and while his arm remained firmly around her shoulders, pressing her forward, Adriana could see no point in arguing with him. Still, she remembered Sally's casual reference to George's future political career. At dinner, the viscount had spoken only of sport. Although Sally had twice mentioned politics and had encouraged Lady Hetta to discourse upon her efforts to protect England from the French, these sorties had proved unsuccessful, Villiers always managing to bring the conversation back to his favorite topic. Adriana could not imagine his wishing to become a great political leader. She put her thought into words as they reached the top of the stairs.

Chalford blinked. "Villiers? A political leader? Utter nonsense, if you ask me."

"But Sally said—"

"Sally is little more than a schoolgirl," he said, "and a foolish, chattering schoolgirl, at that. What does she know of anything, let alone politics? It is not as though she grew up in Melbourne House, as Cowper's little Emily did."

"Sally is a year younger than I am, to be sure," Adriana said stiffly, "but we are both of us older than Emily, Chalford, and well beyond the schoolroom. Moreover, from what I have seen of Sally, she means to have her way about things. Why, even Lady Jersey cannot frighten her, and I can tell you that woman utterly paralyzes me. When Sally chooses, she can appear to be even higher in the instep than the queen. I have seen her."

"Dramatizing," he said, urging her through the sitting room toward her bedchamber. "Sally adores Cheltenham theatrics. Villiers ought to beat her weekly to cure her of such nonsense."

Adriana stopped short in the bedchamber doorway, turning her head to look at him, to see if he meant what he said. He was grinning. She said, "He wouldn't dare raise a hand to her."

"Then, more fool he," said Chalford, still grinning. "Are you going to stand there all night long, sweetheart? Your arms are all over gooseflesh."

"There is no need to change my dress," she said, not moving from where she stood and suddenly determined, like Sally, to go her own road. "The great hall is quite warm if one—"

"If one stands with one's head in a fireplace," he finished for her. "Don't be childish, Adriana. You are going to change your dress if I have to change it for you. You are unaccustomed to the damp air, and I don't mean to lose my beautiful wife to an inflammation of the lungs before I've been married a full week."

"Nor, indeed, until after she provides a proper heir to your precious Thunderhill," she retorted sharply, glaring at him, once again surprised by the strength of her vexation. What was it about the man, she wondered, that stirred her to such emotion? When he returned her glare with an even, unwavering look of his own, she added defensively, "I have never been on this part of the coast before, Joshua, to be sure, but I am never ill in Brighton, which must be much the same climate."

"Brighton harbor is more protected from the elements than Thunderhill," he said.

"All the more reason to go—"

"Go to your dressing room and change your gown, Adriana." The words were measured, and a muscle twitched high in his cheek, but his voice remained cool and steady, and its very steadiness acted as a breeze to her kindling temper.

"I don't wish to change my gown," she snapped. " 'Tis unnecessary. Moreover, Nancy is not here to help me, and if I ring for her, it will be a full quarter-hour before she can get here from wherever it is in this pile that she takes her supper."

"I'll help." Giving her a nudge, he urged her across her candlelit bedchamber into the dressing room, where two oil lamps burned low upon the dressing table, their light reflected in the gilt-framed looking glass. Chalford stepped away from her to turn up the wicks and to open the wardrobe. After riffling through the gowns that hung there, he glanced back at her with a frown. "You must have at least one with sleeves."

"They all have sleeves."

"Don't quibble. You know what I mean. Those little puffs cannot be called proper sleeves, and as for the rest, you'll catch your death if you go about this place with everything above your waist as bare as can be."

"I'll have you know, my lord, that these gowns are all the crack. Even Alston didn't complain of them, except, of course," she added conscientiously, "for their cost."

"He clearly did not think about what our weather is like," Chalford said, frowning heavily at the dresses in the wardrobe.

"If he did, he probably thought it would be as balmy and comfortable as Brighton is when he visits," she retorted.

Chalford looked silently at the floor for a long moment, and she waited, watching, wondering if at last she had pushed him too far. But when he looked up, it was only to turn his attention back to the wardrobe, to search again through the dresses hanging there. Then finally, taking out a dark-green gown, he said calmly, "Here, this one is velvet at least, and you must have some sort of shawl with which to cover your arms."

Her eyes widened. "No one wears shawls, sir, who does not wish to be stigmatized for a dowdy."

"If you do not have a shawl, one of my aunts can lend you one," he said. Then, looking directly into her eyes, he added, "Or if you prefer it, I will find you a woolen cloak to wear."

His demeanor was as calm as ever, but Adriana found herself repressing a shiver, as though there were once again thunder in the air. Swallowing carefully, she nodded and turned so that he could unfasten the many tiny buttons down the back of her dress.

His fingers were nimble, and the task was quickly finished, but when she felt his warm hands on her bare shoulders, felt them pushing the flimsy material aside and down, she stepped quickly forward and turned, clutching at her bodice. "I can do the rest, Joshua, thank you. That velvet dress fastens up the front."

"As you wish, my dear," he said. "I'll wait." He turned, and she thought he meant to retire to her bedchamber, but instead he sat upon her dressing chair.

She opened her mouth to tell him to leave, then shut it again with the words unsaid when she realized that he would refuse to go. Marriage, she decided, had a number of unexpected pitfalls for the unwary. With a sigh, she slipped off the amber dress, stepped out of it, tugged her short silken chemise into place—for she had not altogether ignored the chilliness of the castle's corridors and chambers—and quickly pulled the heavier gown over her head. As she wriggled, she heard him chuckle, and when she emerged from the folds of green velvet, she found him standing again, directly in front of her. Obligingly, he helped her smooth the velvet into place.

"Joshua, really, I—"

"I like velvet," he said, his big hands moving down her ribs to her waist and hips. "It's soft, wants caressing." His fingers touched the lowest gold frog fastening, several inches below her natural waist, many inches below the gown's.

"I can do that," she said hastily, pushing his hands aside.

He let her fasten the first one, then shook his head at her. "You move too quickly, sweetheart. I'll show you how such a task ought to be done if you would please a lover."

She looked at him, saw the amusement in his eyes and something else that made her breath catch in her throat. She found herself unable to resist when he pushed her hands away again, unable to protest when his hands moved beneath the velvet dress to touch the silken chemise, to gather it upward until he could caress her bare hips, her waist, her . . .

"Joshua," she gasped, "Sally and George are—"

"Right," he said. He sighed, straightened her chemise, and turned his attention to the remaining frogs. As he fastened the last one, however, at the point of her deep décolletage, he allowed himself one lingering caress, making her gasp again; and, when she turned her face up to his, he kissed her, putting his arms around her and drawing her body tightly against his.

All wish to resist him vanished, for the moment at least, and Adriana melted against him, savoring the warm sensations that rushed through her. When he set her back upon her heels, she drew another long breath and looked at him.

Chalford smiled at her and moved to the wardrobe again, searching, then reaching for something on the top shelf. When he turned, he held a soft white woolen shawl. Still smiling, this time with satisfaction, he shook it out and held it for her.

Responding automatically to that smile, she allowed him to drape the shawl over her shoulders, catching it up with her elbows, adjusting it until her looking glass told her the effect was not too dreadful. The shawl was old, a little shabby, and certainly unsuitable for evening wear. She refused to think of what Sally would say, but whatever was said, she had no wish to quarrel further with Chalford that night.

More guests arrived the following day and the day after that, including Mr. Dawlish and Mr. Bennett, two young gentlemen who had been favorite flirts of Adriana's in London. Her friend Sarah and Lord Clifford also arrived, and others, but nearly everyone was on his way to Brighton, and with the races starting Friday, no one wished to linger. Even Alston, arriving late Tuesday afternoon with his sister, his wife, and her brother, Mr. Ringwell, would stay only until Thursday morning. The viscount had wagered heavily on one of the entries in the Brighton races.

"Some nag called Houghton Lass in the Somerset stakes," Miranda told Adriana soon after their arrival. "That's the first race, so I've no doubt he's made wagers on others as well. Of course, he has said I may not spend any more money this month. I have spent my allowance, he says, and that is that."

"Well, have you done so?"

"To be sure," Miranda admitted. "Who would not have spent such a pittance? I might have got more out of him, I suppose, only he was angry with me."

Adriana, encountering a grin from Sarah Clifford, engaged some yards away in animated conversation with Sally, grinned back, then said, "In the briars again, Randy?"

"Oh, only for flirting, but he had said I was not to

speak with the gentleman. He was never so strict with you, Dree."

"I obeyed him, my dear. You do not."

"You flouted his authority often! I remember—"

"Ah, but I never did what he specifically told me not to do. His intent might well have been different from his order, like when he told me I was not to demean myself by going with Lady Ashford to a public ball at Vauxhall. After I went anyway, with Miss Bennett and her mama—and her handsome brother, of course—I pleaded confusion over the exact meaning of his order, which made Alston feel superior—to a poor, stupid female, you know—so he forgave me." She smiled. "Mama was used to say that if one put a brick wall before us, I would find a way around it while you would attempt to bash your way through. You haven't changed."

"Nor you, I think. But imagine, Dree, I shall have to be in Brighton a full week before I shall be allowed to purchase so much as a new ribbon. And say what you like, our brother is an unconscionable pinchpenny, and that is all there is about it."

"Come with me," Adriana commanded, nodding and smiling to her other guests as she led her sister through the dining room to the stair hall. Moments later, Miranda exclaimed her approval of the marchioness's sitting room and bedchamber while Adriana moved swiftly through the latter to open a carved wooden box on the table by her bed. "Here," she said, holding out a wad of folded notes. "Buy yourself something pretty."

"Adriana!" Miranda moved forward, not taking her eyes from the money. "Such a lot!"

Adriana grinned at her. " 'Tis less than half of what Joshua gave me, but there has as yet been no opportunity to spend it hereabouts. If we go into Hythe, as I am certain we will, he will go with me, so I shall not have to pay for anything, and since we do not go to Brighton—"

"Are you truly not to go at all?"

Adriana shrugged. "I mean to do what I can to change his mind, but so far he's proved adamant. I flew out at him last night, I'm afraid, after I'd made myself a solemn promise I wouldn't do any such thing. He had come up with me so that I might change my gown for a warmer one, and we no sooner returned to the hall than Sally mentioned Prinny's birthday celebration. When I said that perhaps we might join them on such an important occasion, he contradicted me on the spot. I was mortified."

"Goodness, Dree," exclaimed Miranda, "never tell us you ripped up at him in front of Sally Villiers!"

Adriana shook her head. "Of course not. I am not such a fool. But, I promise you, I did tell him as soon as Sally and George had retired for the night and we were alone that he ought not to have contradicted me as he did."

"And what did he say to that?"

"That I ought not to say things I know are not so if I do not wish to be contradicted. That's when my wretched tongue ran away with me. I told him that no one could blame me for not realizing that he was blind to what he owed his rank and position in society, or that he wanted only to bury himself away from everyone else. I said that to avoid the prince's celebration was to tell him we had better, more important things to do. Then I said he was lucky that princes no longer hold the power of life and death over their subjects, for I was sure that Prinny would take our absence as a monstrous affront to his dignity."

"Adriana, you never said such things to Chalford!"

"I did."

"Then I am surprised you were here to greet us this afternoon. I'd expect, at the very least and regardless of his strong feelings for you, that he'd lock you up in one of his towers on a diet of bread and water for speaking to him so."

Adriana shrugged. "I think you are wrong about his having strong feelings, Randy, though I confess I did expect my tirade to enrage him. It didn't. He stayed maddeningly calm—just told me not to talk nonsense and asked me if I intended to sleep in his room or in my own.''

Miranda, tactfully, did not ask which she had chosen —indeed, there was added color in her cheeks when she turned rather quickly away to look out the window—so Adriana felt no urge to tell her that she had rapidly come to regret her prompt decision to sleep in her own bedchamber, that for several hours she had tossed and turned, her body still tingling from the memory of his earlier caresses. And when the second thunderstorm had come, just as he had predicted it would, she had begun to shiver, squeezing her eyes shut, hugging her quilts to her chin, wishing the curtains at her windows were heavier, that they would shut out the noise and the flashes of lightning.

She had lain there, trembling, for ten minutes—only that, though it had seemed much longer—before the door to her room had opened and Joshua had come in. He said not a word to her, and her attention was so fiercely concentrated upon the storm that she did not realize he had come in until she felt his weight upon the bed. But when he climbed, naked, beneath the covers and drew her into his arms, she took shelter there without thought of protest, grateful for his presence, for his thoughtfulness in remembering that she would be afraid. And when the fury of the storm had abated and his hands had begun to move over her body in a way not meant to solace fear, she had responded at once and with all the passion he could have desired.

Tuesday morning when Nancy had drawn the curtains to reveal gray skies and the promise of more rain, Adriana had felt uneasy when she remembered the things she had said to him before the storm, things to which he had not once referred. Her disquiet deepened when she realized she was alone in her bed. Chalford, Nancy had informed her, had gone riding with Viscount Villiers.

She had not spoken privately with Joshua since then, but she said none of this to Miranda, who was still feigning interest in the view of the Channel from the bedchamber windows. Adriana turned to shut the carved box.

"For goodness' sake," Miranda said then, "just look at that, Dree. Whatever is happening over yonder?"

Hearing a rumble in the distance that sounded a little like thunder, Adriana hurried to her sister's side. "What is it?"

"There." Miranda pointed. "You can see the French coast, despite this dismal weather, and the wind is blowing this way. That must be why we can hear them." She pushed open the window, and another low booming sound drifted across the water. "Do you see them, Dree? Ships, dozens of them. They look like tiny toys. There's another puff of smoke. How long it is before the sound reaches us."

Indeed, the rumbling sound did not come until she had finished speaking, and Adriana found that her stomach muscles had tightened in the meanwhile. So many ships . . .

"Come on, Randy, we must find Joshua." Hurrying downstairs, they found family and guests gathered in the great hall. At the tea table, Sophie was graciously accepting a cup from a tight-lipped Lady Adelaide, while Alston and fair-haired, ruddy-cheeked Claude Ringwell made their careful selections from a plate of sandwiches near Lady Henrietta's chair. Sarah, her husband, Sally, and George were talking with Mr. Dawlish and another gentleman near the north fireplace.

Adriana hurried to Joshua, who stood near the western fireplace, his booted foot resting upon the gleaming fender, his elbow upon the chimneypiece, while he conversed with a large, muscular, older man who was bent over to warm his hands near the flames. "Chalford," she said hastily, "the most awkward thing. Oh, I beg your pardon, your grace." She bobbed a quick curtsy to the Duke of Norfolk, who had straightened and turned at the sound of her voice. "I did not realize you had arrived."

"No ceremony, Adriana, if you please," commanded his grace with a crooked smile. "Give us a hug instead."

She grinned and willingly accepted a lusty hug, glad to note that he had recently had a bath. She had known Norfolk from her childhood, for he had been one of her father's cronies—the one who accompanied the Earl of Wryde into mischief more often than not, she had been wont to think. Though it was said of him that he had no graces other than his title, that he had to be dead drunk before anyone could bathe him, and that as many of his coachman's children were Norfolk's as were his coachman's, she liked him. Nowadays, she knew his grace's energies were taken up as much by architecture as by raking, for though he remained a raffish gentleman, as interested in sport as Lord Villiers was, he was even more interested in the changes being made at Arundel.

"His grace," Chalford said with a smile, "has just been telling me that he wishes Horace Walpole were alive to see what he's accomplished these past years."

"Called the place a heap of ruins when he visited my father in '49," said the duke. "Pity he's dead now. The library is nearly finished. My architect's outdone himself."

"I'm sure he has, sir," Adriana said, turning to Chalford as she spoke and adding urgently, "Joshua, there are ships, dozens of them. We can see them from my bedchamber windows." She glanced around, realizing that she had drawn the attention of everyone in the room.

Lady Henrietta came quickly to her feet. "What is it, Adriana? Ships, you say? Where? Oh, mercy me, what shall we do? Those dreadful Frenchmen!"

"Sit down and compose yourself, Hetta," commanded Lady Adelaide, turning her attention without noticeable reluctance from Sophie's chatter.

"But, Adelaide, they must certainly be French."

"As you thought three nights ago," said Lady Adelaide with a stern note in her voice that could not be misunderstood. When Lady Hetta subsided, abashed, she added, "Much better. You will soon see there is no cause for concern." She glanced at Joshua. "You will wish to send someone to the ramparts to see what it is that has aroused Adriana's disquietude, Chalford. I daresay the alarms the other night will account for it and what she has seen is no more than a French naval exercise of some sort."

Nodding, Chalford left the room, but he was gone for only a few moments. When he returned, he rejoined Norfolk, Adriana, and Miranda near the fireplace. "Someone will report soon," he told his wife in an undertone, "but I daresay Aunt Adelaide is in the right of it and there is no cause for anxiety."

"The ships are very far away," she admitted, looking at Miranda, who had been flirting outrageously with Mr. Bennett.

Miranda grinned. "Goodness, Dree, did you think the French would invade us? Even Orson admits such fears to be idiotish."

"Miranda," said Alston, choosing that moment to step up behind her, "I should like to have a private word with you. At once if you please." His manner was not conciliating.

Miranda flushed and looked to her sister for help.

"Really, sir," Adriana said lightly, "I cannot think what can be of such importance that you must needs speak to her now."

"Miranda," said Alston with haughty emphasis, "is still under my authority, Adriana. Come with me, my girl."

When Adriana made a slight move as though to interfere, Joshua put a restraining hand upon her arm, causing her to turn toward him in protest. Regarding her with steady, slightly narrowed eyes, he shook his head.

She bit her lip and remained still. Glancing then toward her brother and sister, expecting Alston to mock her silence, she discovered that they had turned away and were approaching the door to the entry hall. Before they reached it, however, the second footman entered rather more quickly than was his custom.

His eyes were bright as he sought his master among the company. "M'lord," he said, striving unsuccessfully for dignified undertone as he reached the small group by the western hearth, "they are indeed French ships. Miskin saw them through your glass. Nearer the French coast than ours, m'lord, but he says there be English brigs there too, and it looks like they be engaging the enemy. There be shots bein' fired, Miskin says."

6

Chalford promptly ordered lookouts to the castle ramparts, but as the day proceeded, their reports continued to indicate that the ships showed no inclination to approach England, that they had moved nearer to the French coast instead. By late afternoon the French ships had disappeared from sight altogether, and three English ships had been sighted making slowly for Southampton. Not until that evening, when more guests arrived for dinner, was further information received.

Chalford had suggested that morning that they inform those of their neighbors who might expect to be presented to the new marchioness that she was ready to receive them, and Lady Adelaide had declared that certain persons among them might actually be invited to dine with their other guests that evening.

" 'Tis short notice, of course, but they will be very glad to come, and we will thus attend to several obligations at once," she told him. "We will set back the dinner hour, which will suit our town visitors and likewise make it unnecessary for anyone to be put to unseemly haste." Glancing at Adriana, who had turned from a chat with Sally to listen to them, she added, "Not many of them will provide suitable companionship for you, I fear, but 'tis our duty to condescend graciously whenever possible. We must never appear to snub the local gentry."

"My goodness me, no," said Sally, whose interest had been as marked as Adriana's. " 'Twoud be fatal to snub one's inferiors, particularly since country squires tend, in my experience, to be such very proud persons."

Adriana had no wish to snub anyone, so Lady Adelaide's suggestion was agreed to, with the result that several members of the local gentry—all of those with whom Lady Adelaide could bring herself to associate— joined the houseparty for dinner that evening. Among the first to arrive, after the houseguests and family had changed and gathered once more in the great hall, were Lord Braverstoke and his son, Randall, of Newingham Manor.

Randall Braverstoke caught Adriana's interest at once—and her sister's as a matter of course—for he was a charming, well-set-up young man of some thirty-plus summers, with deep-blue eyes and shining black hair. When he bowed deeply over Adriana's hand, he kept his eyes on her face, his gaze exploring hers while he murmured the usual amenities. And when Adriana smiled at him, his eyes lit with undisguised pleasure and admiration.

"Why do we never meet men like Mr. Braverstoke in London?" Miranda demanded when she and Adriana had moved on to greet other visitors and were beyond earshot of the Braverstokes.

"I like his father, too," Adriana said with a grin. "With those round, red cheeks and that ring of gray hair resting like a halo upon his head, he looks like a plump cherub." When Miranda smiled but faintly in response to this sally, Adriana looked searchingly at her. "I have not had an opportunity to ask before now, Randy, but what did Alston want with you earlier?"

Miranda grimaced. "The usual drivel. He saw me with Mr. Bennett and then heard what I said to you. Said I was insolent."

"Oh, dear."

"It was nothing," Miranda assured her, "but I am tired of his lectures, Dree. Have you spoken to Chalford yet?"

"No, and truly, you cannot wish to come to us, Randy. There is nothing for you to do here. 'Tis nothing like Brighton."

"Believe me, Dree, I would willingly trade a fortnight

of Alston and Sophie's company in London or Brighton for a fortnight of boredom at Thunderhill. Do, please, speak to Chalford."

Adriana nodded, thinking she had best make a push to apologize to her husband for her bad behavior the previous night before she asked favors of him. She felt no urge to explain this detail to Miranda, however, and they were interrupted just then by Sarah Clifford and Sally, the latter demanding to know if the Earl and Countess Cowper were expected to join the houseparty.

"I meant to ask you the moment we arrived," she said with a laugh, "for you must know that I have the most delightful little surprise for them. Only look at this." She began to hold out a small, neatly matted and gilt-framed newspaper clipping, then changed her mind and read it to them instead: " 'From among the fashionable dainties of the season, a young earl, it is said, has given a decided preference to young *Lamb.*' There," she said with a chuckle, "is that not famous? Will it not amuse them?"

"Why would it do so?" Miranda asked.

Sarah, too, expressed puzzlement. "That item was in nearly every newspaper a month ago, Sally. Cowper and Emily Lamb are married now. Are they to visit you, Dree?"

Adriana shook her head. "I believe they intend to spend some weeks at Panshanger, his lordship's house near Hertford. You will have to send your gift to them there, Sally, for I daresay that they, too, will miss Brighton this year."

Sally laughed. "To be sure, dearest Emily is now a proper, dutiful countess, which is all the more reason, I think, to remind her that her affairs must always provide fare for gossip. And this bit came not from just any paper, my dear Miranda, but from the *Times,* which so rarely indulges in gossipy *on-dits.* I clipped the notice at once, thinking to make them a wedding gift of it, but through some cause or other I mislaid the thing and only found it again when we returned to the Prospect Lodge."

"Poor Emily has been providing *on-dits* for all the papers since before her come-out," Adriana pointed out, "but it will be different now, I believe. I have seen her with Cowper. She loves the man to distraction, Sally, and he is so very charming to her. 'Tis like a storybook romance," she said wistfully.

"For the moment, perhaps," Sally said with a grimace, "but Emily is far from being the naive heroine in which story writers delight. She is as worldly as her mama, and no one ever accused Lady Melbourne of being distracted from the main chance by love, though she certainly enjoyed more opportunities than most for distraction. Only wait until Emily becomes bored with Cowper, or he with her. A charming man when he wishes to be, and even more handsome than Leveson-Gower, but Cowper can be as cold and hard as steel, too, and for very little cause." She shivered dramatically, adding, "Goodness knows I wish them well, but marriage . . . Well, my dears, marriage can be very difficult."

Adriana stared at her. Was this the foolish, chattering schoolgirl Chalford had described to her only the previous night? Marriage could, as she was discovering for herself, prove very difficult indeed; however, she could not imagine eighteen-year-old Emily with her large, wide-set brown eyes and pale, innocent face as anything but an adoring young wife. She opened her mouth to say as much, to tell Sally she was being foolish beyond permission to speak so, but the words would not come. A small voice deep inside her suggested Sally might well prove to be right.

"My dears," said Lady Henrietta just then, approaching them with her rapid, clicking steps, her head thrust a little forward as though to carry her more quickly to their sides, "did you hear what Mr. Braverstoke has been saying about those French ships?"

"No, ma'am," Adriana said. "I thought the danger was over."

"Do tell us," urged Sarah; the others nodded encouragingly.

"You had much better hear it from him, for I should most likely make a mull of the tale," said Lady Hetta, signaling to the young man in question to join them. "Tell these ladies what you were telling the others, sir," she said when he came obediently to her side. "He had his yacht out on the water today, you see," she added with a brisk nod.

"Oh, do you have a yacht?" Adriana asked, smiling at him. "What fun that must be. I have always loved the sea, but no one has ever taken me out in anything other than a small sailboat before. I should adore to sail on a yacht."

"Then we must arrange an expedition, ma'am," Mr. Braverstoke said, smiling at her and showing even, strong-looking white teeth. He was of a height nearly equal to Chalford's, but his body was slimmer and his shoulders not so broad. Nonetheless, Adriana thought, letting her gaze drift idly over his form, he seemed well-muscled and fit. She looked up, encountered Sally's look of mockery, and blushed. Fortunately, Mr. Braverstoke's attention had been reclaimed by Lady Hetta, who suggested that he tell about the French ships and never mind puffing off his yacht.

"Chalford has a yacht," she added. "I daresay everyone in south Kent has a yacht."

"To be sure, ma'am," he said, exchanging an amused glance with Adriana, "but I am persuaded that the *Golden Fleece* is a superior bit of craftsmanship, and I should be proud to show her off. You must let me show you her paces one day, Lady Chalford."

"Tell about the French ships, for goodness' sake!" Lady Hetta said so sharply that Adriana would not have been surprised had she stamped her little foot to underscore the command.

"Please, sir, do tell us," she said.

"My pleasure." He smiled at her, then glancing at the others, added quickly, "We had drawn rather nearer the French coast than usual, you see, for it was a fine day for sailing—"

"Indeed, sir?" interrupted Sarah, her eyebrows lifted

in surprise. "I thought the day a dismal one, myself. It looked every minute as though it meant to come on to mizzle."

"Oh, no, not after two o'clock or so," he said, shaking his head. "Indeed, ma'am, we saw the sun several times, and the wind was ideal for sailing. In point of fact, it was so good that we nearly sailed into the battle before we realized where we were."

"So you see," said Lady Hetta triumphantly, "there was a battle, an actual engagement and not a mere exercise."

"Oh, yes," Braverstoke said, "it was a bit of truly smart action—three of our ships against a number of the enemy's large brigs and luggers."

"Good gracious," Adriana said, staring.

Sally's mouth was open, and others were drawing near to hear it again. Lord Braverstoke said eagerly, " 'Twas damned nearly the whole French navy at the first of it. Tell them, Randall."

"Indeed, sir. After watching the French flotilla for six weeks, our people learned it had been joined by reinforcements, and three of our ships went to have a look. Forewarning aside, it must have astounded them this morning to encounter dashed well the whole French fleet just south of Cape Gris-Nez—thirty-four of them, we were told, with eleven brigs, steering south toward Boulogne under the cover of artillery batteries from shore."

"I'll wager they felt safe enough," observed his father. "Our flagship, you say, had but two brigs to assist it."

"Nevertheless," declared Lady Adelaide from her sofa, "I daresay that three English ships is a sufficient force to rout any number of French vessels."

"As you say, ma'am, particularly since they engaged only the ships at the tail end of the flotilla." Again, Randall Braverstoke exchanged an amused glance with Adriana.

"But we won the battle," declared Lady Hetta happily.

"Well, ma'am, we wounded a good many on board the French ships, to be sure, and our grape-and-musket shot carried to the beach as well, but I fear that without having captured a single ship, which we did not, one cannot truly claim victory."

Chalford said, " 'Tis a problem the English navy has faced throughout history, I believe, that the French coast is always so strongly fortified. Every few miles they have a port their ships can put into when disabled."

Norfolk agreed, then added with a smile, "Though of late we seldom succeed in capturing anything, these skirmishes have a good effect by showing the damned French what they may expect if ever they do make a grand dash at us across the Channel."

Lady Adelaide nodded her approval of these words. "To be sure," she said, "England must always prevail in the end."

"I'll not debate that," Braverstoke said, "but our ships took a hammering today from the French shore batteries. My crew and I could do nothing to aid in the battle, of course, but we lingered close, thinking they might be glad of our aid afterward. They were much mauled, the flagship taking on a foot of water an hour, so although English skill may have caused some grief, you will perceive that the *monsieurs* had their share of the fun."

Since Lady Adelaide appeared to enjoy no such perception, it was as well that Benstead appeared upon the threshold just then to announce in his most stately manner that dinner was served.

Norfolk, as the ranking gentleman present, offered his arm to Adriana, saying in a confiding tone as he did so, "Did I ever tell you that Prinny and I are responsible for introducing the civilized habit of dining at this later hour?"

She grinned at him, her eyes twinkling. "No, sir, I don't believe you've ever mentioned that fact to me, but I can assure you that I have heard the tale more than once in my life. My father has been known to describe your dinners with his royal highness as Greek symposiums, with Bacchus as the central god. You will thus approve of Chalford's dining room. The decor provides a veritable temple to Bacchus.''

Norfolk chuckled in appreciation, patting the slim hand resting upon his forearm as he did so. ''Chalford showed great good sense in falling tail over top for you, my dear. You will make an excellent marchioness. Every man should be so blessed.''

''Thank you, sir.'' She could scarcely reply in kind—the present Duchess of Norfolk having gone mad shortly after her marriage to the duke, and it being quite ineligible to mention even one of his many mistresses—so Adriana deftly turned the conversation to his restoration activities.

This topic proved a successful one, since his grace, seated at her right, was perfectly willing to discourse throughout dinner upon his activities. She divided her attention, as was perfectly proper, between this conversation and an enjoyable flirtation with Lord Clifford on her left.

The company was merry, the service excellent, and the hum of conversation droned for an hour before there came one of those odd silences that fall upon every group from time to time, no matter how large or noisy. At that moment, Chalford was informing his butler that several of the guests had expressed a desire to visit the owls after the meal. '' 'Twas plaguily dim in the keep last evening,'' he said, ''so ask the lads to take up some lanterns, but try not to disturb the inhabitants too much. We don't want them all taking flight, after all.''

Benstead replied clearly, with his customary dignity, ''Very good, my lord. Your guests may be interested to learn, in point of fact, that the Prince of Wales has laid an egg.''

There was a moment's stunned silence, followed by a crack of laughter from Norfolk. ''And not for the first time, either,'' he chortled. There was more laughter then, and the merriment grew as guests who understood explained the matter to their neighbors.

Lady Henrietta waited until the noise had abated somewhat before saying brightly, albeit to no one in particular, "That owl must more properly be renamed for the princess now, I suppose."

That brought more laughter and several comments regarding the Princess of Wales's reputation that were less than flattering. Adriana, seeing Sally frown, hoped her friend's customarily strong sense of propriety would forbid her taking up the cudgels on behalf of the Prince of Wales's beleaguered wife as she had been known to do on other, less formal occasions, but Sally remained silent. It was Sophie's voice that could be heard as the laughter died away.

" 'Tis a shocking thing," she said indignantly to the gentleman beside her in a tone loud enough to have been heard above the laughter, "to hear persons of quality making mock of the royal family in such a vulgar fashion."

Another brief silence followed this pronouncement before Lady Adelaide graciously requested her dinner partner to tell her, if he would, a little more about his house in Somerset. The general conversation at once began to hum again, and Sophie, cast into high color, applied her attention to her dinner.

At last it was over. Leaving the gentlemen to enjoy their port, the ladies retired to the great hall, where the conversation became general, ambling from topic to topic until the men joined them there. Lady Adelaide then took matters in hand, suggesting to Chalford that he take those who wished to see the owls straight out to the keep. When they had gone, she urged several young ladies among the remaining guests to display their talent on the pianoforte, and when the others returned, Adriana, Sarah, and Miranda helped her organize tables for games.

Adriana enjoyed herself very much, finding time to enjoy mild flirtations with Mr. Dawlish and Mr. Bennett, indeed with nearly every gentleman present, except of course Claude Ringwell, Sophie's foppish brother, whose fulsome compliments engendered no more response in her than a stronge itch to slap him.

When the tea trays were brought in at half-past ten and the servants began to clear the game table where she had been attempting for some time, unsuccessfully, to recover a mythical fortune lost at Commerce, Adriana got up to stretch her legs. Making her way toward a window embrasure, she encountered Mr. Braverstoke and in the course of a brief exchange of pleasantries reminded him of his promise to take her out on his yacht.

"It will be my pleasure, I assure you," he said with an ardent smile, adding apologetically, "It cannot be for a few days yet, however. My captain informed me when we returned today that there are some trifling repairs that must be made. Now, with the uncertain weather, it is an excellent time to attend to them. I want everything to be in good order when I show you my beauty."

"May a mere husband take part in this conversation?" inquired Chalford, coming to stand beside Adriana. "I have scarcely exchanged a word with you all day, my lady."

She smiled at him. "Mr. Braverstoke has been telling me about his yacht, sir, the *Golden Fleece*. Indeed, he has offered to take me out sailing one day. I should like that very much."

"Perhaps your husband will not allow it," said Braverstoke, regarding the marquess with an air of amused challenge.

"I have no objection," Chalford said. "Indeed, I have heard she is a speedy little craft. I'd like very much to have the opportunity to sail aboard her myself."

"Then," said Braverstoke, resigned but polite, "you must come with us, certainly."

"Oh, yes, Joshua, that would be the very thing."

If Braverstoke did not share Adriana's enthusiasm when Chalford said he would be delighted to join them, nothing in his expression other than a little stiffness in his smile betrayed his disappointment. He assured them both that he would inform them as soon as the ship was ready to set out again.

Once the tea things had been cleared away, Lord Braverstoke and the other local people began to make their *adieux* and take their departure. With this example set, the houseguests too, began to bid their hosts good night. Soon only Villiers, Lord Clifford, and Norfolk were left, the first two of these gentlemen having ruthlessly abandoned their wives to solitary cots in order to sit up with the duke over a game of whist for pound points.

While Adriana teasingly admonished them for their connubial defection, Chalford rang for the third footman. "See to the gentlemen's needs, Jacob. If they play too late, you have my leave to nap in the outer hall. They can wake you if they wish to do so." He looked at the three, who were all grinning at him. "You will not miss us if we retire, gentlemen. There is plenty of port left, or if you prefer, Jacob can serve you whatever else you like. Come, my lady, 'tis bed for us."

Bidding the others good night, Adriana went up the stairs with her husband, then alone to her dressing room, her spirits sagging with the knowledge that many of their guests would depart the next day, the rest the day after, for Brighton. When she had dismissed Nancy, she moved to look out her bedchamber window at the Channel. All was quiet now and a crescent moon cast silvery light on the restless dark waters in the distance, highlighting breaking crests on the rolling waves.

" 'Tis a magnificent view, is it not?"

She had not heard him come in, but she turned now to look at him. He wore a dark-blue silk dressing gown tied at the waist with a long sash of the same material. His feet were bare on the carpeted floor. She smiled at him. "I am glad you came in. You were right in saying we have not talked today. I have not even thanked you for coming in last night as you did."

"You thanked me more than once last night, sweetheart, and thanks were neither expected nor necessary. I knew you would be frightened of the storm."

"But I had not been kind to you, Joshua—earlier in the evening, I mean. When I—"

. "I know what you mean, Adriana. You were angry, that is all. You have every right to express your anger to me."

"But it does no good," she protested. "You do not listen."

"I listen," he said, giving her a straight, rather stern look, "but your anger has not been particularly reasonable, has it? You are vexed because I refuse to follow the mob to Brighton at a time when that city may be counted upon to be full to overflowing, when it will be well nigh impossible to move about the streets for the crowds, and when there are matters demanding my attention here. I have many things to do, and so do you. You ought to spend more time with Aunt Adelaide, for one thing—"

She felt her unpredictable temper stir again and forcibly repressed it. Turning back to the window, she said with a calm to match his own, "I will learn all she can teach me, Joshua, but I have no wish to learn the whole in a week or to demand that she relinquish to me those duties that she enjoys so much. Moreover, I do not believe my vexation stems entirely from your refusal to take me to Brighton, nor do I consider the request unreasonable."

"We are back to that, are we?" The muscle high on his right cheek twitched. "I do not wish to discuss that issue again."

"Nor do I wish it, sir," she said, turning her head to glare at him, exasperated, "but I find your attitude both selfish and arrogant. I have asked for one thing, and you say you are too busy to accommodate me; yet I cannot think what it is you do here that is so crucial that your people cannot manage without you."

"It is my duty to oversee everything that goes on," he said reasonably. "I have been away two months, after all. There is much to learn about what transpired while I was away."

"Brighton is where our friends are, Joshua, and after so many years of being buried at Wryde, years of submitting either to Papa's decrees or to Alston's, is it so unreasonable to wish to share the company of my friends, to share their amusements?"

"You have the company of your friends now, do you not?"

"Well, of course I do, but what good is that when everyone will be gone on Thursday? I shall then be bored to distraction."

"Don't you think you are behaving childishly?"

"Oh," she gasped, "you are always so cocksure, Joshua, so all-knowing, as though you and you alone can be right. You called me childish last night, too, when it was you treating me like a child that made me behave so—if indeed I did. You make me so angry!" She had struggled against her growing fury, but emotion prevailed; and now, without thought for consequence, indeed without thought for anything beyond her outrage, she whirled on him, flailing, her fists pounding against his chest, her angry words punctuating every blow. "I am not a child, damn you!"

Chalford stood there, stunned for a moment, before he made any attempt to protect himself. Then, without effort, he caught her wrists in a firm grasp and said grimly, "I will let you hurl whatever words at me you like, Adriana, but I will not brook outright violence. Such ungoverned behavior merely serves to prove my point, as you must see for yourself. Now, come to bed."

"I shall sleep here tonight," she said, breathing heavily and glaring at him but striving, nonetheless, for a tone haughty enough to match any she had heard from Lady Adelaide.

"I think not," he replied. "You will come with me."

Reluctantly she obeyed him and then, in his bed, found herself fighting unreasonable fury again when he made no attempt to make love to her. She knew from the rhythm of his breathing that he was not asleep, but he made no attempt to speak to her either. In her frustration, she found herself replaying their confrontation in her mind. It was not long before she began to wish very much that the scene had never occurred and to wonder what she could do to make matters better between them.

Finally, after what seemed to be an hour or more of increasing tension, she decided there was only one thing to do. She said quietly, "Joshua, are you still awake?"

"Yes."

She swallowed, wishing this were not necessary. "Perhaps you were right. If I behaved childishly, I didn't mean to do so. It just seems to happen. You must think me awfully spoiled." She paused, drawing a careful breath, then adding in a near whisper, "I hope you are not sorry you married me."

"I am certainly not sorry about that, sweetheart. Nor," he added gently, "do I think you spoiled, particularly. You just found fashionable life in London to your liking and would like to continue that butterfly existence. I understand. Unfortunately, it isn't possible when you are a marchioness with a responsibility to uphold your position."

"But surely we need not remain here throughout the year," she protested, trying hard to sound reasonable and not childish. Really, it was difficult to tell the difference sometimes. "I know of dukes and duchesses who are always traveling about, to country houses, to London, into Leicestershire for the hunting, and to Brighton—like Norfolk, though he lives and breathes for Arundel. No one thinks they are neglecting their duties, Joshua. Surely no one would expect more of us than of them."

"I have never said you cannot ever leave here," he said. His voice had a bitter note in it now. "We will certainly go to London together occasionally and to visit your father at Wryde. I remain here because I prefer to do so, but you may perhaps, from time to time, visit friends by yourself if you like. And you may certainly invite people to visit whenever you like."

Adriana stifled a sigh. Though the conversation had not gone as she had hoped, he had now broached a subject she could not ignore. "I'd like to invite Miranda to stay with us," she said. "She dislikes living with Alston and Sophie, as I did, and she would prefer to come to us. Would you allow that, Joshua?"

"Certainly, although I cannot think it a wise thing to suggest so soon after our marriage. Your brother would no doubt oppose the proposition now, and I believe it would be better for you to become more settled here before you invite her for a long visit. Invite them all to come for Christmas, perhaps, then you can invite Miranda to stay on until she wishes to return to London for the Season, as she surely will."

Knowing she would do well to accept his suggestion and certain she would do herself no good at all by mentioning now that she, too, intended to return to London for the Season, Adriana held her peace.

After a period of silence, Chalford slipped his arm beneath her shoulders and drew her to him. "I know you fear boredom here, sweetheart, but just wait until the others have gone. I'll help you find things to amuse you." Raising himself onto his elbow, he bent over to kiss her, and as she responded, it occurred to her that there was one thing, certainly, that never failed to rout boredom. Their disagreement was soon forgotten.

7

They bade farewell to the last of their visitors before noon on Thursday, and Adriana made every attempt to appear cheerful as she turned back toward the main entrance after waving good-bye to the final coach, but she could not repress a small sigh as she stepped back into the empty entry hall at Chalford's side.

He chuckled. "Go and find a warm cloak, sweetheart. You are going to need it."

She looked up at him, curiosity promptly overcoming depression. "Why do I need a cloak, sir? There is a brisk wind blowing, to be sure, but the air is quite warm today."

"Just, for once, do as I say without question," he told her, grinning, "and put on a pair of sturdy shoes, too. You won't want those skimpy little sandals where we're going."

"And must I change my dress as well?" she asked, looking down at her sprig muslin round gown.

"No need. Since it has no train to get in the way, that one will serve you well enough. Now go!"

Hurrying up the stairs to her dressing room, she quickly donned a pair of stout walking shoes and ordered Nancy to search out a pelisse for her.

"He said to find a heavy cloak, but I haven't got one, as I told him not two days ago, so my Persian double silk pelisse must do. I am persuaded you will have packed it, Nancy."

"To be sure, Miss Adrie, but 'tis not much use against this damp chill, I'm thinkin'. I told you more 'n' once you did ought to have a good heavy wool one made up, with a warm hood, but you never did. 'Tis a wonder 'n' all you've never caught the ague, runnin' about London in naught but such skimpy dresses.''

"No one wears heavy cloaks anymore, Nancy, and one always has furs to wrap around oneself in the coach, so unless one strolls about visiting shops, there is no need for anything heavier than a pelisse or an occasional light shawl.''

"Well, unless I much mistake the matter, miss, you'll be needin' somethin' a lot warmer than that here,'' Nancy said tartly as she extracted from the back of the wardrobe the article in question, an exquisite creation of amber silk with dark-brown figuring, a pattern that was reversed on the inside. "There be a chill in that wind today, sunny skies or not.''

"Well, I am certainly not going to tell Chalford I cannot go with him for lack of proper clothing,'' Adriana said. "He is all impatience, and I confess, my curiosity is sufficiently aroused that I would go with him in my shift if it were necessary. Don't scold,'' she added when her abigail's eyebrows beetled ominously. "I expect to need warm clothes for winter, but Lady Adelaide will know what must be done. Perhaps there is a seamstress in Hythe.''

Flinging the pelisse over her shoulders, settling its wide collar, and tying the silken strings beneath her chin, she took a quick look in the pier glass, then hurried back downstairs to find Chalford awaiting her in the entry hall. He shook his head at the light pelisse but said nothing more than that they had best hurry if they were going to catch the tide.''

"The tide?''

"I thought you might like to see how you like the *Sea Dragon*,'' he said, smiling at her, clearly well-pleased with himself and just as clearly watching for her reaction.

"You are going to take me out on your yacht?''

"Indeed I am. I thought you ought to know what our *Sea Dragon* is like so that you might better compare her with Braverstoke's boat when the opportunity arises.''

Glancing up at him, Adriana eyes twinkled, but she

said nothing of the thoughts tumbling through her mind, thoughts that delighted her and filled her with a warm glow of happiness. She spoke only of her pleasure. "I have always wished to go out upon the sea in a real ship," she said. "This is beyond anything great, Joshua. Where is she?"

"I keep her berthed in a small harbor just above Hythe. We have no dock below the castle. The harbor there is not safe in a storm, and though it is perfectly possible to sail her in, especially when the weather is fine, as it is today, I did not think your first excursion aboard he ought to begin with a climb up a rope ladder to the deck." When Adriana's eyes widened, he chuckled. "We'll save that experience for another time. I do hope your shoes are more practical than that fool pelisse."

She grinned at him. "My shoes are fine." She lifted the hem of her skirt to show him. "Not precisely the height of fashion, but I daresay I can totter about the streets of Hythe without mishap. Indeed, I daresay I could even negotiate your cliff path in them if I had to do so."

Chalford's curricle awaited them at the door, and he lifted Adriana onto the seat, shouting to his groom to "Give them their heads" as soon as he had leapt up beside her and gathered the reins into his hands. The groom did as he was bid, then hoisted himself to his perch behind them as the curricle surged forward. Chalford negotiated the turn from the quadrangle through the barbican gate in fine style, looping his whip and catching the thong with a deft twist of his wrist. A moment later they were across the drawbridge, through the lodge gates, and on their way.

The journey into Hythe was quickly accomplished, and they had nearly passed through the village before Adriana knew where they were. She protested at their speed.

"Nothing much to see here," Chalford told her, slowing his team nonetheless. "Dover and Ashford are the nearest towns of any size, if you are thinking of visiting the shops. The only thing Hythe still has to boast about is Saint Leonard's, which dates from the Middle Ages. It's got a mighty fine chancel."

"But I thought Hythe was a port city," she said. "This is naught but a village."

"In its day it was one of the Cinque Ports," he said, "but its day ended somewhere toward the close of the thirteenth century. Hythe used to spread for two miles along the coast and up the steep slopes behind us, but over the years the sea has spoiled the main harbor and obliterated much of the town."

The private harbor where the *Sea Dragon* was berthed was cup-shaped, small, and picturesque. There were five boats tied to docks there, only one of which was larger than the *Sea Dragon*. Leaving the curricle in the groom's charge, they walked down to the water together. Joshua, carrying a basket he had taken from the curricle in one hand and guiding Adriana with the other placed lightly under her elbow, identified the boats for her. Upon discovering that the larger boat was the *Golden Fleece*, she was pleased to be able to tell him with sincerity that she thought the *Sea Dragon* the more graceful-looking vessel.

Beaming with pride, Joshua helped her aboard. The little yacht gleamed from stem to stern, its woods and brasses polished to a high gloss, its painters and lines coiled neatly in place, its sails tidily furled. The only fault Adriana could detect was an odd and rather over-powering odor of deteriorating fish.

"Welcome aboard, m'lady," said the bearded seaman who hurried up from belowdecks to greet them.

"This is Captain Curry, my dear," Chalford told her. "Are we ready to sail, Curry?"

"Aye, m'lord, the lads are below. Shall I take the basket?"

"Yes, and stow it carefully. 'Tis a picnic for my lady."

"Oh, Joshua, a picnic?"

"Mrs. Motley arranged it when I told her my plan for the day. I daresay we'll enjoy a right good meal." He wrinkled his nose suddenly.

Watching him, Adriana decided with relief that perhaps the odor she had detected was not a normal one. She had been trying very hard to pretend a casual attitude, but now she felt confident enough to ask him what it was.

"I don't know, sweetheart, but it certainly isn't brass polish. Curry, what on earth have you been hauling aboard my boat? Smells like spoilt fish."

The captain shrugged and answered glibly. "As you say, m'lord. The lads found a couple in the hold. Must have been overlooked after you had them gentlemen out fishing several weeks ago. We've throwed 'em out and washed 'er down, but the scent does want t' linger, beggin' yer pardon fer the inconvenience."

Chalford regarded his captain searchingly. "A couple of dead fish, Curry?"

"Aye, sir." Curry gazed back at him, all innocence.

Shaking his head but declining to pursue the matter, Chalford turned the subject to their course for the day, and by the time the crew had come topside to unfurl the sails, Adriana had forgotten the incident altogether. Once they were outside the harbor on the rolling waves of the Channel, with the wind behind them, the smell disappeared and she thought of nothing but enjoying the new and quite marvelous sensations of sailing.

"It's wonderful, Joshua," she said when he joined her at the rail, where she was looking down at the water, watching it rush past the sides of the boat. "Look how the ship makes its own waves at it goes. Oh, it's beautiful."

"I'm glad you like her." He put one arm around her shoulders and, with his other hand, turned her face so that he could look deep into her eyes. "She's a special lady," he said, his voice low in his throat. "I promise you, sweetheart, the *Sea Dragon* is the cleverest, finest yacht on the south coast."

She looked back at him. Her heart was beating faster than usual, but she kept her expression carefully guileless. "I am entirely convinced, my lord, that she is much, much nicer than poor Mr. Braverstoke's *Golden Fleece*.''

"Baggage." He grinned at her, then, staring out to sea again, added ruefully, "I am persuaded that you would find someone to flirt with in a cavern ten miles underground, my sweet, but I could wish you might choose someone other than Randall Braverstoke to work your wiles upon.''

"I think him charming," she said sweetly. "His papa, too. I scarcely remember the other local people I've met, but surely there have been no other men of title. Your Aunt Adelaide, at least, would approve of my favoring the Braverstokes.''

"Well, you're out there," he retorted. "Aunt Adelaide has no great opinion of Braverstoke's title, which is a life peerage only, and considers them both to be a pair of upstart newcomers.''

"Goodness, I am persuaded that Mr. Braverstoke said they had lived in Kent for years.''

"Yes, fifteen to be exact. Upstart newcomers, as I said.''

She laughed. "Well, I suppose that to a family that has been here for seven hundred years, fifteen is like nothing. I daresay we treat people the same in Wiltshire, come to think of it. Papa still calls Viscount Ulster 'that damned new fellow' whenever he mentions him, and I am certain that Ulster must be nearly as old as Papa and has lived at Great Trowley Manor since before I was born. Still he is the first of his family to live on the banks of the Avon, and that is all that counts to Papa.'' She paused, her eyes widening. "Dear me, I have just had the most fantastical notion. Do you think that perhaps Papa and your Aunt Adelaide are peas out of the same pod?''

Chalford laughed. "I believe she would applaud such stuff as his attitude toward the unfortunate Viscount Ulster, but it would be as well for both of us—and for Wryde, too—if she never discovers his affinity for gaming and old port.''

Adriana shuddered as her vivid imagination presented

her with a picture of Lady Adelaide coming upon the Earl of Wryde while the latter was in his cups, but just then her eye was caught by a sail on the distant horizon. She called Chalford's attention to it. "Is . . . is it a French ship, sir?"

"No, sweetheart, just an ordinary trawler. You really mustn't heed Aunt Hetta's megrims. I promise you, we are quite safe from the French. They don't sail this near our coast, for one thing, and if you will remember the tale you heard yesterday, they made no attempt to engage our ships. Rather the reverse, if Braverstoke's story is true, and we've no reason to doubt him."

She relaxed again, giving herself up to the view and the exhilaration of the yacht's movement on the water. The experience was everything she had ever thought it would be, and more. The gentle rocking of the little vessel was hypnotic, the sound of the water against the prow stimulating, and the crackle and snap of the rigging above stirred her imagination. Even the smell of the sea and the cries of the gulls overhead seemed different from this new vantage point. It appeared to be no time at all before Chalford informed her that he was starving and hoped she was ready to investigate Mrs. Motley's picnic basket.

Accordingly, she followed him below, down a cunning ladder to a narrow, hot, and shockingly malodorous companionway that was lit brightly at their end and dimly at the other by the sunlight pouring through the hatch. At the far end of the companionway was a carved door, which opened into a neat little cabin where a linen-draped table had been set out for their meal.

"Here we are, sweetheart. I'm sorry that fishy smell is so strong down here, but I daresay we'll cease to notice it after a few moments. Cozy little place, is it not?"

Adriana had stopped on the threshold and was covering her face with her lacy handkerchief. "Joshua, I can't. I'm sorry, but I just cannot eat a thing." And with that, she turned and hurried back toward the ladder, steadying herself with her free hand against the bulkhead as she went, holding her breath, hoping that if she could block out the dreadful smell, she would make it back to the fresh air without disgracing herself.

She felt his strong hands at her sides before she realized he had followed her, but since he was helping rather than hindering, she made no protest when he boosted her up the ladder and she soon found herself in the open air again, gasping with relief.

"Queasiness takes some people like that," he said after she had obeyed his command to sit down, bend over, and breathe deeply. "They can be as fresh as a daisy abovedeck and sick as a horse when they go below. Probably no more than a reaction to feeling confined. You'll get over the tendency in time."

"It was no such thing," she said tartly, glaring up at him without raising her head. "It was that awful dead-fish smell. I can't think why it didn't make you ill, too."

"Well," he said with an apologetic smile, "I've got a strong stomach, so I daresay I paid it little heed. Are you all right?"

"Yes, of course, and I'm hungry, too, but I simply cannot eat down there with that stench."

"Then we shall have our picnic on deck," he said. "Far better to have a picnic in the open air anyway. I cannot think what possessed me to have them lay it out in the cabin." But then he winked at her, and she laughed, able to guess immediately what his motives had been.

"You can forget that notion this instant, sir," she said with mock sternness, straightening. "If I cannot eat in such an atmosphere, I can promise you I would also be unable to—"

"My lady," he exclaimed, clapping a hand to his chest in affected shock, "spare me my blushes, if you please!"

She chuckled. "I don't believe you know how to blush, sir."

He appeared to consider the accusation soberly for a long moment, then shook his head. "I doubt I ever did know how. You will have to teach me, sweetheart. There must be any number of little things you could say or do to make me blush if you but put your mind to the matter. Ah, yes,'' he added, his lips twitching as he watched the color flood her cheeks, "you have the knack. I daresay you will prove to be an excellent teacher.''

"I wish," she said, carefully avoiding his gaze, "that I had known I would have need of my parasol today.''

"Is the sun too bright?'' he demanded instantly. "I can have them rig a sail over the table if that will help.''

"The parasol is not needed to protect me from the sun, sir,'' she said, giving him a straight look at last, "but rather from the brilliance of a shamelessly impudent husband.''

"Oh, not shamelessly.'' His eyes danced.

"Shamelessly,'' she repeated firmly.

"Then I am to take it you want your parasol in order to rap my knuckles, madam?''

"Rather to break it over your head,'' she said, adding as a second thought, "or perhaps to wrap it around your neck. Indeed, I will give you lessons, sir, if you do not mind your tongue.''

He laughed. "I've married a tartar, sure enough, but before we consider the subject of my lessons more thoroughly, sweetheart, what say you to having our picnic?''

She nodded, completely in harmony with him and pleased with herself for having made him laugh. Feeling fully recovered now from her brief indisposition, she watched with a smile as Joshua, shouting for one of the lads to follow him, plunged down the companionway ladder again. Not long after that, their table, complete with linen drapery, was set up on the afterdeck.

"Sail well into the wind, Curry!'' Joshua shouted. "If you blow my meal into my lap or overboard, I'll have your head!''

"Aye, aye, sir,'' Curry shouted back.

There was silence while they served themselves, but

when Adriana looked up after making room on her
plate for a cold chicken leg, Joshua was frowning
thoughtfully.

"What is it, sir?"

"Curry," he said shortly. "The more I think about
what he said before, the less I like it. I'll speak with him
after we've eaten. I know he lied before, because it's
been two months since I last had anyone out fishing, but
I assumed that the lads had taken her out. Though they
didn't ask my permission, I don't much object because
the fish they catch are cheaper than what they must buy
to feed their families. But if the stench down there
comes from no more than a couple of dead fish
inadvertently overlooked in the hold, I'm a
Dutchman."

Accordingly, once they had finished their meal,
Adriana found herself alone on the afterdeck, watching
while he spoke with his captain. She could not hear what
they said, but she could tell from their expressions that
Joshua was being quietly stern and Curry innocently
defensive. Suddenly, the captain, shaking his head in
agitated denial and gesturing rapidly, began talking
more incisively. Joshua listened, then spoke briefly. A
few moments after that, he rejoined Adriana.

"Had to threaten to dismiss him before I got
anywhere," he said grimly, "but once he realized he was
doing himself no good by playing at this charade, he
told me the whole quick enough."

"Well?"

"Seems my *Sea Dragon* has become a smuggling
ship."

"What?" Excitement gleamed in her eyes at the
thought of actually being on a boat used by free traders.

Reading her expression without difficulty, Joshua's
lips twisted in wry amusement. He said, "According to
Curry, one of the incoming vessels ran into that French
flotilla Tuesday on their way across and was mistaken
for an English ship. Took a broadside before they were
able to raise the Dutch flag, and the ship was sadly
disabled. Knowing they couldn't make England or

Holland with a full load, they waited only until they were out of sight of the other ships before divesting themselves of their cargo. Word came to our local lads yesterday, and they set out in whatever vessels they could commandeer to collect the goods."

"But didn't everything sink?"

"No, of course not. The wines and spirits are shipped in small kegs that float excellently well, and the tea and other goods are well-wrapped in oilskin packets that are also designed to float. No doubt some was lost, but our lads, having equipped themselves with fishing nets, hauled in a good share of the contraband. Whenever they came upon a school of sprats, it seems they employed the nets for their regular purpose, strewing the catch in the sun; and, being small, the things spoil quickly. By the time they encountered a cutter, it was evening, and the *Sea Dragon* appeared to be filled with stinking sprats. Curry said the agents declined to approach the fish at all, fortunately, since the contraband was underneath. I suppose I'd rather they think me a fool for allowing my men to use my boat as a fishing vessel than believe me in league with the free traders."

"Good gracious, what would have happened if the agents had found the goods?"

"I'd have found it damned difficult to prove that my boat had been used without my knowledge or permission."

"What will you do about it now?"

"I have forbidden Curry to take part in such an expedition again," he said. "I believe he will obey me."

"But how can you keep such a man on as your captain, Joshua? Surely you cannot trust him again."

"Nonsense, if I stopped trusting everyone who was involved in smuggling hereabouts, there would be no one left to trust."

"You mean everyone does it?"

"As near as makes no difference. Kent has the highest ratio of persons on the parish of any county in England."

"You mean they get involved in free trading because they cannot otherwise afford to live?"

"Not at all. There are any number of jobs available, but none that pays so well. A man may make from half a guinea to a guinea for a single night hauling goods. He's lucky to make ten shillings a week doing honest labor, and he generally cannot do both. After a night of hauling brandy kegs, he can't stay awake all day to perform the duties of a normal job. He goes on the parish as much to make himself appear to be respectable as to augment his income while he waits for the next run."

"It seems a dreadfully hazardous way to make a living to me," Adriana said. "They must always travel in the dark of night through untraveled, twisting byways, and surely not everyone favors the Gentlemen, even here in Kent."

"Of course not. There are revenue cutters, patrols, and riding officers to be avoided, and from time to time, rival gangs from other areas attempt to infringe upon a local gang's territory. But money isn't the only reward either. The master smugglers—those are the men behind the gangs—not only pay each man for each journey he makes, but also bear all the expenses of eating and drinking for both the man and his horse, if he has one. Each man is also made an allowance of half a sack of tea, the profit from which is equal to more than a guinea. Since they can often count on making as many as three trips in a week, the temptation is such that few men hereabouts can withstand it." He got to his feet and stretched out a hand to her. "Come to the rail. You can see Dover Castle from here."

The white cliffs were magnificent, and the ruins of the ancient castle no less so. Chalford pointed out other interesting landmarks along the way, and the captain even let her take the helm for a few thrilling minutes before the afternoon was done. By the time they returned to Thunderhill, Adriana had discovered in herself an undeniable pleasure to be derived from her husband's companionship, a desire to learn much more about the free traders, and a veritable passion for sailing.

"Never will I get enough of the sea," she told Nancy, who was stirring up the fire when she returned to her bedchamber.

"You get out of them clothes, Miss Adrie," her tirewoman ordered briskly. "Damp as duck feathers they be, and you chilled to the bone, like as not. If you mean to do this ridiculous sort of thing again, you must have some decent, warm clothes made for the purpose, and that's all there is about it."

"I will," Adriana promised her, moving to warm herself by the energetic, crackling fire. "The air turned dreadfully cold before we returned, and I didn't tell Chalford I was chilly because I didn't wish to give him the satisfaction of saying he had warned me. But, oh, this fire feels welcome now. Bring my gown in here, if you please. I'll dress by the hearth."

Nancy nodded, departed, and returned again, carrying the dark-green velvet gown. "You didn't say what to bring, Miss Adrie, but I'll hear no argle-bargle. This be the warmest dress you own, so this is what you will wear. Now, why in the name of all the saints have you not begun to take off that muslin?"

Adriana chuckled. "I managed the pelisse well enough, but I can't reach the buttons on this dress without squirming, and every time I squirm, a cold part of it touches me in a new place. I decided to wait for you."

"Foolishness," declared Nancy. "Going out upon that treacherous water, where no decent Englishwoman ought to go, and thinking you've done something wonderful when all ye've done is get yourself frozen to the marrow. Turn around now and let me see to them buttons. What will you be doing next?"

As much to shock her as to turn the subject, Adriana said demurely, "Well, perhaps I shall go a-smuggling."

"What? You'll never. Smuggling, indeed. I'll wager his lordship would have something to say about that."

"Well, he might, but only because I am his wife, I

daresay. He certainly didn't make much of a fuss when he discovered that his yacht had been used to aid the free traders." She looked expectantly at Nancy, anticipating her reaction.

It was all she had hoped for. The brisk little abigail's mouth dropped open and her hands clutched at the velvet gown she had been about to fling over Adriana's head. "His own boat? Who would dare to do such a thing?"

"My gown, if you please," Adriana said, shivering. She pulled the green velvet down and smoothed it over her hips before she continued airily, "Evidently, anyone who needs a vessel simply commandeers one. This time a cargo had been dumped at sea after the smuggling ship was fired upon by those French ships we saw the other day. The men from Romney Marsh took Chalford's boat to recover their share of the contraband from the sea." She went on to tell about the sprats, and when she had finished, Nancy clicked her tongue in disapproval.

" 'Tis a scandal, that's what it is. A criminal scandal. They ought to be locked up for such impudence, the lot of 'em."

"Then nearly every man in Romney Marsh—indeed, on the south coast—would be locked up. Chalford says they are all in league with the smugglers."

A frown flitted across Nancy's brow. "That Amos, the second footman—you know the one, Miss Adrie. Well, he give me a red silk ribbon yester mornin'. You don't suppose . . ."

Adriana blinked at her. "Amos? Goodness, I shouldn't think so." Then she paused to consider the matter. "On the other hand, I don't see why not. He did seem tired at breakfast, and I daresay that if they went after the cargo yesterday, they would have needed help unloading it and taking it wherever they take such stuff. And they'd have done all that in the dead of night."

The more she thought about it, the more she began to believe that Amos and possibly Jacob, the youngest footman, might well be in league with the local smugglers. She said nothing about the notion over dinner, however, nor did she mention it to Chalford later that night. Believing that he tolerated the Gentlemen, but uncertain as to the exact extent of his displeasure over their use of his boat—and wanting, moreover, to learn a great deal more about the free traders herself—she preferred to feel her way carefully.

8

The following morning, when Lady Henrietta requested her company while she made her rounds to oversee the preparations for the French invasion, Adriana agreed with more alacrity than she might otherwise have felt, hoping that she might thus find an opportunity to discover more about the smugglers. Donning her traveling dress in preparation for the expedition, she wondered if she might more sensibly wear it on future yacht outings.

"I don't think so, Miss Adrie," said Nancy when the suggestion was made to her. " 'Tis wool, sure enough, and warm, but the train'd be a nuisance, and when it gets damp, as it would out on the water all day, you'd begin smellin' like a wet sheep. You'll be wantin' one of a good, heavy silk material instead, tight enough wove that the damp'll just bead up and roll away."

Lady Henrietta agreed when the subject was broached to her a half-hour later in her carriage. "Joshua's mama had such a gown, I believe," she said. "She was forever going out upon the sea. There was a hat of some sort, too, to protect her complexion from the sun. It had a veil that tied down 'round her neck somehow. I might look and see if I can find the hat. The gown would do you no good, of course. 'Tis years and years out of date and much too small. She was a dainty thing, was Eugenia, though to look at Joshua, you'd never think it."

"What happened to her?" Adriana asked. "When I saw her portrait in the long gallery, I asked Joshua about her, but he turned the subject rather deftly and somehow I never quite liked to ask again. I hope it was nothing horrid."

"Death is always horrid," said Lady Hetta with a sad smile, "but it was rather a common ailment when all is said and done. I'm afraid she died in childbirth. Joshua was"—she did rapid calculations on her fingers—"ten years old, I believe. He was away at school, of course, at Harrow. Lord, how that child did hate to go away from Thunderhill, even then. Right miserable he was. But it was worse after Eugenia and her poor stillborn babe were laid to rest. Chalford—his papa, that is—was forced to take extreme measures before Joshua could be persuaded to go back to school." Lady Henrietta paused, reflecting on the past.

"Extreme measures, ma'am?" Adriana prompted.

"He thrashed him," Lady Henrietta said simply.

"How dreadful!" Adriana exclaimed, remembering her feelings when her own mother had died. There had been such a confusion of fury and grief within her that she had been all but unmanageable. She remembered hating Alston and her father for not having died in her mother's stead. Though she had been older than ten years—past twelve, in fact—when she suffered her loss, Joshua, she thought, must have experienced those same feelings.

"That was a dreadful day," said Lady Henrietta, interrupting her reverie, "but in all fairness, I doubt any other method would have answered, and Joshua had been impertinent, a thing Chalford would not tolerate from any of his children. When he died some two years later, there was no one to force Joshua to behave when he came home, for of course he was at school then, too, although most fortunately it was shortly before the long vacation that Chalford died. I doubt anyone could have got Joshua back to Harrow after his papa was laid to rest. I couldn't cope with him at all, nor could dear Lydia, for she was no more than sixteen then herself. So Corbett and Adelaide came as soon as they could to help look after things. But Corbett was a gentle, meek man, not at all the sort to influence a silent, willful, unhappy boy.''

"So it was Lady Adelaide who took control?" suggested Adriana, wondering how that august dame had ever become wed to a man as such her sister described.

Lady Henrietta smiled. "She tried, I suppose, and with regard to the running of the castle, Joshua made no attempt to oppose her at first. Nor did anyone else. But she made little headway when it came to ordering Joshua himself. He withdrew into himself to a truly frightening degree after his father's death, and when Adelaide spoke to him, he would agree with whatever she said and then go his own way. There was nothing she could do about it, because of course he was Marquess of Chalford by then, and no one knew his worth so well as Adelaide. She believed his silence was a sign of maturity, and she applauded what she called his calm demeanor and gentlemanly self-control.''

Adriana winced at the vision these casual words brought to her mind, and she fairly quaked within at another, possibly more pertinent, reflection: Lady Adelaide's opinion, if she ever chanced to learn that Joshua's wife had attempted to batter him to a pulp with her fists out of exasperation with that same calm demeanor and control, simply didn't bear thinking of.

Not wishing to discuss that issue any further, she focused her attention on another point. "Surely he did not leave school altogether at the age of twelve, ma'am.''

"No, of course not. Most fortunately, despite his youth, he took quite seriously his obligations to his brother and sister, and he knew he could not force Ned to go to school if he did not go himself. He went on from Harrow to Cambridge, and when he was done, he swore he'd never live anywhere but Thunderhill again.'' She looked apologetically at Adriana. "Adelaide says I chatter like a magpie. I hope you don't mind my talking like this.''

"Of course I don't. Have you lived here all your life?"

"Yes indeed, though I did travel north the year before Eugenia died to visit Adelaide in Yorkshire—that's where Lord Corbett's home was. Such an exciting journey, and I did so much enjoy walking on the moors each morning. Adelaide didn't fancy the weather there, though, so I cannot be surprised that she never went back after Corbett passed on in the influenza epidemic the year after Aubrey died. Corbett had left his steward to look afer things in Yorkshire, and some cousin or other inherited the estates—for they had neither chick nor child—so Adelaide never returned. She devoted herself to raising Joshua, Ned, and dearest Lydia instead. Lydia married two years later, and then Ned found his Molly the year of that ridiculous peace treaty, and now dearest Joshua has found you." She patted Adriana's knee. "You cannot know how delighted I am that he has fallen in love at last, my dear. He will be so much happier now, will he not?"

"I hope so, ma'am," Adriana said.

"Not that he has been unhappy, precisely," Lady Hetta added quickly, "but it cannot be good for him to have only the castle to occupy his thoughts. He needs a family of his own, and so I told him, but I know he only went to London out of a wish to do his duty. He did not realize the result would be so pleasant."

Fortunately, since Adriana had no idea of how to respond to this, her companion looked away out of the window, seeming not to expect response. How was it, she wondered, that persons like Lady Hetta and Norfolk, who ought to know Chalford, could be so certain that he loved her when she had not the slightest notion herself whether he did or not? For her part, there was just as much evidence to argue that he had merely acquired in her the mistress his precious castle had lacked.

There were moments, certainly, when she thought he felt strong affection for her, moments when she glimpsed a particular warmth in his eyes or when his attitude toward her was notably sensual or protective. But there were other moments when, having thought she understood his motive for something, she discovered it to be something else entirely, like when she first learned that it had been his idea to procure a special license. Even the jealousy she had detected after he had learned of Braverstoke's invitation to sail with him might be explained easily by the fact that he felt possessive of Thunderhill's mistress. Certainly, he had never said anything to indicate that he loved her.

These unprofitable reflections came to an end when Lady Henrietta sat up straight and exclaimed, "Goodness, here we are, my dear! How quickly a journey passes in congenial company."

When the carriage came to a halt in the churchyard in the village of Saltwood and the young footman jumped down from his perch to assist them to alight, Adriana looked about her with interest. It was a small village, little more than the church standing lonely in a field with the high walls of a castle some distance behind it, and a small green surrounded by weatherboarded cottages nearby. Beyond and below them to the east, between their present position and the deep-blue waters of the Channel, she could see the rooftops of Hythe.

Lady Henrietta said, " 'Tis a quaint village, is it not? Saltwood Castle is its only real reason to exist nowadays. But come, we are to meet with the ladies' committee in the rectory."

Adriana soon discovered that Lady Henrietta's helpers were a varied lot. The committee in Saltwood numbered four women. The one at Shepway Cross had but two. And at Burmarsh when they crossed the stream by way of the ancient railed footbridge and entered the church hall, they found but one solitary, plump little lady to greet them.

"Goodness, where are the others, Mrs. Latchmore?" asked Lady Henrietta with a frown.

"Everyone's busy, ma'am, but I've brung the list

from Mary Flack." She held out a crumpled bundle of notes. "That's the lot. We all did our bit."

Moments later, as they recrossed the footbridge, Lady Henrietta said with a sigh, "Adelaide is perfectly right, you know. Volunteers simply must be used up quickly or they cannot be counted upon. There were many more when we began our task, but now everyone is always busy, and we simply must know what goods and foodstuffs there are in order to know what must be done when word comes that the French are on their way."

Adriana gestured toward the notes Lady Henrietta still held in her hand. "It looks as though they have done the job, ma'am."

Her companion shook her head, stuffing the notes into the large reticule she carried. "These will prove to be well nigh illegible, my dear. That is why I prefer to meet with the people who make the lists. Many of them are nearly illiterate, but they are the best their villages have to offer."

Despite the brief time they had been inside the church, Adriana noted as they approached the carriage that both the coachman and the young footman had slumped in their respective places and were dozing in the warm sun. With a twinkling look she directed her companion's attention toward the two.

Lady Henrietta clicked her tongue in annoyance. "Really, I cannot think what comes over them."

"Might there have been a run last night, ma'am?"

Lady Henrietta raised her brows. "Last night? I suppose so, but what would that have to say to the purpose?"

"Well, Joshua said nearly every able-bodied man in Kent is involved in some degree with the smugglers, so I wondered."

Lady Henrietta nodded. "It would explain their impertinence in falling asleep just when they are wanted. Here, Wittersham, wake up!" she cried, jabbing the coachman with the handle of her reticule.

"What are you about, man? And you, Jacob, wake up."

Both men started, then straightened themselves, offering rapid apologies. Jacob, who had been sitting on his step, jumped up, tugging his tunic into place over his long, skinny torso before hastening to help them into the carriage.

They drove on to Dymchurch, the unspoiled little coastal town crouched behind a massive sea barrier built by the Romans and known as Dymchurch Wall. As they passed along the curving main street, Adriana found herself thinking not of Romans or of Lady Henrietta's volunteers but of free traders, wondering how she might discover more information about them.

"Down there by the wall," said Lady Henrietta, "you can see the martello tower they are building to protect the sluice gates. Of course, they ought to have begun work two years ago, only that milksop, Prime Minister Addington, refused to spend any money whatsoever for defense."

"Well, after all, ma'am, he thought he would be able to arrange a lasting peace with the French."

"And so he disbanded our military and stopped all the funds meant to build defenses along this coast," said Lady Henrietta tartly. "I'd no patience with the man. Thank heaven Mr. Pitt is back in power, and none too soon."

"Why is this tower so important?" Adriana asked. She could see that the structure, a round stone form, narrower at the top than at the bottom, already rose some twenty feet above the shore. "And what are the sluice gates, precisely?"

"Why, they control the water level of Romney Marsh, my dear. The whole marsh is below high-tide level. Dymchurch itself is more than seven feet below. Without those gates, the whole thing would be awash in no time. Indeed, that is one of our defense plans, to flood everything if necessary."

"That seems a trifle hard on the inhabitants."

"Sacrifice is often necessary for the greater good, my dear," replied Lady Henrietta calmly.

There was nothing to say to that, and they had arrived at the church, opposite the town hall in a side street. Alighting from the carriage, Adriana followed Lady Henrietta into the dimly lit hall, where a group of five ladies awaited them. Lady Hetta introduced her and was quickly submerged in details of their inventory. Having sat through enough of that sort of thing for one day, Adriana soon made her excuses and went back outside.

Wittersham was pacing up and down near the hedge separating churchyard from roadway, but Jacob lolled against the rear of the carriage again, eyes shut, arms folded across his chest, in much the same position he had taken in Burmarsh. Adriana, shaking her head at Wittersham when he moved to approach her, went straight toward the rear of the carriage, a mischievous grin on her face.

"Oh, Jacob," she crooned softly. "Jacob, do wake up." When he blinked, then straightened so quickly that he nearly lost his balance, her grin broadened. "I daresay you must be very tired, Jacob. Whatever did you do last night when you ought to have been sleeping the sleep of the innocent?"

He glanced in Wittersham's direction, then back at Adriana. "I dunno what ye mean, m'lady."

"Yes, you do, Jacob, and you needn't fear that I am angry with you, for I am not. Not at all. I think it must be dreadfully exciting to be a landsman for the free traders. If ladies could do such things, I should join you in a twink."

The lad looked horrified. "Ye mustn't think such things. Indeed, it ain't fittin' fer such a fine lady." Then, realizing that he had pretty well condemned himself out of his own mouth, he glanced fearfully in Wittersham's direction again. "We oughtn't to speak of such, m'lady."

"What? Will Wittersham squeak beef on you? You see, I know some slang, Jacob. I am not at all nice in my ways, sometimes, and I have a burning wish to know more about smuggling. Pray do not tell me you have naught to do with such stuff. Why, you must be very brave, and very clever, too, to evade the riding officer so easily as I'm told you do. It all sounds most exciting."

He blinked. Clearly he had never thought of himself as particularly brave before. Squaring his shoulders and drawing himself to his full six-foot height, he looked down at her with pride. "It ain't so hard bein' shut o' Mr. Petticrow, m'lady, that it ain't. More like a game it be, us'n agin him. When he's south, we be north, and turn about. Some o' the lads keep watch, o' course, but we knows the route he means to take long afore he's in 'is saddle."

"His lordship said poor Mr. Petticrow has to watch five whole miles of coastline," Adriana said. "It hardly seems fair."

Jacob's look was one of amused tolerance now. "Mr. Petticrow be a nice gentleman, m'lady, and none wishes 'im ill, so it be as well that he have a good, long route and can be kept well out o' harm's way, partikler since 'e won't take gelt fer to turn 'is eyes ter the wall—money, that is, ter look the other way," he added when she looked bewildered. "There's some as ain't so tolerant o' their riding officers as we be."

"It seems odd to me that he never caught wind of the daylight run the other day," Adriana said innocently.

Jacob stared at her. "What be ye knowin' about that, m'lady?" Then, before she could speak, his brow cleared and he said, "Oh, aye, the lads said ye was aboard *Sea Dragon* when the master discovered she'd been out. That were a near thing fer Mr. Curry, that were."

"How do you mean?"

"Well, m'lady, in the general way o' things, the master do look t'other way. But though he don't look ter cross the Gentlemen, he didn't like 'em usin' 'is boat, 'n' that's a fact."

"Why, he didn't seem very angry," Adriana said,

"only a little displeased. I was there, Jacob, and I can tell you he didn't so much as raise his voice to Captain Curry."

The footman grimaced. "He don't never raise his voice, m'lady, but that don't mean poor Mr. Curry weren't shakin' in 'is boots when he realized 'is lordship 'ad discovered he'd been a-helpin' of the Gentlemen, 'n' all. When the master's angry, his voice can freeze the marrow in a man's bones, and that's a fact. So if it be all the same to you, ma'am, I'd as lief ye don't go a-tellin' 'im ye think I be part o' the business. I'm right sorry I nodded off t'day, but 'tis all a man can do to stay awake when he's just a-settin' about in the sun, even if he hasn't been up all hours the night before. I'd not like the master to think I'd been out 'n' about and then shirkin' m' duty."

"Oh, Jacob, of course I shall say nothing to the master, not about anything you tell me, so you needn't trouble your head about that. Tell me more about Mr. Petticrow. Does he not have dragoons he can call upon to help him watch his bit of coast?"

"Only if he knows certain sure that there's a run on, and we take precious care that he don't."

"Here, lad," said Wittersham, coming quickly up to them, his weathered face set in stern lines. "What be ye about, jawin' at 'er ladyship when ye oughta be a-helpin' 'er into the carriage? I'm right sorry if he's discommoded ye, m'lady."

Jacob reddened to his ears, but Adriana smiled at the middle-aged coachman and said, "Pray do not scold him, Wittersham. I asked him to speak to me, for I wish to know something about the Gentlemen hereabouts. Perhaps you can tell me more about their activities than Jacob has been able to. I daresay a man of your vast experience could tell a great deal."

The coachman grimaced. "It ain't fer me to be tellin' yer la'ship what ye ought and oughtn't to talk about, but ye'd do well to keep mum on that subject, ma'am, and that's the truth of the matter, that is. Lady Henrietta be on the stoop wi' some o' her ladies. She'll be right along now, so best ye be lettin' Jacob help ye inside.''

"Very well, Wittersham." Disappointed, Adriana turned again to the young footman, awarding him a friendly smile. "You may give me your hand, Jacob." Inside the carriage, she noted that the coachman followed Jacob around behind, and she soon heard Wittersham's gruff voice, pitched too low for her to make out his words, but carrying unmistakable censure in his tone.

Adriana was sorry that the young footman had been scolded for talking to her, but in the week that followed, as she went about her activities, she found herself watching the castle servants with an eagle eye, trying to determine which ones among them were involved with the Gentlemen and which were not. It was something to break the tedium, although if she had been pressed to tell the truth, her days were full enough that there was little of that.

She went out again with Lady Henrietta to other villages; she went riding each morning with Joshua or with her groom; she appealed to Lady Adelaide to begin teaching her her duties; and she entertained afternoon callers from among the local gentry. The most frequent of these were Lord Braverstoke and his son. They paid their first call two days after the last of the houseguests had departed, and Randall Braverstoke promptly reissued his invitation to take her aboard the *Golden Fleece*.

The outing was arranged for the following day, so on Sunday, after services in the parish church just outside the castle walls, entered from the quadrangle through a fascinating stone tunnel that opened into the family's private chapel, Adriana and Chalford found themselves aboard the *Golden Fleece* heading out into the Channel, while their host jauntily displayed his yacht's amenities. His intention, rather amusingly clear, was to impress Chalford with the superiority of his sloop over all other sloops harbored on the south coast. Chalford responded politely.

Adriana responded cordially, even at times with enthusiasm, but privately she believed that the *Sea Dragon*, though smaller, was indeed the prettier and more graceful of the two, and was kept, sprats notwithstanding, in much better trim. She detected dry wood in several places on Braverstoke's yacht, and although the brasses and the ostentatious gilded medallions that decked the bulwarks at evenly spaced intervals had been polished, the task had clearly been performed in haste. She enjoyed the expedition, but she made no attempt to beguile Mr. Braverstoke into repeating the invitation.

She enjoyed her outings with Chalford, too, and her time with Lady Henrietta, for whom she was rapidly developing a firm affection; however, she could not say that her sessions with Lady Adelaide were altogether successful.

"It is not that she does not wish to instruct me," she confided to Lady Henrietta on Monday morning as they walked together toward Burmarsh, her ladyship having determined to visit Mary Flack in order to decipher the list she had previously been given. "She is very kind, but I cannot help but feel that she believes I should do much better to leave everything to her. And the woeful truth of it is," she confessed with a rueful grin, "that I should like that very well."

"She does not mean to give that impression," Lady Hetta said, turning to smile at her and tugging her hat lower over her forehead in order to protect her eyes from the glare of the sun. "Indeed, she is pleased to have you here, my dear, as are we all. Perhaps she only thinks it better for you to do as you please for a time until you are quite settled in."

"Well, she didn't wish me to come with you today. She said it was not becoming to my station."

"Only because we chose to walk," said Lady Hetta. "She scolded me for inviting you, but really it is too bad to take a carriage round and about, when the path across the marsh is but two miles or so. And after last night's rain, the road is in a dreadful state. The carriage would be a sight when we returned."

"We won't look so well ourselves," Adriana pointed out, laughing. "I don't know whose boots these are that Nancy unearthed for me, but they are certainly better for walking along this muddy path than any shoes of mine would be."

"They are Chalford's. Oh, yes," she said when Adriana's eyes widened in disbelief. "He was only a boy when he wore them, of course, but I daresay nothing has ever been thrown away here. Your Nancy appealed to my woman, you see, so I know. That hooded woolen cloak she found for you is an old one of Adelaide's."

They walked along in companionable silence for some moments after that, enjoying the calls of the birds in nearby hedges and trees. The path twisting across the marsh was one of those convoluted routes described to her by Chalford, and Adriana was having a fine time imagining a line of men and horses laden with brandy kegs in the dead of night, creeping along this very way, silent, ears cocked for the slightest sound in the distance that might herald the approach of riding officer or dragoon. The wind would be moaning through the willows nearby, shaking the leaves on the great hornbeam under which they were passing, moaning . . .

"Good gracious, what's that?" she exclaimed as the sound penetrated at last, wrenching her from her reverie.

Lady Hetta, aroused from a brown study of her own, looked about, blinking. When the sound came again, she pointed. "Over there, beyond that hedge."

But Adriana had already turned from the path. The ground away from the hard-packed trail, thanks to the previous night's deluge, was boggy beneath her feet, but it was not so much so that it hindered her progress as she pushed through the hedge to discover a man, bound and gagged and tangled in the lower branches of the large bush under which he had been shoved.

"Mr. Petticrow!" exclaimed Lady Hetta, jerking her full skirts free of the hedge and rushing to kneel at his side, unconscious of the damage to her clothing. "Dear me, sir, how come you to be in such a dreadful fix?"

"Perhaps if you were to loosen his gag," Adriana suggested, adding when this had been accomplished, "Dear sir, I hope you may not have caught your death." She added her efforts to those of Lady Henrietta, and when the poor gentleman was free of his bindings, they assisted him to his feet.

"Thank you both very kindly," said Mr. Petticrow, who could now be seen to be a man of medium height and somewhat portly stature with light-blue eyes and ruddy cheeks. He began to move his arms and legs carefully, then to stamp his feet. "Stiff as a stick, and not to be wondered at," he said.

"Have you been there all night, Mr. Petticrow?" asked Lady Henrietta. "Are you not very wet?"

"A trifle dampish, thank you, your ladyship, but it didn't come on to rain until after I was stowed, and the bush protected me from the worst of it, I believe. Not that those damned scoundrels— I do beg your pardon, I'm sure, but I find I am a trifle out of temper in consequence of this affront. They'd no intention of providing me shelter by shoving me under there. Meant me to perish unnoticed, that's what they meant by it."

"Oh, surely not," protested Adriana. "Who would do such a dreadful thing?"

"Those dam—dashed smugglers, that's who, ma'am. Don't believe I've had the pleasure," he added with a quaint, though stiff, little bow. "Jeremiah Petticrow at your service."

"This is Lady Chalford, Mr. Petticrow," said Lady Hetta.

"Ah, the new marchioness. Then 'tis a double pleasure, ma'am. Not that I'd say the same of every member of every noble family hereabouts, but your husband is a fine gentleman and it is proud I am to meet his lady. There are those who make it a point to flout the law and those who don't."

"Mr. Petticrow," put in Lady Henrietta, "surely you ought to take off your coat and let your shirt dry in the sun, for you are shivering, and I am persuaded that you will take a chill."

"Bless you, ma'am, I'm not the sort of man to take his jacket off with ladies present. And it takes more than a night's damping to do in Petticrow, as the lads will see soon enough."

"I'm certain no one intended to murder you," Adriana said, giving him a searching look. He was not what she had expected a riding officer to be. There were moments when he spoke like an educated man. Deciding he was merely taking pains to impress them, she added firmly, "You were quite near the path, after all, and I have been told that the smugglers only attempt to make certain you are not nearby when there is a run on."

"Being near to a path that generally no one travels other than the lads themselves hardly shows intent for me to be found, m'lady, and as for keeping me out of the way, I am persuaded it was more than that. This lot was rough-spoken, talked murderous talk, and the odd thing was that I recognized not a single voice among them. I've been led down a daisy path before, more's my shame, but this was different, I tell you."

He could not be shaken from his belief, and both ladies soon ceased to try, putting their efforts instead into persuading him to accompany them into Burmarsh, where he could be sure of finding a cottager willing to feed him and dry his clothes. By the time they reached the village, he swore he was as dry as could be and accepted no more than a cup of hot tea and a bun from Mary Flack before taking himself off.

Their business did not take long, and the two ladies were soon on the path again, making their way back to Thunderhill. Adriana chuckled. "That poor man. It must have ruffled his dignity severely to be found in such a position by the likes of us. No wonder he insisted the men had tried to murder him."

Lady Henrietta clicked her tongue. "You know, my dear, I am sure it is just as you say and the poor man was making more of it than it deserved, but Mary Flack was telling me—whilst you were talking with Mr. Petticrow, you know—that there was trouble last night. She doesn't know the whole of it, but goods were taken and there are rumors of a rival gang attempting to make trouble for the local lads. I do hope 'tis only rumor and nothing more.''

"It sounds exciting," said Adriana.

"Oh, my dear, not exciting at all. Why, I can remember my papa telling us about the dreadful Hawkhurst gang. They terrorized people all over Kent and Sussex fifty years ago, and whenever anyone got in their way, they murdered them. I don't know what we should do if that ever happened again.''

"Well, I am persuaded you needn't fret, ma'am. Surely in this day and age such violence would be scotched at the outset."

So sure was she of what she said that it came as a shock to her a day or so later to learn that more rumors had spread that a gang of smugglers operating out of Sandgate, some miles to the north, was extending its scope of activity. These men were said to be under the control of a master smuggler who advocated violence to force other gangs to bend the knee to his own.

One morning shortly after Adriana heard these rumors, when the family had gathered to break their fast, Jacob burst into the breakfast parlor without ceremony and blurted, "Please, m'lord, they've found Mr. Petticrow staked out on the beach below the castle. He's in a fearful state, sir, and Mr. Wittersham said I was to ask yer permission to bring 'im up."

"Good gracious," said Lady Adelaide with a frown, "I suppose the Gentlemen have been up to their tricks again. 'Tis a pity they will treat the poor riding officer so, but I fail to see how it's any concern of ours, Chalford."

The marquess looked at Jacob. "Was it a prank?"

"No, m'lord," Jacob was pale. " 'E was staked out below the tideline, sir, and when the lads found 'im, the water was near to 'is chin. They'd gagged 'im. He couldn't even shout."

"Tell them to do whatever is necessary for him," Chalford ordered crisply.

9

Once Mr. Petticrow had been tucked up in a bedchamber, the doctor commanding him to stay there until they could be sure he would not fall victim to an inflammation of the lungs, Chalford ordered his family into the great hall and issued an edict.

"Matters seem to have reached such a pass that I have no choice," he said calmly, "but to ask you all to avoid going alone beyond the castle walls until this business has been settled."

"Very sensible," said Lady Adelaide. "If this keeps up, free trading will go quite out of fashion. One already hears complaints that English gold is going into Bonaparte's pockets in exchange for wines and other smuggled goods, and that French prisoners are foolishly being ferried back to France. Of course, ours get home the same way, and it is patently absurd to pay ten guineas the pound for tea when it may be had for shillings instead, or to go without silks merely because the government is so foolish as to impose unreasonable duty. Violence, however, cannot be tolerated. Do you hear, Hetta, you are not to go out."

"But that's ridiculous," Adriana protested. "Oh, not what you said, ma'am," she added hastily when Lady Adelaide bristled, "but, Joshua, you cannot expect us to remain prisoners here."

"That was not my intention," he said. "You may certainly go out whenever you wish, but I can no longer permit you to walk unescorted into the villages or even to drive about the countryside without proper protection. I know it will make for inconvenience, but I trust you will all obey me in this matter. I do not wish to have to worry about your safety."

Lady Hetta nodded briskly. "I shall tell Wittersham to carry a blunderbuss, then, shall I, my dear?"

"More than that, Aunt Hetta. I want armed outriders —at least two of them—whenever you travel beyond these walls." He turned to Adriana. "And you, sweetheart, are not to ride alone, as I know you have done when I have been unable to accompany you. Your groom is no longer sufficient protection. If you wish to ride, you have only to tell me so and I will accompany you."

"Joshua, this is foolish. The smugglers have no quarrel with Thunderhill. Surely they will not molest us."

"The local men are friendly enough, but we have no reason to trust outsiders. You will do as I bid."

Adriana fumed, but she could not with any propriety debate the matter further then and there, so she held her tongue. But when Lord Braverstoke and his son paid a call that afternoon, she took the opportunity afforded by Lady Henrietta's engaging his lordship in conversation to express her feelings to his son. The results were not encouraging.

"I must agree with Chalford," Randall Braverstoke told her apologetically. "One cannot be too cautious. This new gang will do whatever is necessary to collect their goods."

"Not in broad daylight, surely."

"I know little about such things, of course, but they tell me these ruffians have attempted to intimidate the locals into joining them or at least doing nothing to hinder them. That sort of thing can be done by daylight as well as by dark, I suppose. Must hand it to the fellow behind this. He knows his business."

Lady Adelaide, having entered the great hall in time to overhear this last statement, declared, "One does not offer praise to a proponent of violence, young man."

"No, no," said Lord Braverstoke hastily. "The lad didn't mean such a thing. Tell her, Randall."

"Certainly, sir." He smiled at Lady Adelaide. "I was speaking objectively, ma'am. Surely the larger the operation, the greater the profit for all concerned."

"Indeed," retorted her ladyship, "so it is all of a piece, is it, when crime is committed for mere money?"

"Easy for her to say," Braverstoke said quietly to Adriana while his father took punctilious leave of the aunts. "Only let her try to convince a man without it that money is 'mere.' "

Adriana smiled, but since she was out of charity with him for failing to support her against Chalford, she said nothing to lead him to believe she agreed with him. Nor did she intend to stop trying to convince her husband that he was being grossly overprotective. That evening, however, when they were alone, her attempts to beguile him into changing his mind, particularly with regard to her riding, proved singularly unsuccessful.

"Your safety is a matter of primary importance to me," he said, kissing her. "I know what can happen; you do not."

"Then tell me, sir, for I cannot think how I might be in the least danger. This quarrel is not of our making."

"It does not matter whether the quarrel is ours," he said patiently. "The danger is real. Now, come to bed, sweetheart. We've better things to do than to bicker over smugglers."

She obeyed reluctantly, annoyed as always by his casual assumption that he had only to make a decision and she would obey, but as usual, it was not long before he had caused her to forget her discontent. The next morning her frustrations were back in full force, however, for it was a magnificent day, perfect for riding, but when she told Chalford that she would like to have her mare saddled, he shook his head regretfully.

"I know I promised to put myself at your disposal, but I've got my bailiff coming to me at nine o'clock this morning."

"Tell him to come later."

"I am not so capricious. His schedule is more rigid than mine, since he has many duties to attend in a day's time that cannot be as easily put off as mine might be.''

If Adriana had chafed before at being confined, she chafed more now, and when the morning post brought her a sprightly letter from Sally, her spirits sank even lower. According to Sally, everyone who counted in the *beau monde* who was not already resident in Brighton would be so by the prince's birthday.

"Only listen to this bit of her letter, ma'am," she said to Lady Henrietta, who, with a pair of wire-rimmed spectacles perched upon her nose, was busily compiling information from her inventories at the table near the south window. "She writes that Bedford is there, and Mrs. Fitz, of course, and Lord Craven, the handsome Mr. Dawlish—indeed, everyone—but this is the part that made me laugh: 'It is whispered that the Female Jockey Club mean to get up some races of their own, due to a rage for ass-riding which prevails amongst the ladies here. A number of long-eared palfreys may be seen every morning at the end of the Steyne, ready saddled for the morning trot; and, from an early hour, the roads through the Downs and along the cliffs are covered with ladies mounted upon their donkeys, going through their exercises as regularly as any of the grooms on the racecourse.' ''

"Good gracious, what will they think of next?" Lady Henrietta blinked over her spectacles. "Women racing donkeys. I shudder to think of what Adelaide would say to that!"

Adriana smiled wistfully. "It all sounds like they are having a delightful time, does it not?" With a sigh, she rang for Amos to fetch her a standish, whereupon she began at once to answer Sally's letter. When this task was finished and the letter set aside for Chalford to frank, she sighed again, wondering aloud what she could do next to occupy her time.

Lady Hetta suggested that she might like to read a book or help sort inventories with her. "Or, perhaps," she added when neither of these suggestions appeared to stir interest, "you might like to look at some of Adelaide's ladies' magazines to plan your winter wardrobe. She has sent for our seamstress, Mrs. Lymington, to come to us the third week of August.''

Adriana thanked her for the suggestion, agreed that perhaps she would do some such thing one day soon, then excused herself, saying that if she could not ride she could at least get some exercise by exploring more of the castle.

Half an hour later, she found herself climbing the spiral stairway inside the keep, listening to the rustling sounds of the owls in the chambers above. Since callers often asked to see these creatures, she had come to know them rather well, so when she encountered one small, plump specimen perched on the edge of a stair, apparently asleep in a shaft of sunlight from a nearby arrow loop, she stopped and greeted him politely.

"How do you do, Lord North?" When the owl opened his round yellow eyes and blinked at her, she felt her spirits rise and leaned back against the stone wall, careless of her dress and of the penetrating chill. "You look very wise, sir. Can you advise me?" Lord North stared, ruffling the tawny feathers around his neck and moving himself an inch to the right. Having no wish to disturb him further, Adriana sat down on a step below him, rubbing the chill from her arms and propping her chin in her hand as she turned her mind firmly to her problems.

Little thought was necessary to convince her that while she would like to know what Joshua's feelings were toward her—indeed, what his feelings were toward almost anything—there was a matter between them more pertinent to the moment than that. Affection between them would grow or not grow over the years ahead, and she would no doubt learn to read him better as time passed, but in the meantime he had to be brought to see that he could no longer go about making everyone's decisions for them without discussion, without asking for their opinions or considering their desires. While such autocratic behavior might have been all right when he had only siblings, servants, or aunts to consider—

since they all seemed to have been reconciled, somehow, to his way—it would not do for his wife.

After some moments of this reflection, she looked at the round little owl, amused to see that he had closed his eyes again. When she chuckled, he opened one, then shut it. "You are no help, sir," she said. "Indeed, there is no one to help me. Clearly I must take matters into my own hands."

What was not clear was the means by which she might bring Chalford to see that her wishes were not entirely to be ignored, that it was neither selfish nor childish of her to have grown tired of being issued arbitrary orders and to want to have a small part in the process of making such decisions as most affected her. She sighed, muttering to her companion, "Your lordship, there are two things I'd really like to do. One is to visit my friend Sarah in Brighton, and the other is to learn what I can about the smugglers in Kent, but my new lord and master thinks only to bury himself in his castle, away from both danger and amusement, and he expects me to entomb myself with him. I have tried to be an obedient wife; it does not answer."

With an air of great dignity Lord North turned his attention to the removal of a tiny insect from the downy tip of one flight feather, and Adriana, seeing him thus occupied, forbore to burden him further with her problems and politely bade him good day. Descending to the gatehouse entrance, she decided to stroll through the rose garden while she continued her reflections, but when she emerged from the chilly passageway into the warmth of the quadrangle, the first person she laid eyes upon was the young footman, Jacob, striding rapidly in the direction of the marsh gate. The sight of him startled her, for the quadrangle had been deserted earlier and she had not expected to see anyone, and her surprise triggered an idea that flashed into her mind with such speed and force that she gasped at its brilliance.

"Jacob," she called before further reflection might

swerve her from her daring and thoroughly outrageous plan.

The young man stopped and turned. "M'lady? I didn't see ye there in the passage. I'm sorry if—"

"Never mind that, Jacob. Come here. I want to discuss a matter with you, and I have no desire to shout it to the world."

Flushing slightly, the lad hurried back to her. "Aye, m'lady. How may I serve ye?"

"I want you to talk to Wittersham for me, Jacob. I have decided to go to Brighton, and since these rumors have started . . . You know the ones I mean?" When he nodded, she went on quickly, "Well, since there is fear of meeting with violence on the roads, I wish to travel by water. Indeed, to put the matter with no bark on it, I have decided that it will suit me very well, if you or Wittersham can arrange it, to sail aboard a smuggler's ship."

Young Jacob was clearly appalled. "M'lady, I couldn't and Mr. Wittersham wouldn't! I don't mean to be impertinent, ma'am, truly, but the men would never allow such a thing. Why, they don't even travel by daylight."

"All the better, for I am persuaded his lordship would mislike my traveling by such a means, so I shall have to leave by dark, while he is still sleeping."

"Well, they won't do it," said Jacob. "It would be worth my life to ask 'em."

"Nonsense, I am certain that you are very valuable to them and that Wittersham is even more valuable." She paused, giving him a direct look. "Did you not tell me his lordship knows nothing of your activities, Jacob?"

"Aye, m'lady, that I did, and you promised you'd keep mum."

"So I did," Adriana said thoughtfully, "and I should be most reluctant to break my word to you, but I am determined upon this course, you see, so I fear that if you and the others were to prove intractable, I should be forced . . ." She let the pause speak for itself.

Jacob paled. "I could not assist you to defy the master, m'lady. I could not."

"I am not asking you to do such a thing," said Adriana firmly. "Not precisely, in any event. He has never said I may not arrange to visit Brighton on my own, you know. He has only given orders that I am not to leave the castle walls without an armed escort. Surely any escort I might have on a free trader's vessel would be well-armed indeed. You wouldn't wish to deny me an exciting adventure, and surely, Jacob, you don't believe the Gentlemen would harm me, do you?" She regarded him anxiously.

"Our lads wouldn't, but like as not," Jacob said shrewdly, "if master approved, he'd send ye to Brighton on the *Sea Dragon*."

Adriana had to exert firm control over her temper when more than anything she wanted to stamp her foot and shout at him. "Pray do not be provoking, Jacob," she said with forced calm. "Have I not said time and again that I wish to learn as much as I can learn about the smugglers? I think it is wonderful the way they defy the customs officials. Why, if our foolish government had its say, none but the very rich might drink a simple cup of tea, but thanks to the bravery of you and your compatriots, tea, wine, silks, and laces are all available at a cost that many can afford. Don't deny me the privilege of sharing a small part of your adventures. I know I would never be allowed to take part in the actual landing of smuggled goods or the transporta—"

"Gawd, no! Lady Chalford, please, ye mustn't think such things. Not for a moment. Why, wi' the Sandgate lot on the loose, ye might even be killed."

Adriana sighed. "I know. So you see, Jacob, you must arrange this little adventure for me. Your friends may be trusted not to harm me and all they need do is to see me safely ashore at Brighton. If you have trouble with Wittersham, simply tell him that I shall find it necessary to report his activities to Lord Chalford if he does not accommodate me in this matter. No doubt you can all afford to live well on the proceeds of smuggling alone; however, if this new gang prevails, that income may prove unobtainable. And no doubt, Chalford, learning of your activities, will do no more than scold you as he did Captain Curry, but the possibility does exist, I'm afraid, that having already had his temper stirred by Curry, he may lose it altogether when he learns how many of you others are involved. And I have a very good idea how many you are, Jacob.''

The footman said reluctantly, ''I'll do what I can, m'lady. No tellin' when the next opportunity will arise, however.''

''See that it arises soon, Jacob.''

Nodding miserably, he hurried on his way, and Adriana returned to the hall block, reasonably pleased with herself. It was a shame that she had had to threaten to expose the men's illegal activities to Chalford, but she had seen no other course to follow. Now she hoped merely that they had not, in the short time afforded them, learned enough about her to know that she would never do such a shabby thing.

She did suffer some second thoughts after supper when Joshua, in an effort to make up to her for his failure that morning, invited her to ride with him along the beach. The day was still a magnificent one, and as she galloped beside him, she was exhilarated by the smell of the sea, the cries of the shags and kittiwakes overhead, and the sensation of the wind blowing in her face. When Joshua drew up and turned toward her, laughing, she grinned back, well-pleased with him for his thoughtfulness in arranging the outing.

''We can have a fine view of the sunset over the marsh from up there on that ridge if you are willing to wait fifteen minutes for the pleasure,'' he said. ''I've a blanket tied to my saddle, so we may be comfortable.''

She agreed, and leaving the horses on the shingle, they climbed the steep hillside. Soon they were tucked cozily against one large boulder while a second protected them from the breezes blowing off the water.

Chalford pulled her closer to him, and Adriana leaned her head against his shoulder.

"Beautiful, isn't it?" he said when a golden glow appeared in the sky above the western horizon, beneath the descending sun.

"Wonderful," she agreed after a brief silence. "There have been clouds nearly every night since I arrived, you know, so I thought the brilliant sunsets were due to them. But there isn't a cloud in the sky now, and yet there is such color. Look," she added a moment later, "it's nearly pink now."

The sun dipped lower, and the colors above the horizon deepened, growing orange, then red with deep purple streaks slashing through. Adriana sighed with pleasure, watching until the last glow had disappeared, leaving gray sky in its wake.

"We'd best get back," she said. "It will be dark soon."

"We have time. The dusk lasts two hours this time of year."

She glanced around, aware suddenly as she had not been before of their solitary location. "Are we safe here, Joshua? Do you have your pistol?"

"In my saddle holster," he said. "You needn't fret, sweetheart. No one will harm me. I'm too well-known hereabouts, and the trouble that would be stirred up afterward would make such a move unwise, no matter who was responsible. Besides, there will be a moon tonight, I believe. The men from Sandgate are no doubt sitting by their firesides, awaiting the darks."

"The darks?"

"'Tis what they call nights suitable for their activities."

"Well, if they are in Sandgate on a clear night, Joshua, surely they will be in Sandgate during the daytime, any day, and if you are safe, so must I be, so I do think it would be safe—"

"We have discussed that, Adriana," he said, smiling as he rose and helped her to her feet. "I am sorry to restrict your activities, but you must let yourself be guided by me in this matter. As soon as it's safe to do so, you may go riding again without having to depend upon me for an escort.''

''When will that be, Joshua?''

''When I know it is safe,'' he repeated firmly.

Though she knew he meant well, the warmth she had been feeling toward him faded with these words. His protective attitude, rather than making her feel cared for, fretted her independent spirit more than jobations from her brother or father had done in the past. Thus it was that despite his continued kindnesses and the warmth she saw in his eyes whenever they came to rest upon her, not to mention the passion that he could stir within her with the lightest of caresses, Adriana's mind was made up. She awaited Jacob's summons impatiently. Each time she saw him, she hoped he would make some sign or other, but it was not until the following Tuesday afternoon that he did so.

She was curled up in a large chair in Chalford's library, perusing an account in the *Times* of the match at the Lewes races between Mr. Boyce's Bobtail and Mr. Mellish's Lady Brough. The races had taken place the previous Friday and Saturday, but the paper was delivered a day late at Thunderhill.

Jacob entered the library, looked quickly around to assure himself that she was alone, and then, in hushed but nonetheless urgent tones, said quickly, ''T'night, m'lady.''

Flinging the newspaper aside, she leaned forward excitedly. ''What time? And where shall I meet the boat?''

''Wittersham says I'm to meet ye in the hall at three 'n' bring ye to beach.'' He eyed her skeptically. ''He says ye'll ha' to climb the line—the ladder, that be—'cause 'twill be too dark to trust ye to come to no harm in a bosun's chair.''

''I can do it,'' she assured him. Then, bethinking herself of one small detail, she added more diffidently,

"That is, I can if someone else will see to my band-boxes."

"Aye, Wittersham said there'd be one or two, like as not, but he said to warn ye not to fill the boat wi' baggage."

She chuckled. "Never fear, Jacob. I am perhaps a trifle eccentric, but I am not a fool."

Jacob looked nervously over his shoulder at some imagined sound. "M'lady, be you sure you want this? Master's bound to find out, and like as not he'll be fit to knock heads when he do. There'll be the devil to pay then and no pitch hot."

"Well, he won't knock your head, Jacob, so you needn't fear it, and he never gets angry with me. Since he won't know for certain who helped me, all will be well if you just keep a blank look on your face if anyone asks questions. He can scarcely rail at the free traders, after all, if he doesn't know them. I shall leave a message saying I have arranged transport to Brighton and tell him not to trouble his head about me. That should suffice."

Jacob still looked skeptical, but it was not his place to argue with her, and when he had gone, Adriana had all she could do to contain her soul in patience through the rest of the day. She managed to pack two small band-boxes without arousing anyone's curiosity, and though she regretted the fact that she could not take an assort-ment of her best gowns with her, she cheered at the thought that she could buy what she needed in Brighton. That reminded her, too, of the money in the carved box by her bed. Counting it, she decided she might have to hang on Sarah's sleeve before her sojourn was done, but Sarah wouldn't mind.

That evening, after the aunts had retired, she played cribbage with Joshua at a parquetry table in front of the fire in the library. When she pegged out ahead of him for the second time, he grinned at her. "Happy, sweet-heart? You have been looking like a cat at a cream pot all evening."

"Why, sir," she said, meeting his look limpidly, "I am always happy when I win. You owe me two guineas now."

"Must I pay at once or will you have another game?"

"What time is it?"

He drew his watch from its pocket and opened it. "Nearly eleven. I suppose we ought to go to bed."

"It doesn't really matter," she assured him. "We can play another round or two if you like."

He reached across the table to pull one of her curls. "You may play sluggard in the morning if you like, my lady. There is no particular reason for you to get up early. But I am master of this place and thus must arise with the birds. Come to bed."

She had hoped to keep him up longer, for she knew she would do better to stay awake until it was time to leave than to try to waken herself at such an hour, but she had no wish to draw his scrutiny by behaving differently. Bad enough that he had thought her high spirits worthy of comment. She needn't worry, however. There were other ways to see that he didn't sleep too soon.

Indeed, it was nearly one before Joshua fell asleep, and Adriana herself was so relaxed by then that it was all she could do to keep her eyes open. At last, certain that if she remained in bed she would fall asleep, she got up and moved to sit by the window. Knowing from experience that Joshua slept deeply, she did not fear to waken him when she opened the window a crack to let in enough chilly night air to blow the drowsiness away or even when she tiptoed into her room and back, to fetch her watch. She was glad that the night was dark, that the stars and moon were hidden away behind a layer of clouds. Were there moonlight, Jacob had warned her the ship would not come. Surely it was dark enough. She could scarcely see the tiny hands on her watch.

At last, however, it was time to dress. Leaving her carefully written note on the chair and hurrying to her dressing room, she donned her traveling dress, Lady Adelaide's hooded cloak, and Chalford's cast-off boots. Then, pulling her bandboxes from under her bed, where they had been hidden from sight by the bed curtains, she carried them down the stairs, through the dining room, to the hall. The rooms through which she passed seemed larger and more mysterious in the dark, but she dared not light a candle. For one thing, she would have been hard-pressed to carry one without losing her boxes. For another, she feared, however nonsensically, to waken someone with the light.

Jacob was waiting for her, and they went quickly. At one point, after they had crossed the drive, he stopped her with a hand on her arm, pointing toward the barbican as he pulled her into the shadows. A glow shone briefly in the gateway passage, and a moment later a watchman swinging a lantern strolled into the quadrangle. He paused, looking up as though the weather were his first concern, them from side to side. Seeing nothing amiss, he went on past the keep toward the rose garden.

Quickly, Jacob urged Adriana toward the marsh gate. "He'll come back the same way," he muttered. "Best we make speed."

The trip down the steep, pebble-strewn path to the beach was a harrowing experience. At every step, despite her sturdy boots, she feared to slip and fall, but at last they reached the tall boulders that marked the edge of the beach. Their feet crunched on the shingle as they made their way toward water's edge, but Jacob no longer seemed to worry about any noise they made.

She could see the dark bulk of a medium-sized sailing vessel some fifty yards out, and the rowboat was waiting, drawn up onto the sand, with two burly men standing by to man the oars. Jacob made no attempt to introduce her as he helped her aboard, and Adriana could not feel that the men would welcome amenities, so she held her tongue and took her seat in the stern.

The rowboat was efficiently launched, and the journey to the ship took but a few minutes. When they reached her, the rowboat drew alongside with a thump, and the men shipped their oars.

The rope ladder looked thin, narrow, and altogether unsuited to its purpose. Adriana eyed it askance.

"We'll keep it taut fer 'e, m'lady," said one of the oarsmen in a gruff voice.

"Will you, now?" she retorted. "And will you also fish me out of the sea when I tumble in?"

"Mayhap y'd prefer me to carry you up—over me shoulder like," the second man suggested, amusement clear in his voice.

"No, thank you. I shall do." She hitched the front hem of her long skirt up under her chin, hoping the darkness would cover her. Then, grasping one side of the ladder firmly in each hand, she placed a foot on the bottom rung and let herself swing free of the rowboat. There was brief panic when her body seemed destined to crash into the side of the vessel, but the men grabbed the ladder, steadying it. She took a deep breath and began to climb. After that it was no time at all before willing hands were assisting her onto the deck of the smuggler's vessel.

Still no introductions were made or requested, but when the commander of the vessel suggested that she would prefer the privacy of his cabin belowdecks, she assured him that she wished to stay on deck and would do her best not to trouble anyone.

"This is an adventure, Captain, and I mean to enjoy every minute of it," she said.

He grunted, but she heard a chuckle or two from his crew, and one of them showed her a pile of coiled rope that she could use as a seat. There were no proper benches. Clearly, this was no nobleman's yacht, commandeered for the purpose.

As the sails were raised, Adriana bethought herself of the booms guarding the mouth of the harbor, but the ship sailed out with no difficulty at all. There was a brisk breeze out of the northeast, so they moved with speed, and once again she felt the exhilaration she always felt on the sea.

"Comfortable, mum?" It was the captain.

Though she knew it was too dark for him to read her

expression, she smiled. "This is beyond anything great, sir. I cannot thank you enough."

He grunted again, then moved forward several yards. The water looked lighter now, she thought, standing to look over the rail. She could see white horses riding the waves. Overhead she beheld a patch of stars, quickly hidden by scudding black clouds. A moment later, the half-moon peeped through that same break in the clouds. She heard the captain swear beneath his breath.

"Up wi' ye, Wee Donal'," he ordered in a low but carrying tone. "Keep a sharp eye out."

The clouds above appeared now to be separating, breaking apart. The moon appeared more often, but briefly, only to disappear again seconds later. The little ship sped on.

"Sail ho!" came a shout from the rigging not a half-hour later. " 'Tis a big 'un, Cap'n, straight off to stern."

"Cutter?"

"Most like," replied the disembodied voice from above.

"Oh," gasped Adriana, "is it revenuers?"

"Aye, mum," the captain replied wearily. "More o' yer adventure, I'm thinkin'. We'll just pray it ain't more 'n ye've bargained fer altogether."

10

For a moment, Adriana feared the cutter would catch them, but mercifully, the clouds overhead thickened again. The captain hoisted all sails and headed seaward, away from the coast. The little ship seemed to fly then, for she was built for speed with a light hull and lines at bow and stern like those of a racing yacht, and she soon showed the cutter a clean pair of heels.

"Will we be able to sail into Brighton?" Adriana asked the captain an hour later when he came to assure her that all was well. "I should not like to be responsible for new difficulties, you know. If it is too dangerous for you and your men, you must do as you think best and never mind me."

For the first time, he chuckled. "Earlier, that would ha' meant feedin' ye t' the fishes, ma'am, and hopin' fer best afterward. But ye've got courage, I'll say that fer ye. Not a squeak out o' ye did we hear, e'en when their cannon roared. We'll see ye in t' Brighton, right enow, and should we sight yon cutter again, we'll do what we done afore, which is t' say we'll put up our lady's helm, present 'er stern side to 'is majesty, and run before the wind."

"Why did you run at all?" she asked. "Surely, you unloaded any cargo you carried earlier. What could they have found?"

"Aye, mum, cargo be safe ashore, but we've our own share o' the goods below and"—he screwed his weathered features in what was clearly meant to be a wink—"our fair passenger besides. We'd have a time explainin' yer presence, that we would."

She nodded, realizing she had no wish whatsoever to

have to explain to his majesty's customs agents her presence aboard such a vessel. Not, she thought mischievously, that it wouldn't be worth something to see the look on Chalford's face when they sent for him to fetch his wife. She couldn't help but worry about the free traders, however. "It is getting light," she said. "That must make it more dangerous for you than ever—landing, that is."

"Nay, mum, for the wind's a-shiftin' an' that'll mean we can hoist our spinnaker. 'Tis a fine bright-striped sheet, she be. Only wait till ye clap yer peepers on 'er. We'll rearrange our rigging a trifle as well, and even if we run onto the same lot as chased us earlier, they'll never guess us t' be the same vessel. Nor will they suspect us fer what we be wi' so noteworthy a sail as yon red-and-white spinnaker a-flyin' afore us." He peered at her, his head to one side. "We was meant t' make landfall after daybreak, mum. Had ye not thought upon what a night landing would mean t' ye, all alone as ye are?"

She had not. Indeed, she realized now that there had been a rather large gap in her planning. "I imagined myself landing in darkness," she admitted, "but then I simply imagined myself cozy and warm, tucked up before a fire in my friend's house. I never considered how I would get there from the shore. I daresay you must think me a ninnyhammer."

The captain grunted. "Mr. Wittersham, fortunately, had his wits about him, ma'am. There be a gig laid on fer ye on the cliff above where we'll put in. The lads'll see ye up the cliff and the driver's a man ye can trust. What ye tell yer friends be yer ain concern, but I trust ye'll be namin' no names."

"Why, Captain," she said demurely, "I could not an I wished to, for I've not heard a single name other than Wee Donald's, which is scarcely sufficient to identify him. Moreover, I've seen no face clearly save your own, and that by early twilight."

"Ye'll see us all clear enow afore we make landfall, howsomever, for we've fallen behind our time."

Indeed, they had traveled far out into the Channel in their effort to elude the revenue cutter, and it was nearly nine before they dropped anchor and lowered a boat. When Adriana realized the ship would not tie up to a dock, she dreaded the impending descent of the rope ladder, but she was spared this ordeal. Instead, she was lowered in a bosun's chair, a rigging of straps and ropes that enabled her to maintain most of her dignity and to descend to the rowboat without mishap. Once there, she was helped out of her harness by one of the same two sailors who had rowed her to the vessel in the first place, while the other held them away from the side of the ship. She recognized both from their voices when they spoke to her.

The path up the cliffside was clear of pebbles and thus not as difficult to manage as its counterpart at Thunderhill, and the gig was waiting as promised at the top, in the charge of a small, wiry man, perched stiff-backed upon the seat and dressed in buff-colored stockinette breeches, boots, white gloves and neckcloth, and a long-tailed dark coat similar to that worn by gentlemen for riding. A dark beaver hat sat squarely upon his grizzled locks.

Adriana regarded this personage with amazement.

"Stir yer stumps, ye lunkheads," he snapped, making no effort to descend from his perch. "Ain't I been a-waitin' on ye this hour an' longer? What ye think—I got time ter waste? Think I be a sluggard like yerselves, 'n' yon lot aboard ship? Snip-snap, then! Toss them cases under the seat, 'n' give the lass a hand-up. I've aired me poor 'orse long enough, I thank 'e."

" 'Her ladyship' to you, twiddlepoop, so mind yer tongue," growled one of the two sailors who had brought Adriana ashore.

"Twiddlepoop, is it? A fine way to address a man of important affairs, such as myself. Me name is Flood, m'lady," he added with a dignified tip of his hat and nod of his head once the second sailor had helped Adriana onto the seat beside him. "Mr. Horace Flood, me acquaintances style me. An' proud I am t' be of

service to ye. Where will we be a-headin', if ye please?"
When, before replying, she glanced back over her
shoulder to thank her two assistants, he snorted,
"Leave 'em go. 'Tis beneath yer notice they be, the pair
o' them."

"I'll give you notice, Horace Flood," said one of the
sailors menacingly, taking a step back toward the gig.

"Nay, leave go," said the other. "He's no use to
anyone with his bones all broke. Good day to ye,
ma'am. 'Twas a lively trip, this'un, 'n' no mistake."

Mr. Flood sputtered in impotent fury while Adriana
made her grateful *adieux,* but when she turned to him
contritely afterward and begged his pardon for making
him keep his horse standing, he shrugged eloquently,
clicked his tongue at the horse, and said, " 'Tis all one
t' me, I suppose. Yer direction, ma'am?"

"Lord Clifford's house in the Steyne," she said,
grabbing hold of her bonnet as the gig leapt forward
and began to rattle along the Marine Parade at a rapid
pace. "You know it?"

"Out o' course, I do," he replied with a sniff of
pride. "Guess I knows near about every 'ouse in
Brighton. Lived 'ere all me life, I have. Be there in the
shake of a lamb's tail."

"I suppose the town is as full as it can hold right
now," she said.

"Well, yer out in yer supposin', then," he told her.
"The place is pretty nigh deserted, thanks t' the races
bein' over."

"Dear me, I hope everyone is not gone. I am persuaded Lord Clifford must still be in residence, and
Lord Villiers, and perhaps Viscount Alston, as well."

"Oh, aye, and 'is royal 'ighness be still at the
Pavilion, sure enough. Had one o' 'is 'select parties' last
night. Laughed m'self fit t' split atterward."

Enjoying Mr. Flood hugely, Adriana willingly
accepted this broad hint and begged him to tell her what
had happened.

"Ye'll recall 'twas a night as dark as the devil's backside?" When she nodded, he said, "Well, a gennelman

was a-driving 'is tandem up North Street atter enjoyin'
isself at 'is 'ighness's party, when 'is lead horse, wi'
more spirit than caution, as one might say, endeavored
to open a new passageway through a stone wall. Failed,
o' course, 'n' the gennelman ended up sprawled in the
road, a-blessin' 'is soul an' askin' them as came to 'elp
'im up, was 'e 'ome so quick as all that, and would they
kindly 'elp 'im to 'is bed?''

Adriana chuckled. "I hope the horse was un-
harmed.''

"Just a mite dizzy, me lady. Here we be on the Steyne
now. That be Lord Clifford's 'ouse on the right
ahead.''

She was glad to see that few people were about. The
sky was still overcast, which perhaps accounted for the
lack of activity, for it was nearly ten o'clock, and she
knew that on a sunny day, the grassy area in the center
of the roadway would be filled with strolling ladies and
gentlemen and laughing children. The sandy beach
would likewise be crowded.

There was a housemaid on the front steps of Clifford
House, polishing the brass knocker. As soon as she
realized that the gig was drawing to a halt before the
house, however, she whisked the rag beneath her apron
and disappeared inside.

A moment later, as Mr. Flood, still on his dignity,
condescended to step down to the flagway in order to
assist Adriana to alight, the door of the house opened
again to reveal the porter and a liveried footman. The
footman hurried down the steps to the pavement.

"Your ladyship!" he exclaimed.

"Yes, it is I, indeed, William, and you've no need to
inform me that your mistress is not expecting me. I
mean to surprise her. Those two bandboxes beneath the
seat are all my baggage. Will you take them for me,
please, and see that Mr. Flood is well-recompensed for
his kindness in bringing me to you safely?''

"Certainly, Lady Chalford. Her ladyship is in the
morning room, ma'am. Mr. Porson will show you the
way.''

"Oh, I remember the way," said Adriana, turning to mount the steps. "I'll go straight up to her now."

Lord Clifford's butler greeted Adriana in the narrow entry hall, nodded when she said she would announce herself, and inquired as to whether she had enjoyed a pleasant journey.

Since he had been a footman at Sarah's father's estate in Wiltshire before rising to his present lofty position with Lord Clifford, Adriana had known him for years. She grinned at him. "I had an adventure, Porson, and if you are very good, I shall tell you all about it presently. But now I must find her ladyship and inform her that she has a houseguest."

The butler shook his head as she turned away, and she had no doubt that if he had a confidant in the house, he would soon be regaling that person with incidents from her childhood that were better left untold. She had little time to think about that, however, for she fairly flew up the stairs to the morning room. Flinging open the door, she beheld her friend, curled up on a brocaded French seat in the window embrasure, framed by yellow satin curtains, sorting through her morning post.

"Adriana!" Sarah's letters went flying as she leapt to her feet and hurried to hug her visitor. "What on earth brings you here? Has Chalford relented, then? Is he below? Oh, my goodness, you dreadful girl, you might have sent me warning. You are both most welcome, but I needn't tell you that. Oh, how I wish Mortimer had not already gone out. I believe he has walked down to Donaldson's Library to read the papers. I can send my page to fetch him in a trice, however, so that needn't signify."

"Sarah, Sarah," Adriana protested, freeing herself with a laugh. "You chatter too much and give no one else a chance to speak. You may leave Mortimer in peace. Joshua is not with me."

This last announcement effectively silenced Lady Clifford. She stared at Adriana, a myriad of emotions playing across her expressive face. Finally, she said, "Dearest, you haven't."

"Haven't what?"

"Left him, of course. You cannot have done such a thing to such a kind man."

"I haven't left him," Adriana said. "Do sit down, Sarah, and ring for tea or something. I have had no breakfast and I promise you I am starving."

"No breakfast!" Sarah rushed to tug the bell. "But how is this? Surely, you put up at an inn somewhere for the night. Did they not feed you before you left this morning?"

"I stayed at no inn, Sarah. I was delivered to your door by the drollest little man in a beaver hat and split tails."

"Mr. Flood! He is quite a personage in Brighton these days. He was used to perform various services for the summer visitors, but since his cousin became a footman in a noble house, Mr. Flood has acquired new habits of dress—his cousin's master's castoffs, I daresay—and set himself up as a hackney coachman. I must tell you, dearest, though he would certainly disagree, his gig is not quite the mode of transport one associates with a marchioness, to say the very least of it."

"Then you will no doubt disapprove of the mode of transport I employed from Thunderhill to Brighton, Sarah. I came on a free trader's ship, and Mr. Flood met me on the clifftop when we'd made landfall and drove me to your doorstep."

"Free traders!" Sarah was shocked. For some moments, in fact, she was rendered speechless, and when she opened her mouth at last, she had to close it again when the door opened to admit the footman and a maidservant with a tea tray.

"Mr. Porson, knowing your ways, m'lady, had already ordered tea," William said, moving to take Adriana's cloak and gloves.

Blinking in bewilderment at the untimely interruption, Sarah recovered her wits long enough to say, "Pray bring Lady Chalford some food, too, Liza. She has not broken her fast this morning."

"Toast and jam will suffice," Adriana said, eyeing her friend with undisguised amusement.

"Yes, m'lady. At once." The maid stared at her for a moment until recalled by a small noise from the footman, whereupon she flushed and hurried out.

Adriana waited until William, having informed her that she would find her things in the blue bedchamber, and having ascertained from his mistress that nothing more was wanted, left the room before she said, laughing, "Your maidservant seems to disapprove of me. She is new, is she not?"

"She is, but that is not why she stared, Dree. Have you chanced to look at yourself in a mirror?"

"No, how should I have done so?" Adriana inquired, sitting and pouring out a cup of tea for herself and another for Sarah as though she were in her own house. In point of fact, so familiar was she with every house Sarah had ever lived in that it was nearly the same thing. "Do I look a disgrace?"

Sarah burst into laughter, reaching to find a chair and sitting as though her knees were too weak to support her. "Oh, Adriana, one would think you still fourteen, instead of nearly two-and-twenty. Remember when you rode by yourself to watch the sunrise at Avebury Circle?"

"It was the summer solstice. I thought there would be something to see. How angry Papa was, to be sure, but I had asked him, you know, and he had said I might go one day."

"He hadn't meant that day, however, or that you should go alone. You ought to have been here for the donkey races, you absurd creature. How you would have enjoyed them!"

"So Sally wrote," Adriana said. "I wish I had been here."

"Well, you are here now, and you have not explained how that comes about. If you have not run away from Chalford, how is it that you took passage on a sailing vessel of dubious repute? And of greater import than that, are we to anticipate the arrival of a furious husband? I need hardly tell you that Mortimer will be displeased if such a thing as that should come to pass.''

"Oh, no, I am persuaded that there is nothing to fear from that direction. Chalford has no violent temperament. He is as placid and kind as . . . as a sheep. Really, Sarah, I am all out of patience with the man.''

"Dear me.'' Sarah fell silent again when the door opened to admit the maidservant with Adriana's toast and jam on a silver tray, but when the maid had gone, she continued as though there had been no interruption, "I cannot think what ails you, Adriana. You knew what Chalford was when you married him.''

"I hardly knew him at all,'' Adriana protested. "Indeed, I sometimes think I know him no better now.''

"Don't equivocate. You know precisely what I mean. You knew Chalford for an obliging gentleman of amiable temperament. I believe you described him as 'self-possessed' and 'mild of manner.' You said nothing about sheep then that I can recall.''

Thoughtfully, Adriana spread jam on a piece of toast. "I don't know how it is,'' she said at last, "but there is something about that mildness that makes me want to shake him, particularly when he issues arbitrary orders and simply assumes everyone will obey them. I get so angry. You know my wicked temper, Sarah, but I can control it with Alston, who is *not* mild of manner. Chalford has only to say that things must be as they are to stir the coals. He never argues. One time I became so frustrated with his calm manner that I actually flew at him with my fists, and all he would do was to catch my wrists and tell me I must not resort to violence.'' She grimaced at the memory. "I can tell you, Sarah, I felt prodigiously like murdering him after that.''

"And so you ran away rather than murder him? How considerate of you, dearest.''

Adriana's gloomy expression promptly cleared and she laughed. "Is that how I made it sound? No, I didn't run away. That particular episode wasn't even what induced me to leave. I wanted to come to Brighton to see everyone, and Chalford has positively interred himself in that castle of his. You saw how proud he is of Thunderhill when you were there? Well, I decided it was going to take a charge of gunpowder to blast him out, and I didn't wish to wait for that, so when I got fed to the teeth at last, I came to you on my own.''

"You mean for him to come after you, and that's the truth of the matter," Sarah said flatly.

"Is it?" Adriana considered that viewpoint as she smeared jam on another piece of toast. "Perhaps you are right. I truly had not thought that part of it through. Indeed, I scarcely thought any of it through. Had our coachman not had the forethought to arrange for Mr. Flood, I should have had no means of getting to this house from the clifftop.''

"Your coachman knows of this start? Good God, Adriana—''

"Oh, he is one of the smugglers," Adriana explained.

"One of the smugglers! Your own coachman?''

"Indeed, they are all of them in it in one way or another. Even Chalford does not seem to know how many of his servants are in league with the Gentlemen. So long as they do their work at the castle, he pays no heed to what else they do. I was as astonished as you are, but smuggling is quite the thing in Kent—or here in Sussex, as well, for that matter.''

"I find it difficult to credit that Chalford does not know.''

"Well, he may know, of course, but since it is his habit to keep most of his thoughts and feelings to himself, his people, most fortunately for me, all think they have kept it dark. Thus, when I threatened to betray them to him, they agreed to do as I asked, which was to bring me here aboard a smuggling ship.''

"Adriana, you are a menace. I believe your whole purpose is to discover the limits of what Chalford will tolerate. Your brother will say you deserve to be whipped, and for once I almost believe I agree with him.''

"I hope you do not see much of Alston and Sophie,''

Adriana said, ignoring the rest of Sarah's statement. "I have no wish to listen to his upbraidings."

"Well, unless you mean to stay hidden indoors, in which case I fail to understand why you came to Brighton at all, you will see him. The town is thin of company, so if you go out, there will be no crowds to conceal you. People will begin to arrive at the end of the week for Prinny's birthday on Monday, but I doubt that even then you can avoid your family. You certainly cannot mean to stay hidden from Miranda; she visits me every day. In fact, she is coming this afternoon. She will find it difficult to avoid mention at home of your presence here."

"I'd not ask her to do that," Adriana said. "I shall just have to make the best of things, I suppose, and trust Alston to have washed his hands of me now that I am Chalford's wife." She yawned. "I'll tell you what, Sarah. If you can keep them all at bay long enough for me to get some sleep, I'll be a deal more capable of behaving sensibly. I didn't sleep at all last night."

Sarah leapt to her feet. "Then not another question will I ask you," she said, pulling the bell. "You will go straight upstairs and I shall give orders that you are not to be disturbed until you ring. And my Lettie will attend you then. I daresay she will scold you for coming off without Nancy—"

"Not so much as Nancy will scold when I return," Adriana said with an amused grimace. "That is another detail I didn't think through. She will forget her place entirely. I think I would rather hear what Alston has to say than listen to Nancy."

"Well, get you gone for now, my dear. Take her ladyship to the blue room, Liza," she said to the maidservant, "and see that she has whatever she needs. She is going to rest."

In less than a quarter-hour Adriana was out of her wrinkled travel dress, tucked up, and sound asleep in the comfortable blue bedchamber overlooking Lord Clifford's tiny back garden. She slept undisturbed, and when she awoke, it was nearly three o'clock. Ringing for Sarah's tirewoman, she accepted that bustling dame's assistance, freshened herself with the aid of a pitcher of cold water and a basin, and changed into one of the frocks she had brought with her—a sprig muslin round gown that had been pressed and hung up—and a pair of light-blue sandals. Then, when Lettie had brushed her hair into a neat pile of curls atop her head, she hurried downstairs to the drawing room, overlooking the street, where she knew she would find Sarah.

Her hostess was not alone. Miranda jumped up from her place on the claw-footed, green satin sofa and ran to greet her sister. "It has been all Sarah could do to keep me from going upstairs to roust you out of your bed!" she exclaimed. "What do you mean by coming to Brighton without so much as a word to me?"

Adriana laughed. "I didn't know when I was coming. Indeed, I decided to come only a few days ago. Did Sarah tell you?"

Sarah said, "I wasn't certain how much I ought to say."

Adriana frowned. "I never thought. I did promise to keep silent about my voyage."

"Voyage?" Miranda stared. "You came by boat? Sarah did tell me you came without Chalford, but surely you did not take his boat, Dree, without his leave. He will be furious. You ought to have thought about the consequences to his captain."

Adriana laughed. "How unlike you, Randy, to consider consequences, but there will be none of that nature, for it was not Chalford's boat. You must say nothing of this to Alston, or indeed to anyone. If I did not know I can trust you to keep your tongue between your teeth, I would not tell you at all, for the safety of a number of persons might depend upon our silence."

Miranda's eyes widened. "Goodness, Dree, what have you done? You know I shan't say a word to Alston."

"Or to anyone," Adriana insisted.

"Very well. Tell me."

"Free traders brought me to Brighton. We had to outrun a revenue cutter, and it was the most exciting thing imaginable."

"Good gracious," Miranda said, awed. "Were you not afraid of them, Dree? I would have been terrified. Surely, they were rough, dangerous men."

"Oh, pooh," said Adriana. "They were men, that is all. There was no reason to fear them. Indeed, they were very kind to me and took excellent care of me."

"They didn't feed you, however," Sarah put in dryly.

"Oh, that was nothing, but I am hungry again, now that you put me in mind of it. Is there tea in that pot by your elbow?"

"Not a drop. I shall ring for more in a trice, however."

Miranda said, "Even knowing nothing of the smugglers, Alston will split a seam in his new coat when he discovers you are here without Chalford. What will you tell him about your journey?"

"Oh, if I must, I'll say I came with friends, which is true enough. I felt they counted me a friend when the trip was done."

"You will not prevaricate with Chalford, however."

"No, but he presents no difficulties. He may be a little displeased if he actually feels impelled to come after me, but I left him a letter, explaining that I was coming to Brighton for a fortnight or so and inviting him to join me here if he found himself able to do so. He never actually forbade me to come on my own, you know, so I daresay he will not scold, even if he should come. He never does so," she added simply.

"I daresay you have never given him so much cause before," said Miranda, grinning. "Did you ever ask him about my visiting Thunderhill, by the bye?"

Adriana explained what Chalford had said about Christmas, and after her tea had been served, she revealed her more pressing needs. "I must have some clothes, Sarah. I brought little with me, as you might guess, and though I do have some money, it will not be enough, so I hope you have not outrun the constable, for I mean to borrow whatever I must."

"We can have the carriage out this afternoon, if you like," Sarah said. "My dressmaker here is a most obliging woman who does not shut her doors until after six o'clock. Do you have something suitable to wear to the theater tonight? Prinny has ordered a comedy, *Speed the Plow*, and Mortimer wishes to attend. We have been rather dull since the crowds moved on to Lewes, and nothing has occurred to enliven or awaken us, save donkey races and a storm the whole of Saturday night. The Steyne has been deserted these past two days, and there has been little noise save the occasional braying of an ass or of a solitary cracked French horn from the petit orchestra at Donaldson's Library."

"The fact is," Miranda said, "that the regular summer residents hardly ever muster strong until the races are over and the mobocracy, as Sally Villiers calls the bourgeois element, are quite dispersed. Alston comes here for the races, of course, and cares little for crowds or anything else, including plays, I fear, but Sophie, thank heaven, convinced him that the Monday-night balls at the Castle are not to be despised."

"Did Alston win any money at the races?" Adriana asked.

"Not so much as he lost," Miranda said with a grimace. "There has been no living with him, believe me, since the outcome of the Somerset stakes was announced. Consider his elation when Houghton Lass came in the winner. Mr. Mellish's Lady Brough, I must tell you, was the favorite in that race, so Alston thought himself very clever to have backed Houghton Lass."

"But you said he didn't do well," Adriana protested.

Miranda and Sarah exchanged wise looks, and Miranda said, "It was reported that Houghton Lass and the horse coming in second had both run on the wrong side of the post. Controversy raged until the following day, when it was decided by the Jockey Club that his highness's Orville had won. Only conceive of Alston's fury when the results were announced. He fared no better with the other races, and I fear I may have made matters worse by trying his temper more than once."

"Particularly," said Sarah, grinning, "when you went to the races after he had absolutely forbidden you to do so."

"That settles it," Adriana said flatly. "I must avoid Alston at all costs."

Miranda chuckled. "Well, I cannot say I blame you, but you won't do it. Some well-meaning tabby will inform him of your presence here within half an hour of your setting foot outside. For that matter, someone may well have seen you when you arrived, or the servants will have passed the word. Your best hope is to meet him publicly, somewhere where he may be counted upon to hold his nose in the air and not take you to task."

"That will only postpone the reckoning," Sarah pointed out.

Adriana sighed. "I will not stay hidden away like some cowardy cat. Let us visit your modiste, Sarah. I do have a gown I can wear to the theater tonight, even one that would suffice for a concert or a ball if you will lend me some jewelry, but I do not have much of anything else to speak of. I did feel I ought not to trust the free traders near my jewels."

Accordingly, they set out to visit the shops, and Adriana was able to order several gowns, bonnets, and other necessary articles. Lady Clifford's modiste, Madame LaPlant, a thin, flat-bosomed Frenchwoman with a bubbling personality and an air of practicality, promised faithfully to deliver the first of these within two days' time, and Adriana was well-satisfied.

They dined at home, and Sarah told her husband that Adriana had accepted an impromptu invitation from friends to carry her from Thunderhill to Brighton, and that Chalford might or might not find himself free to follow her in a day or two. The amiable Lord Clifford, a tall, lanky gentleman with bony shoulders, narrow hips, and a lean face nearly always enlivened by a broad smile, took no exception to this glib explanation, saying only that he was always glad to see Adriana.

The fact that Brighton was temporarily almost devoid of entertainment made it less surprising, despite Miranda's assurance that Alston never went to plays, that practically the first persons they saw at the theater in the New Road were Alston, his Sophie, Sophie's brother, Claude, and Miranda herself, seated in a box opposite the Cliffords'. There was no hope of avoiding Alston's eye. Indeed, that he had seen them the moment they entered was only too apparent.

"Is that not your brother opposite?" asked Clifford. "Why's the fellow glowering so?"

"Dyspepsia," replied Adriana promptly.

Sarah chuckled.

"Daresay he's offended by the fact that you've chosen to stay with us rather than with him," Clifford said comfortably. "Can't say I like the fellow much, Adriana. Hope that don't distress you. Oughtn't to say such stuff, I suppose."

"Nonsense, sir, you may abuse Alston with my goodwill. I daresay he intends to make himself unpleasant." She did not let her brother's glowers overset her, however, and settled back to enjoy the play and the farce that would follow. When Miranda, on the arm of an admirer, visited their box at the second interval, she informed Adriana in an undertone that Alston had no intention of seeking her out that evening.

"Well, the Fates be praised for that," said Adriana.

"He will call at Clifford House tomorrow morning instead," said Miranda sweetly, "when he trusts he will find you at home."

11

Porson's voice was carefully devoid of expression the following day when he entered the morning room to announce Viscount Alston's arrival, but his countenance, when his gaze met Adriana's, spoke volumes. She was sitting upon the French seat in the window embrasure, the latest issue of the *Lady's Monthly Museum* spread open upon her lap. Sarah, at a nearby table, was writing a reply to one of her many letters.

Alston brushed past the butler into the room, dismissing with a gesture the suggestion that he might care for refreshment. "Sarah," he said abruptly, looking down his nose at her, "I stand upon no ceremony with you. I wish to be private with my sister."

"Do you, indeed, sir?" Sarah inquired with a lifted eyebrow. "This is still my house, I believe."

Adriana shook her head. "Don't expose yourself to his ridiculous temper, dearest. He can scarcely eat me, after all."

"Very well," Sarah said, rising to her feet. The skirt of her blue muslin gown swirled about her legs as, moving toward the door, she turned just before she reached it to speak again. "Porson will be just outside if you need him, my dear."

"I have never been more shocked in my life, Adriana," Alston announced before the door had clicked shut behind Sarah and the butler. "Whatever are you about?"

"Do sit down, Alston," she said calmly. "I've no wish to strain my neck looking up at you."

"Your wishes, dear sister, are of the supremest

indifference to me," he said, moving several steps nearer. "You are behaving badly, and I mean to see that you cease to do so at once. Where is your husband?" When she did not speak, he snapped, "A home thrust, is it not? But I will have answers, my girl, and I will have them now. Then you will return to your home. First, I wish to know who was so misguided as to assist you in this latest start of yours. Tell me that, if you please."

"No, I will not," she replied, her temper rising to meet his, as it had always done. "That information is of no concern to you. And as to where Chalford is, I presume at Thunderhill, unless he has begun his journey to Brighton. As Miranda no doubt informed you, I do not know precisely when he will join me here."

"I should be most surprised to learn that he even knows you *are* here," Alston said. "Does he?"

"Yes, of course he does."

"Then, pray inform me as to when he changed his mind about allowing you to visit Brighton. It is not so long since he apologized to me for denying you this pleasure, my dear. I told him not to distress himself, that forgoing a pleasure would do you good. How do you like that, eh? I'll wager you did not know he had confided in me, did you?"

He was so near now that he loomed above her, and Adriana knew that if she did not move, she would lose her temper altogether. Flinging her magazine aside and getting to her feet, she said, "You seem to forget, sir, that you no longer have the right to call me to account for my actions. Only Chalford has that right, and what he does or doesn't do is no business of yours." She turned away, her demeanor as haughty as his own.

Alston's hand shot out before she took a step. Grasping her hard by the shoulder, he spun her around to face him. "You'd like me to ignore your starts, wouldn't you? But things are not always what we like. I am still your brother, and I still have every right to force you to behave in a manner that does not disgrace our family. When you offend me and mine, when you hold us up to public ridicule, then you may well believe that I will hold you to account. Indeed, you deserve to be beaten for your folly in showing yourself here at this house without Chalford.''

"Take your hand off me, Alston. I haven't the least notion what you are talking about.''

"Oh, don't you? Well, that's all of a piece with the other, I suppose. How do you think it looks for my sister to show herself, alone, in Brighton without my so much as knowing she meant to come here? Answer me that. You came to Clifford's house, avoiding mine. How do you think the tabbies will respond?''

She managed to pull away at last, her eyes sparkling with greater wrath than ever. "I don't care what they say. I came where I knew I would be welcome and where no one would question my motives. And what, may I ask, is so dreadful about my being here without Chalford? I am sure I am not the first wife to live outside her husband's pocket.''

"What you do after you have produced an heir for him is one thing, but having developed a reputation as an unconscionable flirt, despite my attempts to curb you, you dare not compound matters by behaving loosely so soon after your wedding.''

"Oh, not an 'unconscionable' flirt, surely,'' Adriana said, her voice now dangerously calm.

The note of warning impressed the viscount not a whit, however, its only effect being to inflame his already lacerated temper. He was an articulate man, and he did not spare her, but she merely bowed to the storm, knowing from experience that his fury would blow itself out. His description of her actions and her character might have reduced a weaker woman to tears, but Adriana would have scorned to cry. Nonetheless, by the time he finished his diatribe and took his leave of her, her hands were clenched into tight fists and her face was drained of color.

It was thus that Sarah found her. "My dearest,'' she exclaimed, "what has he done? I ought never to have left you.''

Adriana drew a long breath. "Your presence would

not have deterred him," she said, her voice perfectly normal. "If I look a trifle pulled about, 'tis from no more than the effort to restrain my own temper. Sarah, I have never seen him so angry, though God knows I have infuriated him time and time again."

"But he has no right to come the master over you anymore, Dree, so whatever he said, you need not heed him. No doubt that is why he seemed angrier than usual. He recognizes his impotence, his lack of authority."

"You may be right about that," Adriana said with a rueful look, "but I own there was a deal of truth in the things he said, and he does not know the whole. Chalford will know." She grimaced. "I may get that whipping yet, Sarah. Alston said I deserved one, just as you predicted he would, and I have just rather uncomfortably recollected Chalford's once suggesting that George ought to beat Sally frequently. He said he— George, that is—was a fool if he didn't take a firm hand to her."

"Well," said her friend with a look of fond amusement, "Chalford will not beat you. I daresay he will not be best pleased over the way you got here, but you have said yourself that he never even raises his voice to you. And you have given him cause before, have you not? More than once, I'll be bound."

"You know I have." Adriana bit her lower lip. "The fact is that he wants a nice submissive wife, willing to bow to his every wish—indeed, willing to throw herself heart and soul into his precious castle. I cannot. I spent too many years confined at Wryde with responsibilities that . . . well, that . . ."

"That were too great a burden for any young girl to carry," Sarah finished for her when she hesitated. "You tried to become mistress of Wryde and mother to Miranda, all at once."

"Well, Papa was grief-stricken—"

"Port-stricken, more like," Sarah interrupted acidly.

"And Alston," Adriana continued as though there had not been an interruption, "could scarcely have been expected to come down from Oxford just to take us in hand. He did what he could during his holidays, of—"

"I remember how it used to be when he came home," Sarah interrupted, "so you needn't try to make me think him a pattern card imposed upon by circumstances. You used to flee to us almost the moment you heard his horses' hoofbeats on the drive. Mama was used to say you and Miranda would have been better to have lived with us or with some relative rather than at Wryde."

"Papa would never hear of any other plan, and indeed, I felt it my duty to stay, particularly after he gave himself up to his gout and began to remain at home. Even so, the place nearly went to rack and ruin before Alston married Sophie and finally was able to take charge. You know," she added thoughtfully, "I never before thought about how kind it was of him to take us to London. Perhaps, like Joshua, he would liefer have stayed at Wryde."

"Stop it, Adriana, you are becoming maudlin." Sarah's voice was sharp. "If you think for one minute that Sophie would prefer ruralizing in Wiltshire to puffing off her consequence in London or Brighton, then you must be all about in your head."

Adriana gave herself a shake. "Forgive me, Sarah, I am talking pure nonsense. I know it as well as you do. The fact of the matter is that I will babble about anything and everything rather than consider what is really on my mind. Since Alston took his leave, all I can think about is that Joshua may soon be here, perhaps in as much of a fury as Alston was, which I confess has me in something of a quake, since I don't know what form his fury takes. Or, worse than that, he might not come at all."

"Goodness, why would he not come?"

"Because he often does not do the things I think he will do," Adriana said candidly. "Whatever shall *I* do, Sarah, if he simply makes up his mind to the fact that he chose a bad wife? What if, having left, I find I cannot go back?"

Sarah, hiding a smile, did what she could to soothe these fears, but Adriana refused to allow herself to be consoled. Insisting that she would be but poor company, she saw her friend and Miranda off that afternoon to pay calls without her. Though Sarah had agreed that some solitude might do her good, she had insisted that Adriana not allow herself to fall into the sullens.

"We have been invited to a concert at the Pavilion this evening, and I mean to see that you go with us," she said firmly. "Alston won't let anyone else see his displeasure with you, of course, but you will give the tattlemongers food for scandal if you hide yourself away now that they know you are here."

Adriana agreed, deciding that the best way to deal with the emotions still churning within her was to take a good long nap. Thus, she retired to her bedchamber, slipped out of her muslin gown and into her bed. When the sound of the door opening, then shutting again, awoke her two hours later, she stretched, opened her eyes, and turned over, expecting to see Sarah's tirewoman.

Chalford leaned back against the door, his arms folded across his chest, his eyelids drooping as he surveyed his wife. "Are you enjoying your stay in Brighton, my dear?"

"Joshua!" She sat up so quickly her head swam. "My lord, what . . . that is, how. . . ?"

"Perhaps you believe I ought to have had myself properly announced," he suggested gently.

She stared at him, trying to see into his eyes, hoping they would give her a clue to his mood. She had read that eyes were like lamps, like windows of the soul, but where Joshua was concerned, the lamps were too often dim, the windows shaded. Even when he straightened and she could see his dark-gray eyes clearly, there was no more than a sort of flintlike look to indicate that he might be angry.

"I certainly didn't expect to see you just now in this

room, sir," she said, striving for that same calm and wishing her heart weren't thudding in her chest. Surely it pounded so hard, he ought to be able to hear it.

"I told Clifford's people that I would announce myself. The footman kindly showed me the way to your door so that I might surprise you." He moved toward her.

Adriana felt as though her thudding heart had suddenly leapt into her throat. She reached for the fallen blanket, thinking to cover herself, but her hand stopped of its own accord. "Joshua, please, my lord, I know you must be angry, but—"

"I was not overjoyed to find you gone," he said, cutting in with that same even tone as he came to a halt beside the bed, "but your note explained your feelings well enough. I had not realized I had been behaving selfishly. I apologize. I never intended to force you to such drastic action."

"Oh, no, it was not like that, truly!"

"No? Then you must explain to me how it was."

She stared up at him, wide-eyed. "Joshua, are you or are you not angry with me? Have you come to take me back?"

"Why, no, my dear, on the contrary, I have brought your abigail, albeit under some protest, and your clothes."

"Then, you don't want me back." She fell back against her pillows. "I was afraid that you would not."

"What nonsense is this, Adriana? I will grant you that since I have been in the habit of directing persons who expect to be directed, I am out of the habit of considering wishes other than my own. When you first accused me of behaving selfishly, I thought you merely a trifle spoilt through having had so little parental guidance over the years, and I did not take your words to heart. I ought to have listened. You have succeeded in making that fact quite clear. I brought your clothes because I knew you could not have carried many with you on such a hasty journey—certainly not enough for a fortnight in Brighton." He paused, smiling down at her.

"I can't be away that long, I'm afraid, but I can spare a sennight to please you, I believe."

"D-do you know how I got here, Joshua?"

He looked out the window. "An ill-judged choice of transport, certainly, but I daresay, in view of my prohibitions, the only one you could manage. I didn't know you numbered any of the Gentlemen among your acquaintance. You will no doubt laugh when I tell you that my first thought was that Braverstoke had conveyed you here aboard the *Golden Fleece*. Had he not chanced to call soon after Miskin discovered your letter, which had been blown to the floor by a draft from an open window, I should have labored under that misapprehension rather longer than I did."

"But how then did you discover—?"

"Young Jacob is not yet sufficiently practiced in the art of deception to sustain a prolonged interview," he said. "I'd have been here late last night, but we were becalmed near Bexhill."

"You brought the *Sea Dragon*?" When he nodded, she knew why Nancy was with him under protest. Sitting up again, she looked at him searchingly. "Joshua, are you truly not angry with me?"

His mouth tightened a little before he said, "I believe I understand your actions. I don't pretend to applaud them."

She had a sudden urge to beg his pardon for what she had done, but she ruthlessly suppressed it, telling herself it was only because he had stirred her compassion by seeming a little upset to think he had behaved selfishly. The fact was that he had behaved, if not selfishly, then certainly with arrogance. Lessons were often painful, but if he had learned one and had done so without a fuss, so much the better.

When her conscience suggested to her that she was miffed at having failed to arouse his temper by her actions, she turned a deaf ear. It would have been easier for her, certainly, if he had reacted as predictably as Alston had, or as her father would have reacted under similar circumstances, but she told herself firmly that she was grateful not to have enraged Chalford and proceeded to act accordingly.

There was no question of removing to another house, first because every house in Brighton was bespoken for the rest of the summer, and second, because Sarah and her husband made it clear that they would be mortally offended if Adriana and Chalford went anywhere else. After the Pavilion concert, they returned to Clifford House, where Adriana and Joshua bade good night to their host and hostess and went upstairs. At the door to the blue bedchamber, Joshua said briefly, "Come to me after you dismiss Nancy. I am in the room next to this."

She had first to endure a severe scold from her abigail, the effect of which, added to Joshua's casual command, was to make her rather wary when she entered his room. He greeted her warmly and dismissed his man, but once in bed, with her head upon his shoulder, he asked gently, "What happened at the Pavilion tonight to set Alston goggling at me in such a way?"

"I think he was surprised to see you," she said carefully. When he did not respond, she tried to explain. "He was angrier with me than you are. He said I acted improperly in coming here without you, so no doubt he expected you to be angry, too, or not to come after me at all. He suggested, in fact, that you did not even know my whereabouts. When he saw you so cheerful tonight and being so attentive to me . . . well, I daresay he was surprised, that's all." She waited, hardly daring to breathe.

"I must continue to surprise him," Joshua murmured, turning his head to claim her lips.

It was all she could do not to bite him. If he noted her stiffness toward him at all, however, he treated it only as a challenge to his skill, and his skills being what they were, it was not long before she responded to them. If, by the time they slept, he had rather more scratches across his back from her long fingernails than he had ever suffered before, he no doubt put those down to his lady's unbridled passion.

By morning Adriana was feeling stimulated and not a little challenged herself, for a night's reflection had convinced her that Sarah had been right. Teaching Joshua a lesson had not been enough. She had felt little satisfaction at hearing him acknowledge his failure in the past to heed the wishes of others before making decisions on their behalf. The fact was that she had known exactly what to expect from Alston when he discovered even part of what she had done, and she had not had the least notion what to expect from Joshua, though he knew the whole. That, in a nutshell, was what challenged her now. He was her husband; she ought to know him better.

There was a certain amount of euphoria to be enjoyed, too, of course, for not only had Joshua followed her, but he had promised her a week in Brighton, and she was certain she would convince him, before the week was out, to stay longer. In the meantime, she decided, it would not be entirely out of the way to attempt to discover the limits of his tolerance. Therefore, when Clifford bore Joshua off with him to Donaldson's Library, informing the ladies that they would take a dip in the sea before returning, Adriana promptly suggested another expedition to Madame's little shop. Sarah laughingly agreed but warned her not to draw the bustle too tightly.

"I mean to purchase as much as I can in the time we are here," Adriana informed her. "I've no idea when the next opportunity will arise, and I have little faith that a Hythe seamstress will please me as well as Madame does. And do remind me, Sarah, if I forget, to have the bills directed to Joshua."

Not only with regard to her wardrobe did Adriana give herself free rein. As the days passed, the town began to fill with members of the *beau monde*, and the amusements to which the Cliffords and their guests were invited grew in number. Adriana blithely turned her attention to the enjoyment of every pleasure.

On Friday the four joined a riding party, including George and Sally Villiers, Miranda, the handsome Mr.

Dawlish, and a number of others, for an outing on the cliff. That evening the gentlemen dined with his royal highness at the Pavilion, where they were later joined by their wives for tea and coffee, with entertainment provided by his royal highness's own band.

On Saturday morning at eleven o'clock the town was suddenly alarmed by the reports of two signal guns, followed immediately afterward by the drums of the Gloucester Regiment beating to arms. Within a quarter of an hour Brighton was in a complete state of defense. At the first shot, Adriana and Sarah had leapt to their feet, but Joshua and Clifford had both laughed at them, telling them it was merely one of Prinny's attempts to test the readiness of his troops to defend against invasion.

"He's enjoying the threat as much as Aunt Hetta is," Joshua told Adriana. "He explained the entire plan to us over dinner."

" 'Tis a pity," Sarah said tartly, taking her seat again, "that he did not warn the town. I daresay that any number of people will have been frightened out of their wits."

But although many persons they met that day talked about the incident, none seemed particularly alarmed by it. The general reaction was approval of the speed with which the troops had responded. That night at the theater, the prince was cheered by the crowd when he entered his box with his party.

Seated far to the left of the royal box with Sally, George, the Cliffords, and Joshua, Adriana expected to enjoy the evening quite as much as she had enjoyed her previous visit to the theater. Having paid no heed to the billing, she noted with some dismay that the title of the play was *The Provok'd Husband*, but the antics of Sir Francis Wronghead and Lady Townley soon had her laughing as hard as anyone else in the audience. By the last interval she was recovered enough to enjoy agreeable flirtations with Mr. Bennett and Mr. Dawlish when they paid their respects, and after the play, when the Clifford party adjourned with some others to the

Villiers' house on the Marine Parade for a late supper, she conversed animatedly with her supper partner.

Twice before supper ended, she encountered Joshua's steady gaze from across the table. The first time, he smiled at her. The second time, just after she had patted her dinner partner's hand by way of emphasizing some small point or other, she thought when she looked up quickly that he looked a little hurt. The look vanished so quickly, though, that she could not be sure, and when they returned to Clifford House, he behaved so normally that Adriana wanted to shake him.

"You ought to be thoroughly shaken, Dree," hissed Sarah when, going up ahead of the gentlemen, they met briefly on the landing. "If I were ever to behave as you have been behaving these past days, Mortimer would throttle me."

Smiling ruefully at her friend, Adriana sighed and went to her bedchamber, to give herself up to Nancy's ministrations.

On Sunday they attended the Chapel Royal and tnen joined their friends to observe a military review on the cliff, after which they attended an al fresco supper, retiring early so as to be refreshed for the prince's birthday celebration.

On Monday morning, they hurried through breakfast, for the festivities were to begin soon after ten o'clock when a roll of drums announced a general military review of troops from the surrounding counties, all of whom began gathering on Newmarket Hill. When Adriana and Sarah met Lord Clifford in the hall, Joshua was not with him.

"Still in the morning room," said Clifford in reply to his wife's query. "Glaring at his post. Bills, I reckon."

"Nonsense," said Sarah, glancing anxiously at Adriana. "He does not glare."

"Frowning, then," said her amiable husband. "I'll fetch him." He did so, and Chalford came at once, apologizing with apparently unimpaired cheerfulness for having kept them waiting.

The review itself began at noon, and the Clifford

House party arrived well beforehand in order to enjoy conversation with their friends before the Prince of Wales's arrival at one o'clock. His highness, mounted upon a splendid bay charger, was accompanied by his brothers, the Duke of Kent and the Duke of Clarence, as well as a numerous cavalcade of military officers, private gentlemen, and foreigners of distinction.

"A splendid spectacle, all in all," pronounced Lord Clifford afterward in the carriage on the way back to the house.

"Indeed," agreed his lady, "much grander than yesterday's. So many handsome men in uniform . . ." She sighed ecstatically, casting a look of twinkling mischief at her husband before adding hastily, "Then, too, to hear 'God Save the King' sung by such a vast crowd must always stir one's patriotic fervor."

Joshua chuckled. "They say Prinny enjoys pomp and ceremony, so he must have liked this occasion very much."

"Well," said Sarah more seriously, "I for one wish he had a proper hostess in Brighton, for I think it very unfair that only the gentlemen may be invited to his birthday dinner. You ought to be ashamed, sirs, leaving us to our own devices, as you will."

"Nonsense," said Clifford bracingly, "you will enjoy yourselves quite as much as we will, cutting up characters with Sally Villiers at her ladies' dinner party."

"And when we all meet at the Castle afterward for the ball," put in Chalford, smiling at his wife, who had remained silent during this exchange, "I trust you two will have managed to save at least one dance for your husbands."

Adriana returned his smile. "I will save a country dance for you, sir, if you are not too late, but Sarah is right. It is unfair to leave us out of the best of the festivities. You will all drink too much and eat too much and no doubt forget all about us. His highness needs a woman to control his debauches."

"Well," Joshua said, "you can't expect Prinny to

stomach having his wife in Brighton when he comes here to avoid her as much as for any other cause. And although his relationship with Maria Fitzherbert has received something akin to approval from their friends, it would scarcely be appropriate for her to act his hostess to ladies of quality for his dinner parties."

"No," said Adriana thoughtfully, "though I think she has been treated abominably by all the royal family, his highness included. I cannot think why she agreed to reconcile with him. She must love him very much, which is rather amazing, I think—that anyone could, I mean."

The hint of a frown creased Chalford's brow. "You would do as well, however, to keep that opinion to yourself, I think."

Sarah chuckled. "You've no need to fear that Adriana would do anything so silly as to say such stuff to anyone but us, sir. She may be outspoken, and an outrageous flirt, but she would never create that sort of scandal, I promise you."

"Goodness, Sarah," Adriana exclaimed, "you ought not to make such promises as that. According to Alston, you know, I created that sort of a scandal merely by coming to Brighton."

A tactful silence followed this statement, but Adriana was watching Joshua, and she felt a stir of excitement when she saw the muscle high on his right cheek jump. She thought it was entirely possible that she had vexed him, but she was not altogether sure, and nothing more came of the incident, for by the time they reached Clifford House, it was time to dress for their late-afternoon and evening activities. Nancy and Lettie were waiting to attend to Adriana and Sarah, so the gentlemen adjourned to Clifford's library to refresh themselves and then to their own dressing rooms. Two hours later, Adriana, with Nancy in silent attendance, was adjusting her headdress of diamonds and gilded feathers when Chalford entered her bedchamber.

"Very becoming," he said, regarding her elegant robe of brown and gold tissue over a petticoat of brown crepe richly embroidered in gold and trimmed with gilded lace and diamonds. "I have not seen that dress before, I believe."

"Goodness no," she replied, meeting his gaze a little defiantly in her looking glass. "You would not expect me to wear something I have worn before, sir. Not tonight, when everyone will be looking to see what I have on. This gown was delivered only this afternoon." She stood and turned, giving him the full effect. Nancy adjusted a diamond loop fastening on one sleeve, and when she had done, Adriana said, "Just fetch my gloves now, and then you may go. Do not wait up for me."

Chalford waited until Nancy had handed Adriana a pair of gold net gloves, curtsied, and left the room. Then, quietly, he said, "Is that gown not a trifle more splendid than one expects to see at a ladies' dinner party or a ball at the Castle Inn?"

"'Tis the prince's birthday ball, Joshua," she reminded him. "Indeed, everyone will be dressed to shine. You would not wish your wife to be thought a dowdy on such an occasion, surely."

"No, sweetheart, certainly not, but if the bills I received in the post today are any indication, you have been wasting the ready with careless abandon ever since you set foot in Brighton."

"Oh, is that why you were frowning over your letters this morning? I wondered when Mortimer mentioned it but did not care to ask then, of course, and we have not been private with each other till now. I hope you are not vexed that I had the bills directed to you. At first, when I did not know whether you would come, I meant to borrow what I needed from Sarah. She is like a sister to me, after all, so you need not look so disapprovingly."

"Surely, you had money of your own."

"A little, not nearly enough." She saw that he was frowning again and added innocently, "I lent half of what you gave me to Miranda because Alston was in one of his squeeze-penny moods and refused to allow her to buy anything when they first arrived. Truly, Joshua, I have bought no more than I need. I ordered warm clothing, because I shall need it at Thunderhill, and

jewels, for I didn't know you would be bringing mine.
And, of course," she added casually, "I ordered new
gowns for Lady Berkeley's and Maria Fitzherbert's
routs on Thursday and for the Duchess of Bedford's
drum on Friday."

"But we leave Wednesday," he reminded her, "so
you can cancel those orders. You will have no need of
such elaborate gowns at Thunderhill, and you will want
to purchase new ones in the spring if we should go to
London."

"We can't leave on Wednesday," she said patiently.
"I know that you said we would stay only the sennight,
but surely you would not wish to offend Lady Berkeley
or Maria Fitzherbert, and I have already accepted their
invitations. You would not have me cry off now. The
prince leaves next week to visit his parents at
Weymouth, you know, so I shall not mind then if you
insist—"

"We are leaving Wednesday morning, just as I said
we would," Joshua said firmly.

"Joshua, we can't. You don't seem to understand.
Everyone else only just got here, and the amusements
have barely begun. Please, sir, say we may stay through
the week, and I promise I shan't complain about the
dullness at Thunderhill ever again."

"I am sorry you think it dull," he said, tight-lipped,
"but with the situation as unsettled and potentially
dangerous as it is at home, I am acting against my best
judgment in being here at all. We go home Wednesday
morning. In the meantime, you will, if you please, be a
little less free with your spending. If you insist upon
keeping the gowns you have ordered, I will say no more
about them, but there is no reason to be extravagant
merely for the pleasure of it, which I must say is what it
appears has been the case with you of late."

"Oh, you are impossible!" she cried. "You said you
would pay more heed to my wishes, and now just listen
to yourself!"

"That's enough," he said.

"No, Joshua, it is not nearly enough," she said

furiously, turning away from him toward the door, "but it is all I dare say to you now, for I have no intention of missing a moment of the festivities tonight." At the door she turned back, unable to resist a parting shot. "I hope you choke on your dinner, sir!" And with that she stormed from the room.

12

By the time the cavalcade of carriages from the Villiers' house turned off East Street into Castle Square and deposited Adriana, Sarah, Sally Villiers, and the other ladies at the tall, red brick building with elegant arched windows on the northeast corner, Adriana had recovered her temper and was looking forward to the ball. Sally's party had been a success, for she had put herself out to provide the ladies with as fine a dinner as any the prince might set before his guests. There had even been a band of Scots Guards to entertain them, and the wines flowed as freely as they might be expected to flow at the Pavilion.

Though the elegant ballroom of the Castle Inn, with its forty-foot arched and vaulted ceiling, was eighty feet long and forty feet wide, it was already so crowded by the time the ladies arrived that the lovely plaster reliefs, medallions, scrolls, and delicate moldings that graced its walls could scarcely be seen without standing right up against one. Adriana and Sarah moved through the crush to the long row of columns forming the boundary of the ballroom opposite the entrance, where there was a space perhaps six feet deep between the columns and the windows beyond them, providing a corridor of sorts. They had engaged to meet Miranda by the second column from the south end.

"There you are!" she exclaimed as they approached her. "We have been here nearly an hour already, for"— she glanced quickly over her shoulder, then moved to stand beside Adriana, lowering her voice—"Sophie and her odious brother were afraid they might miss seeing would not put in his appearance before half-past nine at the earliest, but they would come. How was Sally's party? I do wish I might have gone, but Sally could scarcely invite me without—''

"It was delightful." Sarah, who was facing the other two, spoke quickly, with a warning note in her voice. "We both had too much wine, however."

"Nonsense," said Adriana, ignoring the warning. "We are perfectly all right. Just a trifle above par, as Alston might say. Gracious, what a crush this is! How will we ever dance?"

"You will find a way, Adriana, I am sure," said a cool feminine voice behind her. "I collect that you have purchased another expensive new gown. 'Tis becoming, of course, but it prompts one to hope that Chalford is really as wealthy as we believed him to be."

Flushing at this unwelcome reminder of the unpleasantness with Joshua, she turned to find her sister-in-law, draped in silver lace over a petticoat of pink tissue. Sophie's look of strong disapproval gave Adriana to realize that she had been standing there long enough to hear nearly everything that had been said, as had Mr. Ringwell, who stood behind his sister, grinning. Greeting them both with as much politeness as she could muster, she asked bluntly, "Where is my brother?"

"At the Pavilion, of course," Sophie replied, attempting to cool herself with the pink feather fan that matched her opulent headdress. "Where else would he be, for goodness' sake?"

"Well, since he does not approve of the Prince of Wales, I imagined he might be anywhere else," replied Adriana.

"He knows his duty, I suppose," Sophie said with a lofty air. "I do think he might have taken dearest Claude with him, though Miranda and I are grateful for his escort, of course." Her attention was claimed just then by a lady unknown to Adriana, and since Sophie did not immediately present her, she and Sarah took the opportunity to slip away.

"For I tell you, Sarah," she muttered the moment they were beyond earshot, "even to please Miranda I cannot and will not suffer that odious woman tonight. It was all I could do not to tell her precisely why Alston did not dare to take her loose-fish brother with him to the Pavilion. Can you imagine what Prinny would say if he were to clap eyes on Claude? And did you see how Sophie looked at my dress? Depend upon it, she will describe it to Alston down to the last stitch and diamond. I only hope he will not consider it his duty to speak to Joshua about my ruinous extravagance. I promise you I have had enough lectures today."

Sarah's eyebrows raised slightly. "Lectures, my dear? Not that you haven't deserved them, mind you. But from the unflappable marquess? How is this?"

Adriana shrugged. "It was not so bad, but he said, as you did yourself, that I have been spending too freely, so I'd as lief he hear no untimely complaint from Alston. More important than that is that he insists we must leave Wednesday, though I had hoped to persuade him to stay till the end of the week. He will not even discuss the matter. As always, he has simply made his declaration and assumes that I will abide by his decision."

"And so you lost your temper." Sarah grinned at her.

"How well you know me," Adriana said wryly. "Heaven knows I did not mean to do so, but when he was so placid about thwarting my wishes, so imperturbable in his assumption that all would be as he desired, he made me want to scream." She sighed. "I confess, Sarah, that just as you suggested, I have been trying to discover his limits, but whenever I try to finesse him into expressing what is in his mind, he takes the trick by infuriating me instead. There are times, you know, when I am nearly certain he is displeased. A muscle twitches in his cheek, and his lips fold together tightly. But then he speaks, and he is as calm and unruffled as ever. How I wish I knew a way to disturb that damned composure of his without sacrificing my dignity!"

Sarah shook her head but could say no more, for her attention was claimed by a young man who stepped up to ask if she would honor him later with a dance. A moment afterward, Adriana greeted a gentleman acquaintance of her own, and by the time the prince's party arrived at half-past nine, she had encountered a number of young men with whom she was acquainted and had begun to enjoy herself quite tolerably.

The crowd was so great by then that she was unable to see the prince or any of his companions. Only the altered, more harmonious sound of the musicians' instruments, which they had begun to tune sometime earlier, gave warning of his arrival. The opening notes of the first dance initiated a spirited attempt to clear the center of the floor, but room could be made to form only two sets, and the dancers, their progress constantly impeded by the encroaching crowd, had great difficulty getting through the pattern. Rumor had it that the number of persons attending the ball had reached six hundred.

Adriana saw Chalford at last just after the musicians had struck up for the second dance, for which only one set was attempted, everyone else giving themselves up to conversation. She was chatting with Mr. Dawlish when she espied her husband making his way toward them through the crush. Her smile broadened winsomely and she leaned toward her companion, placing her fingers lightly upon his arm.

"I declare, sir, I am perishing for thirst. Is there not a punch bowl set out in the card room on these occasions?"

Responding warmly to her smile, the auburn-haired young gentleman shook his head. "They are setting up tables in the card room for the supper tonight, my lady, there being so many. Perhaps there will be something to drink in one of the two smaller rooms, however. Shall we see?"

"I shall be forever in your debt, sir," she said, giving his arm an involuntary squeeze when the crowd parted briefly to give her a clear view of Chalford, who was looking in her direction, frowning slightly. She turned quickly away with her companion.

Dawlish did indeed find a punch bowl in the little supper room, and Adriana thanked him graciously if rather vaguely, for she was attempting to see if Joshua had followed them. He had not done so, however, and when Dawlish, regarding her more amorously than before, led her back to Sarah, Lord Clifford stood beside his wife, but of Joshua there was no sign.

"Your husband was looking for you, Adriana," Sarah said, raising one eyebrow in silent query. "He and Mortimer were afraid we'd not get good places for supper if we don't make a push to be part of the first dash."

"Mr. Dawlish was so kind as to fetch me some punch," Adriana explained, turning then to the young man to add with a decidedly flirtatious air, "You must join us for supper, sir."

When he politely demurred, she would have none of it, insisting gaily that he would not be intruding in the slightest. "I daresay my brother and his wife, and my sister, and possibly my brother's wife's brother— dear me, what a tangle that sounds! Truly Mr. Dawlish, you would be doing us the greatest favor by joining us, for families, you know, ought not to be left to their own devices lest they bore one another to distraction. Please do not abandon us to such a fate, sir. Come with us, do."

Laughing, Dawlish agreed, and soon after that, Chalford appeared, accompanied by Alston, Sophie, Miranda, and Mr. Ringwell. The latter bowed low, winking at Adriana as he did so.

"Ah, so here you are," he said archly. "Chalford found he had misplaced you, and we quite thought you must have been spirited away by some blackguard. My sister was distressed when you slipped away, you know. She quite expected you and Lady Clifford to join our little party, at least until your respective husbands arrived. I fear you are in for a scold, my dear."

Ignoring him and turning to Chalford, she said

blithely, "Mr. Dawlish rescued me from thirst, sir, and has kindly agreed to take supper with us as his reward. Is it time to go down?"

Chalford acknowledged Dawlish politely enough, but Adriana was certain for once that he was annoyed. Despite his customary, unruffled demeanor, she detected a glint in his eye steely enough to give her a brief qualm when his gaze rested upon her. But when he moved to her side and said quite matter-of-factly that it was indeed time to go down, she placed her hand defiantly upon Mr. Dawlish's forearm, offered the young man a brilliant smile, and strode off with him, leaving Joshua to follow in their wake.

The supper was a splendid one, lasting until nearly two o'clock in the morning. Chalford, although seated at his wife's left, made no attempt to engage her attention, and Adriana, deciding that she had been mistaken earlier about seeing any odd glint in his eye, found herself rapidly growing as resentful of his inattention as she was of her brother's frequent disapproving looks and barbed remarks, or Mr. Ringwell's ill-bred compliments.

Throughout the meal, the inn servants saw that no wineglass went empty. Consequently, she allowed herself to flirt more freely than usual with Mr. Dawlish, her behavior growing more outrageous with every passing moment, reaching its zenith when she allowed that increasingly responsive gentleman to feed her grapes from his own plate. By then, thanks to the glow she felt from the wine, it had become easy to ignore Alston's comments and even Sarah's warning looks. She paid no heed whatsoever to her husband, or she might have noted both the muscle tightening in his cheek and a growing whiteness around his lips.

The orchestra began to play for dancing again at two o'clock, and when they returned to the ballroom, they discovered that the prince and a number of others had departed, making it possible to form a normal number of sets for dancing. Adriana promptly accepted Mr. Dawlish's invitation to join one of these.

The dance was a spirited Scotch reel, and by the time it was over, her head was spinning as much from the energetic activity as from all the wine she had drunk. Dizzily, she clutched at Mr. Dawlish's arm as he led her from the floor toward the long row of columns. Not until they had nearly reached them did she realize they were at the wrong end of the room.

"My party is at the south end, sir," she said, putting her free hand to her head in an attempt to steady it. For some odd reason it had felt these past few moments as though it were too heavy for her neck to bear.

Dawlish paid no heed to her words, drawing her closer to the columns instead and looking down at her, his eyes bright, his expression nothing less than moon-struck.

Adriana's eyes widened as she became aware of his intensity. "Sir, you must take me back to my family," she said hastily. Looking around, she realized that though there were people nearby, no one was looking in their direction. All were trying to watch the dancers taking their places. When Dawlish attempted to draw her toward the corridor beyond the columns, she resisted, digging her heels in, wishing her head would clear so that she might think rationally. "Mr. Dawlish, please take me back."

"You needn't pretend now, my beautiful lady," he murmured, lowering his head, his hands clasping her upper arms as he attempted to pull her nearer to him.

Adriana didn't move. "Mr. Dawlish, I never intended—"

"Your intent has been dashed clear all evening—for days, in fact. Knew your man, too. Been mad about you since London, but your flirting was always so casual a fellow didn't take it seriously. Married women have much more freedom, do they not?"

"Sir, let go of my arms," she commanded, trying hard to sound firm but well aware that she had slurred her words.

He ignored her, yanking her sharply forward and lowering his mouth to hers without further ado.

Twisting desperately, she tried to free herself, tried
even to use her fingernails to good purpose; however,
since both she and Dawlish wore gloves, those efforts
were useless. Finally, she brought her heel down hard
upon his instep, causing him to gasp with pain and to
relax his hold upon her arms enough for her to break
free. One or two persons turned, then looked discreetly
away again when she shot them an angry look.

"How dare you, sir!" she demanded, rounding on
Dawlish furiously, her arms akimbo.

"How dare I?" he repeated, rubbing his injured left
foot against the back of his right leg and glaring at her.
He made no effort to lower his voice. "You've been
playing fast and loose with me all evening, my
lady—aye, and on previous occasions as well. 'Tis plain
as a pikestaff you're not indifferent to my attentions.
You welcome them, in fact."

Adriana spoke quietly in the hope that he would take
the hint. "Sir, you have mistaken the matter. If I was
friendly—"

"Is that what you call it? Dash it, Adriana, you can't
go about making up to a fellow for days on end,
granting him favors in place of your own husband, and
then simply say 'no' when he takes you at your word."

"You've no right!" she cried furiously, lifting her
hand.

He caught it in a strong grip, forcing it back to her
side. Then he grabbed her upper arms again, giving her
a rough shake and saying vehemently, "There's a word
for females like you, and although until tonight I
certainly didn't take you for one of them, I have been
brought to recognize my error. You're no more than a
damned flirt, a tease—indeed, madam, not to mince
words, I tell you to your face that you are an
unconscionable cockchafer and deserve to be taught a
lesson." His hands tightened upon her arms bruisingly
as he forced her behind the columns into the corridor.
Though she struggled, she knew that this time it would
take more than a heel to his instep to make him release
her.

Suddenly, another, more powerful hand clamped her left shoulder, wrenching her free of the startled Dawlish's grasp and sending her spinning into the nearest column with a force that stunned her. She was not so dazed, however, that she did not recognize her rescuer and thrill to see him there. Nor did she fail to observe—indeed, to revel in—the heavy blow that knocked Dawlish to the floor. He lay there, unmoving, but Joshua did not stay to see what damage he had wrought. Instead, he turned on his heel and made straight for his wife, ignoring the gasps and gapes of a rapidly increasing group of astonished onlookers.

He was upon her before she could gather her wits or close her mouth, and no matter how strongly she might wish she could become one with the column behind her, there was no way to elude him when his hand shot out to grab hers. Jerking her forward, he clamped her hand into the crook of his elbow, bending to mutter coldly and for her ears alone, "He was right about one thing, madam: you deserve a lesson, and so help me God, you'll get it here and now if you defy me. We are leaving."

Shocked to her toes by what he had done to Dawlish and sharply aware now of their interested audience, Adriana flushed scarlet with embarrassment but didn't for a moment consider arguing with him. Indeed, it was all she could do to keep up with him, for Joshua strode across the ballroom toward the entrance without looking to right or left, the crowd parting before him like wheat before a whirlwind as whispered reports of what had happened flew ahead of them.

Outside in the square, he brusquely ordered the Clifford carriage to be brought around, and while they waited, Adriana, no longer feeling the least effect from the wine, attempted to compose herself. Joshua said nothing.

Inside the carriage, as they passed from Castle Square into East Street, she turned to him, anxious to explain the whole thing to him. "Please, Joshua, I—"

"You will keep silent," he said abruptly, with so

much ice in his voice that a chill raced down her spine, causing her to shift uncomfortably on her seat. The journey back to Clifford House was accomplished in glacial silence.

When they arrived, Joshua sent the carriage back to the Castle to await Lord and Lady Clifford, for Adriana and Sarah had sent their phaeton home upon arriving at the inn, having expected to return in the larger carriage with their husbands. Inside the house, the porter, after taking one look at the wintry marquess, said not a word as they passed him on their way to the stairway.

When Adriana hesitated on the first landing, Chalford said in the same frigid tone he had used earlier, "We are going up to your bedchamber. I do not wish to be disturbed."

His words triggered a vivid memory of Mr. Dawlish as she had last seen him, making her marvel at the fact that she had ever mistaken her husband for a placid, nonviolent man, and reminding her of his suggestion that Villiers ought to beat his Sally. When next she remembered what he had said to her before their dramatic exit from the ballroom, she experienced a frisson of fear. She had wanted to discover what would put him in a rage and she had certainly accomplished her purpose, but the result was much more than she had bargained for. Though his frosty anger was nothing like the fury she was accustomed to igniting in her brother or her father, it was a good deal more frightening. She shivered again when they reached the door to her bedchamber. What on earth did he intend to do to her?

Joshua pushed the door open and Adriana hurried inside the dimly lamplit room, moving quickly to the far side, where she turned, her back against the wall. "Please, Joshua, you must let me explain. It wasn't what you thought!"

He shut the door with a snap, and his chilly gaze met hers across the room. "You are mistaken," he said, making no attempt to move from where he stood. "It was precisely what I thought."

"He misunderstood my flirting. He tried to force

me," she protested. "The things he said! You cannot know—"

"I heard exactly what he said," he interrupted coldly, "and I know that you deserved to hear every word. You led him to expect that he would find you an easy conquest, and when he responded to the lures you had been throwing out to him all evening, you chose to be offended. The name he called you was not a pretty one, certainly, but tonight it fitted you very well. This is not the first time I have been privileged to witness such behavior from you, but I will tell you here and now that it had better be the last. I have made allowances in the past—for your youth, your boredom, and for your lack of a mother to guide you in such matters—but I'll make allowances no longer."

Her eyes were like saucers. "You're really angry with me."

"Can you be surprised if I am?" he demanded. "Do you dare to tell me that you do not deserve my anger?"

She didn't want to answer. If he was going to scold her, she wanted him to shout, to bluster—in short, to do the thing the way she was accustomed to having it done. She would bow her head before his wrath, and when it was spent, she would apologize and explain, and that would be that until the next time.

"Well?"

She swallowed uncomfortably, but he only waited, looking at her with that steely glint in his eyes, his very silence demanding a response. "I didn't think you would get so angry," she said at last. "You said nothing at all when I let him take me down to supper. When you spoke as you did after you hit him, I thought you were angry with him because of what he said to me and a little angry with me because people would talk about such a scene . . . about me. Was it all me from the beginning, Joshua?"

"I hit him, not you," he said, "but I'll not deny that I was angry with you. I had already decided it was time for us to leave. Had he not put his hands on you—" He broke off, then demanded swiftly, "Are you proud of your behavior tonight, Adriana? Are you proud that you drank too much wine, that you allowed your foolishness to carry you beyond the line, that you behaved in fact precisely as Dawlish said you behaved?''

"Please, Joshua," she said, taking a hesitant step toward him, "I don't want to talk about it like this anymore. If you're angry with me, then say what you have to say or do what you have to do, but don't—"

"Don't what, Adriana? Don't make you think about what you did? Don't make you see how unbecomingly, how shamefully you behaved? Can you imagine what it was like for me to watch my wife casting out lures to a puppy like Dawlish?''

"No!" she snapped, suddenly as angry as he was. "No, Joshua, I cannot imagine, because I never know what you think. Even when I let him take me to supper, I couldn't be sure you were angry. You are always the same, always composed, always so certain that everything will be done the way you want it done. Even Lady Adelaide bows to your wishes, does she not? Other people's wishes, other people's needs are as nothing to you.''

"That isn't so, Adriana," he said quietly.

"It is!" she shouted at him. "Only look at you now. The minute I oppose you, you go all calm and self-possessed. Your face becomes a mask that I, for one, cannot read. I never know what you think about what I do. You expect me to be a mind-reader. If I behaved badly tonight it was because I was angry, too. No, not angry, that's the wrong word. Frustrated is the right word. Sarah said I was trying to discover what you will tolerate. I think I was trying to discover if you had any feelings to express at all. You behave like some sort of omnipotent ruler at Thunderhill, and you make me feel like your concubine, tossing me an occasional visitor like a bone to—"

"That will do, Adriana." The chill this time was greater than ever, and it stopped her midsentence, sending the icy shivers racing up and down her spine again. "We will not discuss my behavior at the moment, only yours. If you are not happy with things as they are, we can talk about that tomorrow if you like, on our way back to Thunderhill, but now we will discuss your actions, and we will discuss them thoroughly." With that, he proceeded to do so, and if the discussion was entirely one-sided in that he no longer paused to demand answers from her, it was nonetheless emotionally annihilating.

As he methodically ticked off point after point—deploring her flirting, her extravagance, her refusal to submit graciously to his commands, her subornation of his servants, her foolhardy association with smugglers—Adriana grew whiter and more wretched. There were tears in her eyes before he was done, but they had no effect upon him. At one point she put up both hands and said in a small, wavering voice, "Don't, Joshua. Please, don't say any more." But that had no more effect than her tears. He continued to shred her character until he could find no more to say. Then, adding only the recommendation that she "think about that for a while," he turned on his heel and left the room.

She stood where she had stood through it all, feeling unable to move, shaken by his chilly condemnation as she had never been shaken by any of her brother's or father's blustering scolds. The tears spilled over at last, coursing down her cheeks, and with a gasping sob, she collapsed onto her bed and let them come, crying until she could cry no more.

When her tears had run dry, she tried to summon anger, even resentment. She tried to tell herself that he had been wrong, that he had deserved what she had done. But his words came echoing back to her, spinning through her mind until she thought she must scream, and she knew that in trying to push him to his limit she had gone too far. She knew, though she despised herself with the knowing, that nearly everything he had said of her was true.

Then, and only then, did she remember that he had said they would return to Thunderhill "tomorrow."

The memory shook her, but she could scarcely blame him for his decision. After the scene she had caused, there wasn't a tattlemonger in Brighton who would not be in possession of all the distasteful facts by dawn. One of the faces she had seen most clearly when Joshua dragged her from the ballroom had been Sally's, and already that young lady had achieved a notable reputation as a gossip. "Silence" they called her, and her friendship with Adriana would no more stop her tongue than her even closer friendship with Emily Cowper had stopped her from talking about that young woman. No doubt Joshua would wish to put as much distance between himself and the gossips as he possibly could.

At last, she sat up and blotted her tears, knowing she would have to apologize and knowing, too, that the apology this time must be sincere, not a sop to soothe a gentleman's temper or to ease tension. Thus, the sooner it was done, the better it would be. Suiting thought to action, she disentangled her headdress from her hair and flung it aside, blew out her flickering lamp, and without taking time to wash her face, went to find him.

When she opened his door, it was dark inside. "Joshua?"

"I'm here." There was the sound of flint against a tinderbox, then sparks and the glow of cotton, and in a moment the candle on the table by his bed was lit, casting a glow over the little room with its lavender curtains and spread, and its polished floor. Joshua sat on the high bed in his shirt sleeves. He had taken off his coat, waistcoat, neckcloth, and boots, and it was clear from the resulting disarray that Miskin had neither waited up for him nor been awakened.

Now that she was with him Adriana didn't know how to begin. She picked up his embroidered waistcoat from the floor and put it on a chair, collecting her thoughts, determined not to let him put her out of countenance again.

Joshua said nothing, but he watched her through narrowed eyes. Instead of disconcerting her, this time his silence gave her courage, and finally, blurting the words, she said, "You were right, sir. My behavior has been reprehensible, particularly tonight, but I shall endeavor to do better in the future if you can find it in your heart to forgive me."

He still said nothing, but the hard glint disappeared from his eyes, and taking courage from this sign, she moved to stand before him, clasping his large hands between her smaller ones, looking at him with her heart in her eyes. "Please, Joshua, won't you help me put this night behind us? I'll try very hard not to flirt anymore, and I'll learn all there is to learn about my duties at Thunderhill, and I'll never associate with smugglers again, and I'll be as obedient as I know how to be, and—"

"Would you repeat that last part, please?" he asked gently.

"I said—"

"I know what you said."

To her vast astonishment, she realized he was amused. She stared at him, wide-eyed, then said indignantly, "I meant every word, Joshua. Truly!"

"I believe you," he said more seriously, pulling her nearer so that she stood between his open thighs. "At least, I suppose you must believe this affecting apology of yours, but I don't believe for one minute that you will be able to make it good. You can no more stop flirting than you can fly, and I very much doubt that you have the least notion of obedience. The minute someone is foolish enough to give you an order, you set about determining the quickest, most effective means of flouting it."

"I don't!"

"You do," he said, reaching for the diamond fastenings to her robe and beginning slowly to undo them, "and you are, despite what you believe to the contrary, just as accustomed to ordering your life to suit you as I am to ordering mine to suit me. But I shall say no more on that head. Indeed, I have said all I mean to say tonight and probably a deal that I did not mean."

She looked at him. "Truly, Joshua?"

"I store things up," he confided, bending his head to kiss her neck. "When I get really angry—which fortunately is a very rare occurrence—I blow up and everything comes out all at once, the large and the small. By then they all seem the same size, and even though the storm nearly always blows over quickly, I have been known to say more than I ought to say."

"You were very angry with me," she said softly, drawing her finger provocatively along his jawline. "You frightened me."

His hand moved inside her robe, caressing the soft breast beneath, making her gasp with pleasure. "You deserved to be frightened, sweetheart," he murmured. "Did you not?"

She melted against him, encouraging his kisses as she wriggled to free herself from the last folds of her clothing. Clearly, though the worst was over, it was still going to take some time to placate him; however, if she did the job thoroughly, perhaps by morning he would change his mind about returning immediately to Thunderhill.

13

Adriana discovered the error of her thinking late the following morning when she returned to her own bed-chamber to discover Nancy packing her things. Joshua had wakened before her and, according to her abigail, had given orders for their departure at one o'clock. She dressed quickly and went in search of him, finding him in the breakfast parlor, discussing a large underdone beefsteak, grilled kidneys, and potatoes.

Sarah, sitting opposite him, was watching with wonder approaching awe. "Good morning," she said to Adriana. "I have just suggested to your husband that he ought to arrange for the demise of his breakfast before it comes to table. I shouldn't be at all amazed to see that animal get up and walk off the plate."

"Don't be vulgar," Adriana said, nodding when the footman preparing her plate indicated a bowl of sliced fruit. "Muffins, too, William," she said, taking her seat. "Instead of condemning Chalford's eating habits, Sarah, you ought to help me convince him that it is quite unnecessary for us to return today."

"I hope," said the marquess, giving his wife a direct look, "that she won't try to flog a dead horse. I've already explained to her that we must leave soon if we are to catch the tide."

"But, surely—"

"No, Adriana." There was an implacable note in his voice that she had come to recognize, but she was feeling unaccountably carefree that morning and would have pressed harder had not a spark of amusement lit his eyes when he added, " 'Tis as well we did not make any wagers last night, is it not? You'd be run off your legs mighty soon, sweetheart, if you had to pay a forfeit every time you proved me right.''

She bit her lower lip, then looked up to thank William and to ask him to bring her a pot of tea. When the footman had gone, she grinned at Sarah and said, ''I promised to be obedient, and Joshua said I'd never manage to do it. Foolish of me to make his point for him so quickly, was it not?''

''I wish you could both stay with us longer,'' Sarah said wistfully. ''It won't be the same without you.''

''Quieter,'' murmured Chalford, ''no juicy scandal to delight your neighbors and set the tabbies twitching.''

''Oh, fiddlesticks,'' Sarah said, laughing. ''What scandal? Nothing happened last night that won't be eclipsed within a day or two by some incident of greater interest. Now, if you had knocked Adriana to the floor instead of poor Mr. Dawlish—''

''Poor Mr. Dawlish!'' exclaimed Adriana. ''Well, I like that. Let me tell you, Sarah Clifford—''

''The less you say about what passed between you and Dawlish, the better I shall like it,'' Joshua said quietly.

She smiled, in charity with him again. ''I confess, sir, I hope no one else was close enough to hear what he said to me.'' Then, noting the look of interest on Sarah's expressive face, she said, ''You needn't think I'm going to tell you now, for I won't. Joshua,'' she added, turning abruptly back to him, ''if we must return today, can we take Miranda with us? She can be ready in a trice, and she would very much like to go. She does not wish to wait until Christmas, and neither do I.''

''Your brother will never hear of it,'' he said.

''Perhaps not, but we shan't know if we do not invite her.''

''Very well, but don't be cast into gloom when Alston says she may not come.''

Pleased though she was to find him so reasonable, Adriana had no more expectation than Joshua did that her brother would allow Miranda to escape his protection, so no one was more surprised than she was when at a quarter-past noon, Viscount Alston's carriage drew up before Clifford House and deposited the Lady Miranda Barrington and her maid upon the doorstep.

"Can you credit it?" demanded Miranda the moment she crossed the threshold. "Nothing was ever more providential. That odious little bounce, Claude Ringwell, has been making the most absurd advances, and dear Alston, having observed his attempt to fondle my backside on the stair this morning, was actually moved to agree that I shall be safer at Thunderhill."

"And how long," Sarah asked sweetly, "did you have to wait on the stairway for your victim to present himself?"

Miranda chuckled. "Nearly half an hour, and then I had to shriek like a banshee to be certain Alston would hear me, but he simply erupted from his bookroom, and there was Claude, looking as guilty as a fox with feathers stuck in his whiskers. I thought," she added sagely, "that you might decide to leave today, so I decided it would behoove me to be ready, just in the event, you know, that you should ask me to go with you."

"It seems to me," said Joshua thoughtfully, "that in such a case, Alston would have been more likely to have banished young Ringwell from the house than to have allowed you to leave."

"Oh, he could not do that," said Miranda airily. "Sophie, for some reason known only to herself, quite dotes on Claude. Besides," she added with a wicked grin, "Alston thinks me a paragon at the moment, compared to Dree. I have never sunk so far beneath reproach as he now thinks she has."

Adriana grimaced and glanced at Joshua, but when he smiled at her, she smiled back, finding it impossible in the face of her sister's cheerful teasing to be as downcast at leaving Brighton as she had thought she would be. Their return journey aboard the *Sea Dragon* was uneventful, and once they were back at Thunderhill, Adriana had the odd feeling that she had

never left it. Almost immediately, the excitement of life
in Brighton faded into memory, like a dream, as though
she had never gone.

The aunts were there to greet them, Lady Hetta full of
news and her sister as stately and awe-inspiring as ever.
Adriana, replying to Lady Adelaide's request for news
of some of her friends in Brighton, hoped silently but
nonetheless fervently that her ladyship would never
know about the voyage on the smugglers' ship or the
incident at the prince's birthday ball. If Lady Adelaide
had heard a word about either one, she did not say so.

"Only think of it," Lady Hetta was saying
indignantly to Chalford when Adriana paused in her
own account to draw breath. "To have been taken
captive and borne off to France, then simply abandoned
there. The poor man!"

Chalford, noting Adriana's bewildered look,
explained, "She has just been telling me that Petticrow
has come to grief again."

"Mercy, what now, ma'am?"

"Those detestable smugglers—not ours, I think, but
the others, the new ones—carried him off to France and
left him there without any identity papers or food or
anything. He could have been killed by those dreadful
French or starved or goodness knows what. It was an
appalling thing to do to the poor man."

"Indeed, it was, ma'am," Miranda agreed, "but how
do you know that is what happened?"

"Why, he told us so! Mr. Braverstoke rescued him,
you see, and Mr. Petticrow came here at once to tell us
all about it."

"Braverstoke rescued him!" Chalford repeated.

"Pure foolhardiness," pronounced Lady Adelaide in
measured tones of disapproval. "The man had no
business to involve himself in so dangerous a venture."

"Indeed, it was no such thing," said Lady Hetta. "It
was the most fortunate circumstance."

"Encroaching," insisted Lady Adelaide. "He and his
father." Encountering a look from her nephew, she
added, "Perhaps you will say I ought not to speak so,

Joshua, but you know it is perfectly true. The son is a ne'er-do-well and the father a bumptious little man, the last person one expected to inherit Newingham Manor or to have the impertinence to come courting at Thunderhill. What, a fourth cousin with a title for life and not a penny to bless himself with, if the truth be known, for the stipend accompanying such titles is never princely. I do not like for him or that young man to be running tame here, and I devoutly hope you will not continue to encourage them to do so."

Chalford waited politely until s.e had finished, then turned to Lady Hetta. "Pray continue your tale, ma'am."

She smiled gratefully. "You know how dear Mr. Braverstoke enjoys taking that yacht of his out, Joshua, and sailing as near as the devil himself to the French coast—really, a most dangerous pastime, I agree, but very brave of him, Adelaide, not foolhardy at all. Well, someone from shore carried word to the *Golden Fleece* —no doubt some of the French smugglers, if the truth of the matter were known, since our people must deal with someone over there, after all. In any event, someone did, and Mr. Braverstoke's people were able to collect him."

"That was fortunate, certainly," Chalford said. "How long ago did this occur?"

"They brought him home yesterday afternoon. We gave him a good meal, and he is sleeping in his old room right now. I insisted upon that. The poor man simply could not go home alone in the state he was in. He hadn't slept for three days!"

"Well," said Chalford, "Petticrow does seem to be prone to adventure. We must hope he will tell us all about it."

The riding officer was only too willing to comply with this request when he joined them that evening for supper. His clothes had been brushed and pressed, and he was fully refreshed, but his temper was not entirely mended. He cast a sidelong look at Joshua when Adriana and Miranda began to pelt him with questions.

" 'Twas the most damnable thing, m'lord," he said, looking squarely at Joshua, then turning back again to apologize for the intemperance of his language. "It would try a saint, m'ladies, in truth it would. I was taken like the veriest amateur. They came up behind me when I was watching Strawberry Cove—north of Hythe, you know. There are cliffs there, so the lads don't attempt to unload cargo, as a general thing, but there are caves in the cliffs, so when things get hot, they sometimes unload there until the coast is clear again. I spoiled a run a sennight past, so I expected they'd be wary for a time. There I was, waiting for them, and they must have known I was, for the next I knew, I'd a sack over my head and was trussed up like a bag of hops ready for the oasthouse. They rowed me out to the ship and stowed me in the stern hold. All the way to France they took me, and all the way I listened to the damned sound of their blasted stern mast above me, creaking and wailing in the wind like fingernails on a slate. Like to drive a man to Bedlam."

"How dreadful," said Miranda, "but how fortunate Mr. Braverstoke was able to rescue you and bring you home again."

"Aye," the riding officer agreed, but there was a note of doubt in his voice, and after a moment's silence, he looked at Joshua again and said, "I'd know that ship again, I believe, m'lord. Got free of the trussing before she'd cleared the French harbor, and it was dawn by then. Only saw her from astern, but I could hear the screeching of that stern mast, so I know it was the right ship, and she'd got a pair of carved wooden panels mounted on the stern bulwark in the same place as the *Golden Fleece* has those garish gilded medallions."

"But nearly every ship has some decoration of that sort, sir," Adriana protested. "Why, the *Sea Dragon* has heraldic devices in exactly those same places, though neither she nor the *Golden Fleece* can be the ship you describe, of course, since both are sloops and have but a single mast. But even if you identify the ship, how would you catch your men? The owner may know nothing of the use to which his boat is being put. Why, it could be a situation exactly like when—"

"That's a point," Chalford said, cutting in. "You know as well as I do, Petticrow, that the Gentlemen tend to 'borrow' what they need. They'll leave a keg or a sack of tea to pay for what they borrow, but they have no scruples against taking a prize horse right out of a man's stable if they need it for a run."

"And you know, m'lord, that that don't excuse anyone," Petticrow said severely. "A man's boat being used without his knowledge don't mean the revenuers won't hold him to account if the boat is seized with contraband aboard. Not," he added, "that that signifies for much when we don't know the man or his boat."

"If you could identify the ship beyond a doubt—"

"Ah, but that's what I can't do, m'lord. Only seeing her from astern, I never saw her lines clear. And if I was to keep an eye on every private yacht I suspect of taking part in nefarious doings," he added with a sharp look, "I'd need a hundred eyes just for my own five-mile bit of coast, and no mistake. What with the Sandgate gang moving in on the locals hereabouts, as they are, I've enough on my plate without seeking more trouble, and that's the nut with no bark on it."

When the ladies left Joshua and Mr. Petticrow to enjoy a glass of port after supper, Miranda said, " 'Tis the drollest thing, you know. I have never before sat down to supper with a riding officer. Only think what Alston would say, or Sophie, with all her bourgeois gentility—how she would stare!"

"I am sure I cannot think why," said Lady Hetta, looking quite as bewildered as she sounded. "Mr. Petticrow's antecedents are perfectly respectable, you know."

"Are they, indeed, ma'am?" Adriana shot her a twinkling look. "I must say, one doesn't expect a riding officer to speak like an educated man, as he often does, although I never knew a riding officer before, so perhaps I am being unfair about that."

"Geoffrey Chaucer was a customs agent," said Lady Hetta, "and he was certainly an educated man."

"But not," said Lady Adelaide acidly, "a man whose works a lady of quality ought to read, Hetta."

Lady Hetta squared her thin shoulders. "I daresay Mr. Petticrow speaks as he was taught to speak, you know. His papa is a squire in Berkshire, and he told me once that he was expected to go into the Church—for he is the younger son, as anyone can tell merely by looking at him. I cannot think why younger sons are always so much better-looking than their more eligible elder brothers, but such is always the case." She blinked myopically. "What was I saying?"

"He was supposed to enter the Church," Adriana prompted, avoiding Miranda's eye and stealing a glance at Lady Adelaide, whose attention was now riveted on the needlework in her lap.

"Oh, well," Lady Hetta said, following her glance self-consciously, "he thought he would prefer to do something more adventuresome, you know, though not the military, because there was nothing much doing to interest him when he was of an age to join. And since he disapproves of smuggling—although to do him credit, he blames the government quite as much as he blames the smugglers for its existence—he became a riding officer."

Adriana repeated this information to Chalford that night after they had gone to bed, certain he would enjoy hearing about Geoffrey Chaucer in particular. She lay with her head upon his shoulder, anticipating his amusement, but instead of chuckling, he sighed. It was a long sigh, even a long-suffering sigh. She turned her head, trying to read the expression on his face.

"You disapprove, sir?"

"There is nothing of which to disapprove. I was just wondering if, having learned what an eligible *parti* old Petticrow is, you will now wish to add him to your list of conquests."

"Detestable man," she said, applying her elbow to his ribs, "and I do not speak of Mr. Petticrow. You know, though," she added musingly as another thought struck her, "I shouldn't be at all surprised if your Aunt Hetta has an interest there."

He snorted. "Don't be nonsensical. Aunt Adelaide would forbid him the castle if she suspected a thing like that."

"Well, I shan't suggest it to her, then. Would you mind?"

"The question won't arise. Aunt Adelaide, I can tell you for a fact, is much more concerned about Lord Braverstoke. Seems he's been haunting the place. But neither he nor Petticrow will win the day. Aunt Hetta has had numerous offers since her come-out, but she told me once she'd never met a man who could offer her more than she has here. Very proper sentiments, I thought."

"You would," said Adriana.

"By the bye," he said then on a more somber note, "Petticrow informs me that the disturbances between the Sandgaters and our local people have escalated in number and degree of violence. A Burmarsh man was beaten nearly to death in a scuffle last week, and the batmen carry more than lumber now to protect their runs."

"Batmen?"

"The landsmen consist of tubmen and batmen," he said. "The tubmen collect the goods from the ship, and the batmen stand guard over the whole business, start to finish. Generally, they are armed with clubs, but of late they have not worried so much about noise as about losing goods to the Sandgaters. There have been, Petticrow says, a number of skirmishes. Several men have been threatened, pressed to join the Sandgate gang."

"Joshua, are you trying to suggest more subtly than usual that your restrictions will stand with regard to our going outside the castle walls?"

"Nothing to be subtle about," he said. "I've already given the orders, and I expect you to relay them to your sister. And, Adriana, please, for once in your life, don't attempt to circumvent my commands. Just obey them."

"Yes, my lord," she replied submissively.

Joshua raised himself onto his elbow, looking down at her, and though the room was too dark to read the expression in his eyes, Adriana could feel its intensity. "I mistrust you most when you sound like that, sweetheart," he murmured gently, "but you would be well advised to obey me in this. You have had but a single taste of my temper, and you didn't like it. I can promise you, you will like the outcome even less if you cause me to lose it again. You are to take outriders with you if you go out in daylight, and you are not to go out at all after dark. Agreed?"

"Oh, very well," she said, wishing she could sink further into the mattress, away from him, until he relaxed again. "I'll tell Miranda, too, Joshua, so will you please stop looming over me like that?" She put out her hand to caress his bare chest, moving her fingers lightly, teasingly, until she had distracted him from anything else he might have wished to say on that uncomfortable subject. But half an hour later when they lay back, sated, against the pillows again, it was she who returned to it, saying curiously, "Why do you not simply request assistance from the dragoons if you are so concerned for our safety? Surely, they would come if you asked them."

"They have fifty miles of coastline to patrol, sweetheart, so whether they would come at my command is not the question. They are too few in number and they are needed everywhere. We cannot keep a squadron sitting on the beach here hoping for a convenient confrontation. Moreover, there are indications that this new gang intends to unite the Gentlemen all along the south coast, so the patrols will no doubt be particularly busy now."

"Then you ought to organize your own patrols, sir."

"My men will protect the castle and the lands surrounding it to the best of their ability," he said, "but I will ask no one to risk his life unnecessarily. If the trouble increases as I anticipate it will, there will be questions asked in Parliament soon, and no doubt the military patrols will be increased accordingly."

She thought his attitude distressingly nonchalant, and found herself wishing he would exert himself to more assertive action against the intruders. Not surprisingly, she discovered the following day that her sister shared her views.

"One would expect him to fight buckle and thong to protect this place," Miranda said when they found themselves alone in the breakfast parlor. "Lady Hetta has said he cares for nothing so much as Thunderhill. Indeed, you have said the same."

"True," said Adriana, adding with a sigh, "I believe his passion for this castle may exceed any other feeling he has."

Miranda stared at her, then said suddenly, "What does one do to amuse oneself here when there are no houseguests?"

Adriana gave herself a shake and grinned. "I warned you. Pray, do not tell me you are bored already."

"No, of course I am not, only I hope you mean to do something to entertain me."

Adriana wrinkled her nose. "I suppose that once Prinny leaves Brighton we will have visitors again, and Joshua has said that his sister, Lydia, will come in September with her children, although, with the troubles, he may put her off for a time. Sally and George are going straight to Prospect Lodge Saturday, because Lord and Lady Jersey expect to meet them there for George's birthday on Monday, so they won't come at all."

"We must arrange our own entertainment then," Miranda said archly. "We'll begin by inviting Mr. Braverstoke and his cherubic papa to dine with us. That will annoy Lady Adelaide, but I think we must encourage Lady Hetta's romance with his lordship, do not you? I say, Dree," she added with an arrested look, "do you think Mr. Petticrow suspects Mr. Braverstoke or Chalford of being in league with the free traders?"

"Of course not." Adriana laughed. "He may have

noticed something about the ship that took him to France that put him in mind of their yachts, but you will remember that he mentioned a second mast, and neither the *Golden Fleece* nor the *Sea Dragon* has one. Moreover, I believe that if either yacht was used, it was used without their knowledge, just as the *Sea Dragon*—''

"Goodness, smugglers dared to use the *Sea Dragon*?"

Nodding, Adriana proceeded to describe that occasion, and Miranda's reaction was all that she might have hoped it would be.

"Good gracious," she said, "Chalford must have been livid!"

"No," said Adriana, "Joshua never becomes heated."

"Tell that to your Mr. Dawlish," recommended Miranda.

Adriana smiled. "Even then his anger was the icy sort. Joshua never shouts like Alston or Papa. Indeed, I didn't think he was angry at all about the *Sea Dragon* being used, but his people said the captain feared for his place. If I recognized his displeasure at the time, I thought it had to do with the sprats and the awful smell, not with their having used the boat."

"Well, then, I believe we must encourage Mr. Braverstoke and his father to call as often as they like," Miranda said, grinning. "I find them perfectly charming."

Adriana agreed, but she discovered that it was not necessary for them to do anything to encourage Randall Braverstoke. He had already learned of their return to Thunderhill and that very afternoon found him a guest in the great hall, having come to pay his respects and to discover the news of Brighton.

"For you must know by now," he confided, taking his seat and acknowledging that he would welcome a glass of wine, "that my father does not follow the fashionable crowd about anymore. He was used to enjoy gaming in London or supper parties in Brighton as much as the next man, but he has become more sedentary these past years and does not like to be cooped up in a carriage for extended periods of time. And my time, of course, is taken up by the business of running the manor. He has never paid particular attention to everyday details, so the burden falls to me."

"But you still find time to enjoy your yacht, sir," Miranda said, smiling at him, "and surely, if you have time to sail to France, you have time occasionally to sail to Brighton."

"The distance is much greater to Brighton, my lady," he reminded her, chuckling.

"Adriana and I once thought it to be a mere hop and skip from Thunderhill to Brighton," she said, adding with a confiding twinkle, "Sir, I must tell you, we have heard how, on your last voyage, you rescued Mr. Petticrow. That was very brave of you."

"Not at all," he said. "Not much to it. He had got a French fisherman to take him out into the Channel in hopes of running across an English ship. We merely took him aboard."

"Why, we got the impression that you had sailed right into a French harbor," Adriana said, surprised.

He winked at her. "That sort of behavior is frowned upon by our ships of the line, ma'am, being as how England is at war with France. I'd as lief you didn't mention such notions in company."

She thought she understood him very well, but she found herself unable to respond to his wink as she would have done only weeks before. Although he was as charming as he had ever been, it was not so much fun to flirt with him as it had been, and she was content to leave him to Miranda. At first she thought her attitude was due to Miranda's expressed liking for him and a wish to leave her sister a clear field, but after less than a week at home, she discovered that she had no desire to flirt with any of their gentlemen callers.

The number of these was greater than one might have expected, for not only were those young gentlemen who lived in the vicinity motivated to pay calls, but an astonishing number of young men found it convenient to pass by Thunderhill on their return to London from Brighton.

"You have developed quite a following, my dear," said Adriana to her sister a week after their return, when they had seen three of these young men on their way. "I am quite cast in the shade, for they certainly do not come to see me, although my husband does not believe as much, I fear. He was moved to suggest only last night that I ought to wear a sign, pointing out the fact that I am no longer a prize on the Marriage Mart."

"That is only because he chanced to enter the hall yesterday afternoon just as that absurd Mr. Fancourt offered to fight a duel with Mr. Braverstoke to determine who would sit beside you on the green sofa."

"I have the most lowering suspicion that it was the loser who was meant to sit next to me, however," Adriana said with a melancholy sigh. "Can you deny it? They both of them sat nearer to you than to me, when all was said and done."

"On account of Chalford looking daggers at them."

"Pooh," retorted Adriana. "It was no such thing. Mr. Braverstoke, at least, has not been visiting nearly every afternoon for the purpose of staring into *my* eyes, minx."

Miranda grinned at her. "No, he accompanies his papa, who comes to visit Lady Hetta, and he passes the time by very kindly instructing me in the ways of the Kentish smugglers."

"Miranda, you never asked him if he thought his boat might have been used by the Gentlemen!"

"Well, no, not precisely, though I did say I'd heard that they sometimes use whatever boat is handy. Just hinting, you know. And, Dree, he pokered up like anything. I think it would be as much as a man's life is worth to take the *Golden Fleece* out in such a way. Mr. Braverstoke does not approve of smuggling, and he dreads the violence, which is why he is so careful to accompany Lord Braverstoke when he visits here."

"Fustian," said Adriana, laughing. "He comes to flirt with you, my dear. And do tell me, please, just when did you discover this fascination for smuggling? You never sympathized in the least with my interest in such activities."

"Well, I wasn't interested, if you must know," admitted her sister, "but I have never seen a free trader, Dree, and you have. You have even sailed on one of their ships without coming to grief. But you have never seen them in real action, and Mr. Braverstoke says he has. And," she added with a wicked little smile, "this Saturday night is when the darks will begin, Dree. There will be no moon at all. And Mr. Braverstoke has heard a rumor that there is to be a large run right here at Thunderhill."

14

Adriana stared at her sister. "Miranda, you cannot think for one moment that you are going to watch a smuggler's run in progress. Good God, Alston would kill us both if I allowed such a thing. Not only would it be foolish beyond permission but extremely dangerous as well. We might be caught, even killed."

"Alston will never know the least little thing about it, and we won't be killed if we have a gentleman to protect us," Miranda said persuasively, before adding quickly, "I have not asked Mr. Braverstoke yet, of course, but I mean to do so, Dree, and I believe he wishes to impress me, so I am certain he will agree to escort us. Unless," she suggested with a twinkle, "you would prefer to ask Chalford to lend us *his* escort."

"He wouldn't," Adriana said flatly. "If he heard so much as a whisper of what you suggest, he would lock us both in that tower you mentioned weeks ago and throw away the key. It will not do, Miranda. Put the thought straight out of your head."

"Oh, very well, if you are afraid. I did think that, interested as you have always claimed to be, you would snap at an opportunity to discover precisely what happens when the goods are brought ashore, but I shall be the last person to castigate you for a coward, Dree, if marriage has made you too cautious for such adventures. I quite understand why you might be afraid of Chalford after what happened at the Castle Inn."

"I am certainly not afraid of Joshua," Adriana said indignantly. "I merely think it would be wise to obey him in this instance. Does Mr. Braverstoke even know which gang of smugglers is involved in this particular run? What if it is the Sandgate gang? And how does he come to know of such things, anyway? Answer me that."

"Oh, he says one hears whatever one wishes to hear when one keeps an ear to the ground. No one expects any of the local inhabitants to betray the Gentlemen, after all, so if one is interested . . . Well, you know yourself how much you discovered through merely asking a few questions."

"And through a little discreet blackmail," Adriana reminded her. "Still, I suppose you are right, and if a large run is to be landed here on the beach, it must be the local people who will be involved. Even Joshua says there is no need for us to fear them. But I did promise we would both obey him this time, Randy, and I've no wish to vex him. He has given strict orders that we are not to go outside the castle at all after dark."

"Well, for goodness' sake, it is not as though we are proposing to follow the goods into Romney Marsh. I have looked about and I am persuaded we can see all we might wish to see from a vantage point at the foot of the cliff path. There are large boulders there, you know, and some tall scrub as well. I daresay that if we dress sensibly in dark clothing, we can hide behind the boulders and see without being seen."

"How will we see anything if there is no moon?" Adriana demanded. "The smugglers will scarcely be dancing about with torches or candles, particularly since they once frightened Lady Hetta by showing lights and must know of that incident by now."

Miranda shrugged. "We will see nothing if we make no attempt, that is certain. If there is starlight, we will see a great deal, for the sand and shingle are light in color and the men will be moving about. And we will see the outline of a ship, at least. And there will be sounds of movement, and the knowing of what is going forth, and . . . Oh, Dree, you will not turn spoilsport at such an exciting opportunity. Say you will not."

Adriana said nothing of the kind, telling herself as well as her sister that she was determined to show

Joshua that she would obey him when his command was
a reasonable one. Her curiosity was overwhelming,
however, and the more she thought about the smugglers
going about their business just below the castle, as they
had been doing her first night there, the harder it was
not to give in to Miranda's continued persuasions. Her
resistance, over the next few days, grew weaker, and
when Miranda, informing her triumphantly that Mr.
Braverstoke had agreed to provide armed escort for the
expedition, added the casual rider that Adriana's refusal
to go would not by any means put an end to the matter,
Adriana demanded to know what she meant.

"Why, only that I shall take my maid with me if you
are so disobliging as to refuse to go."

"You shall not. I'll tell Joshua what you plan to do.
I'll forbid Maisie to accompany you."

"Pooh, you would never betray me to Chalford, and
Maisie would only promise to obey you and then do
precisely as I tell her to do, for she loves adventure as
much as we do."

"Then I shall tell Mr. Braverstoke that he is not to
encourage you in this madness."

Miranda shook her head. "It will not do, Dree. You
have had every opportunity this week past to tell him
not to heed my entreaties, and you have done nothing of
the kind. Confess now, you have been wanting to see the
smugglers in action ever since you arrived at Thunderhill. Can you deny it?"

Adriana stared at her younger sister in acute dislike,
but Miranda only grinned at her. "Don't look so
smug," Adriana said at last in a resigned tone. "It
doesn't become you."

"Never mind that. You cannot have changed so much
that you will not revel in an adventure of this sort. Do
say you will come, Dree. No one else need ever know the
least thing about it. Surely, you don't think Chalford
will discover us."

"No, he did not stir the night I crept out to meet
Jacob and the smugglers," Adriana admitted. "Indeed,

he sleeps as one dead, once he sleeps. But if he should ever find out—''

"He won't," Miranda said quickly when Adriana's unwelcome reflections expressed themselves vividly in her countenance.

Adriana still had second thoughts, and when an announcement in the Friday *Times*, delivered on Saturday, threatened to put a stop to the plan, she could not be sorry for it.

The paper was delivered to Chalford's place at the breakfast table, and it was he who read the notice and exclaimed over it.

"The Earl of Jersey has died!"

"Good gracious!" Adriana said. "How? What happened?"

Obligingly, Chalford read the account. " 'On a visit to Viscount and Viscountess Villiers, Lord Jersey, upon returning to Prospect Lodge from drinking the waters at Tunbridge Wells, fell down in a fit whilst walking with his son, and expired at once.' "

"Oh, dear," murmured Lady Hetta in distress, "as if the poor man had not had troubles enough to plague him these past years what with his disputes with the king and Frances's naughtiness."

"Jersey was never bad in himself," pronounced Lady Adelaide austerely. "He was merely weak and overindulgent to that little bewitching wife of his. Her unbecoming behavior with the prince and Jersey's inability to control her are what made him appear to a good many persons to be sadly wanting in sense."

"We must go to Prospect Lodge at once, Joshua," said Adriana. "There will be any number of things we can do to make things easier for poor Sally. She has Lady Jersey— Good gracious, *Sally* is now Lady Jersey! How odd to think of her so. But her mama-in-law will be driving her to distraction, and there will be guests, and all the details to look after—''

"Frances will not like being a dowager countess," observed Lady Hetta thoughtfully.

Chalford's lips twitched, but he said with his usual calm, "We will do as you think best, sweetheart, but it would be as well to write first to discover what Sally means to do. This is yesterday's paper, after all, and his lordship died on Thursday, so certain matters must already be in train. If you write immediately and send your letter by messenger, you can have your reply tomorrow or by Monday at the latest."

"Oh, yes," agreed Miranda quickly. "One would not wish to be behindhand in one's obligations, Dree, but you cannot want to rush off so precipitately. Certainly not today!" The look she cast her sister was a speaking one, and as soon as they were alone, Adriana took her to task for it.

"You will have us both in the basket if you make such improper remarks, Randy. I didn't know where to look and I was certain Lady Adelaide, if not Joshua himself, must have asked you what was so special about today."

"Oh, nonsense, they will have thought nothing about it other than that I was trying to keep you from rushing off."

"Well, you would not want me to desert Sally at such a time, either. And do not tell me that she will have George's sister Charlotte to assist her, for if Charlotte gives a thought to anyone but herself and her megrims upon losing her papa, it must be for the first time in her life."

The argument might well have continued indefinitely had not an express arrived from Sally that same afternoon, warning Adriana not to set out in haste. "She knows I will have had the news by now," Adriana told her husband as she scanned Sally's elegant copperplate, "and as she is well-acquainted with my generous and impulsive nature—"

"Particularly impulsive," Joshua interjected dulcetly.

She wrinkled her nose at him. "Odious man. In any event, *as* I was telling you before you interrupted me, George's papa having expressed a wish to be buried at Middleton Stony, they leave . . . No, they have already departed this morning. 'An imposing cortege,' Sally calls their cavalcade."

Joshua smiled at her. "You cannot convince me that Sally will need either of us in Oxfordshire."

"No, for her stepmama will meet her there. Indeed, she will have a houseful, for Middleton Stony is much more centrally located than the lodge. I shall write to her, of course."

"Say everything from me that is proper, if you will."

"Of course."

Joshua looked at her rather more closely than before. "Are you feeling quite the thing, sweetheart? You've seemed a trifle out of sorts these past few days."

Adriana flushed but forced herself to return his look. "I am fine, Joshua, truly. A little tired after all my dissipation in Brighton, perhaps, but that will pass. She smiled at him.

Though he returned the smile, he continued to regard her searchingly. "I hope you would tell me if something were wrong," he said gently.

"Of course I would," she replied. "Why would I not?"

He did not press her, but the exchange did nothing to salve her conscience. Since their return, she had felt closer to him than ever before. She missed him when he was attending to his duties, and she looked forward to their private moments together. She wanted nothing to happen that might weaken the growing bond between them. But when she attempted to explain the situation to her sister, that young lady nodded casually and said she quite understood and would make no further demands upon her.

"But I warn you, Dree, I mean to see this run. I have not turned fainthearted. Moreover, one of us must certainly keep the rendezvous with Mr. Braverstoke. We can scarcely entrust one of Chalford's footmen with a message to him at this late hour."

Adriana didn't agree with this last statement. To leave Mr. Braverstoke waiting in vain at the bottom of the cliff path would have cost her no loss of sleep. But since she knew Miranda would go with only her maid for protection, and since she had protected her sister from the consequences of such folly for as long as she could remember, there was nothing for it now but to go with her.

She had made up her mind long before bedtime that she could not sleep with Joshua without betraying her guilty conscience, so it was with relief rather than disappointment that she accepted his suggestion that she retire early and to her own bed.

"A night's rest will do you good," he said gently as he took her into his arms and kissed her good night. "Let your Nancy tuck you up with a hot posset or a warm brick or whatever will bring the color back into your cheeks, and sleep the night away."

"Yes, sir," she murmured, snuggling against him with thought for little else other than the gentle caresses of his hands on her body.

"So obedient," he said. "If I didn't know better, if I hadn't seen for myself that you are beginning to be content in this dull place, I might suspect you were up to something."

"I am content, Joshua," she said quickly. "Thunderhill is beginning to feel like my home, too. Truly, sir, it is."

He smoothed her hair back from her forehead. "I know. The place grows on a person, does it not, sweetheart? I thought it would if you would but give it half a chance."

She agreed, glad when he did not tease her more, fearing she would somehow give herself away. The night's intended expedition no longer felt anything like an adventure, for there was only guilt, none of the exhilaration she was accustomed to feeling when she was up to mischief. She needed to make no effort to stay awake, finding it impossible to sleep, but hoping fervently that Miranda would sleep through the night.

The room was very dark when her sister came in. "Get up, Dree," she hissed. "I thought you would be dressed. Hurry!"

Then, for a time, with Miranda's excitement to spur her on, it did seem like other times. She scrambled into her clothes, and the two of them slipped down the stairs to the hall and out into the quadrangle. Remembering her previous experience, Adriana pulled Miranda into the shadows, but they saw no sign of the watchman. They went quietly through the marsh gate and made their way down the path.

"Beware pebbles," Adriana whispered, "and keep silent."

There appeared to be no activity on the beach yet, and for that she was grateful, for she was sure their progress on the path must be noted by anyone within earshot. Her eyes had adjusted to the darkness and she could see the path. There were clouds overhead, but the stars shone brightly through the spaces between them, and as Miranda had predicted, the shingle and sand showed clearly below.

They reached the bottom of the path without mishap and moved toward the large boulders. Even though she had expected him to precede them, Adriana had been so certain the beach was deserted that when Braverstoke loomed up ahead of them, she had all she could do to stifle a scream of surprise.

"Shhh," he whispered. "We'll crouch down over there. You will see everything much better."

"I don't want to get far from the path," she said.

"We won't, but you'll want to be farther over to see the marsh path, so you can watch where they take the goods."

Knowing she couldn't stand there arguing, Adriana agreed to let him lead the way, but the farther they moved from the cliff path, the more nervous she became. "This is far enough, sir," she muttered finally. "With all the shrubbery at the edge of the shingle, we shan't see much anyway, and we won't have nearly so much cover for ourselves if anyone should show a light."

He only grunted and moved a few steps farther, but Adriana, catching her sister by the elbow, drew her back into the shelter of the tall boulders. A moment later, where the shrubbery was darkest, they saw a flash of yellow sparks, as though from a tinderbox. The signal was answered by a tiny blue light offshore. The yellow sparks glittered twice again.

"Watch the mouth of the harbor now," whispered Adriana.

The bulk of the two-masted ship could be seen clearly against the starlit horizon as she sailed silently in.

"Lady Hetta said the harbor was boomed," Miranda murmured.

"The captain is a spotsman, my dear," Braverstoke said, crouching beside them, keeping his voice low. "He can find any place along this coast, I daresay, without so much as a light to guide him. The booms do not trouble him at all."

"Well, I am persuaded he must prefer a decent, sandy landfall," Miranda retorted. "He wouldn't land just anywhere."

"Nearly anywhere," he said quietly. "Indeed, it is essential for the success of the trade that any beach may be used at any state of the tide. Otherwise it would be relatively simple for the authorities to police a few favored spots. A good captain can land anywhere. If the beach is steep, he will run right into the shingle before he drops anchor. Here, where he can expect the tide to drop and where the beach slopes out and is sandy, he will use skiffs to run the tub lines in. Watch."

The ship anchored well off, out of danger of grounding, and within moments her sails were down and the thud and squeak of a tub boat being lowered over the side could be heard. The sound of its oars came next, and a number of shapes separated themselves from the shadows surrounding the shingle. Men whose presence had only been suspected but moments before moved down to the beach to meet the boat. Braverstoke murmured a running commentary, explaining what was transpiring below.

"Rowboat's got the tub line," he said. " 'Tis a stout warp, like a huge necklace, with pairs of half-ankers roped together on it every few feet. The lads from shore'll cop hold as soon as the boat reaches the beach."

"What's a half-anker?" whispered Miranda.

"The tubs. Can't cart regular brandy kegs about without a great deal of difficulty, so the French very kindly put the stuff in half-barrels that can be managed more easily. The dry goods and fine stuff will be in the boat, as it goes back and forth."

There were flashes of starlight on steel at the tideline the minute the boat rubbed onto the sand.

"They have knives," Adriana said, startled.

"And a good many other weapons," Braverstoke muttered. "But the knives are to cut the tubs loose from the line. They'll pick up every piece of rope and yarn, too, so as not to leave a clear message they were here."

Speed was essential, and the men on the beach moved in a line with rapid, well-practiced motions, slinging tubs onto their shoulders and moving from the shore back to the shadows as others moved forward to take their places.

"I keep expecting to hear a horse whicker," Miranda said.

"They don't use horses here in Romney Marsh," Braverstoke said. "Easier to use humans, because of the narrow, twisting paths. On good roads, they use ponies, but here where the easiest way to elude the authorities is by throwing a plank across a dyke and picking it up on the other side, they don't want horses. There are, moreover, lots of nearby storage places the authorities will never find. Takes a lot of men for a run of this sort, though," he added thoughtfully.

Just then the breeze, which had been drifting idly through the cove with barely enough force to stir the leaves in the shrubbery, began to blow harder, and Adriana became aware of a high-pitched sound from the water, a near screeching wail. As it increased, the sound became irritating to her nerves. A memory stirred but would not take form in her mind.

The skiff had returned to the ship and was being

rowed back to shore again, and she could see the
shadow of its prow against the night sky as the men
strained to bring it over the crest of the last in-rolling
wave. Just then there was the sound of a heavy thud
from the direction of the ship. She looked up in time to
see light from a temporarily unhooded lantern glinting
on a large, familiar gilded oval medallion. She heard
Braverstoke gasp beside her, then utter a curse. The
lantern still gleamed strongly long enough for her to
realize that men were lifting something, a heavy cover of
some sort, back into place.

"That's the *Golden Fleece*!" she exclaimed, leaping
up and forgetting to keep her voice down. "They simply
covered up the medallions with carved wooden panels."

"Nonsense," Braverstoke snapped. "She's a two-
master."

"But I've seen how rigging can be changed to make
one style of boat look like another," Adriana said.
"Perhaps that mast squeaks so because it is not a
permanent fixture. I know that's your boat, sir. Surely,
you know her lines, even in the dark. Why, Chalford
says that any man can recognize his own boat."

"That's ridiculous," Braverstoke said angrily. "Any
sloop looks like any other sloop, and that is not a sloop,
moreover."

"There is something in a Shakespeare play about
protesting too much, sir," Adriana said then, quietly.
"I can think of only one reason for you to refuse to
recognize your own ship, and that explains your
knowing so much about what was planned—"

"Enough!" he snapped. There was a flurry of
movement, and she saw the glint of metal in his right
hand at the same moment that Miranda cried out
sharply in pain.

"Let go of me!"

"Stay where you are, Adriana," he ordered roughly.
"I've a pistol in my hand and I won't hesitate to use it."

But Adriana, at the first gleam of metal, had leapt to
her feet and stepped back, feeling with her hand for the
boulder behind her. She backed against it now and

moved carefully around, hoping that in the darkness he couldn't see her clearly.

She could hear Miranda struggle, cursing him in words that would have brought either a smile or a reprimand to Adriana's lips at any other time, but for the moment she was only glad that her sister distracted him.

Braverstoke shouted, "Where are you, damn you? I'll kill her, I swear I will, if you so much as mention my name to anyone. Do you hear me, girl? You keep mum, or she's dead!"

"He'll kill us both if he can, Dree. His secret's out if he doesn't. Run! Get help!"

Moving as silently as she could and as quickly as she dared, Adriana made her way back toward the cliff path. She was heading for the foot of it when she heard him shout orders to his men.

"Find the bleeding wench! Don't let her escape. And get the goods away, whatever happens."

Changing her route, certain that anyone who searched for her would also make for the path, Adriana began climbing, hoisting her skirts out of her way and grasping at rocks and scrub to haul herself up the hillside beneath the marsh gate. Turning once to look over her shoulder, she saw Braverstoke outlined against the shingle, dragging Miranda from the boulders toward the tideline. There didn't seem to be anyone immediately behind her, but there were many shadows moving on the beach, and she could hear men shouting to one another as they tried to find her. Someone lit a torch, but a gruff voice shouted at him to snuff it out again.

Grabbing hold of a rocky outcrop, she heaved herself up another foot or so, then looked up to see how much farther she had to climb before she would reach the top of the hill and the safety of the castle. A shadow loomed above her. A brawny hand grasped her wrist and began to haul her upward.

Had she had any breath left, Adriana would have screamed. As it was, she barely had the strength even to try to free herself. She struggled, not certain whether it would be worse to fall down the hill or to be murdered by the villain above her.

"Damn it, m'lady, let be!" The voice sounded familiar, but all her concentration was focused upon freeing herself. She dug her knees into the hillside and tried again to pull free.

"Lady Chalford, it's me, Petticrow. Damn it all, ma'am, I'm trying to help. Don't fight me or we'll both go tumbling."

Gasping her relief, she came nearer than she had ever been in her life to fainting, but Petticrow was able to get his hands under her arms then and hauled her up to sit beside him. As she struggled to catch her breath, she became aware of more sounds, including several shots, from the beach below.

"Miranda!" she exclaimed. "Braverstoke's got Miranda!"

"Aye, in the tub boat," her companion agreed. "They have nearly reached the ship by now. We were waiting till all the goods were landed. You caught us a bit off guard, m'lady."

There were scuffling sounds from the beach now, more shouts and sounds of fighting. She heard horses, too.

"You've a squadron with you?"

"Not a squadron precisely," he said. "The nearest was beyond Dungeness Point and would have come too late. We'll hope the cutter made good time, though. Look yonder."

She followed his gesture toward the mouth of the harbor. The sails on the *Golden Fleece* were up and she was making for the opening, but there was another dark shape, a smaller, more graceful ship that seemed to dance tauntingly in her path.

"The *Sea Dragon*," she whispered, her pounding heart fairly stopping the breath in her throat. "That's the *Sea Dragon*!"

"Aye," said Petticrow, "and if his lordship can just manage to throw the other captain off his stride, mayhap he'll run into one of the booms and save the cutter a deal of trouble.''

But it quickly became obvious, as Adriana watched in terror, that the commander of the *Golden Fleece* had no intention of being outmaneuvered. The roar of cannon shocked her into momentary silence. Then she cried, "Joshua! My God, he'll be killed!"

"His lordship's prepared, m'lady. Ah, and there's his majesty's cutter, right on the mark. Now we'll see some action, ma'am. They'll blow the *Golden Fleece* right out of the water."

The answering roar of cannon from the *Sea Dragon* was accompanied by an echoing boom from the cutter. Adriana felt now as though her heart had stopped beating altogether. She grabbed at the riding officer's arm, shaking him out of his triumphant state. "Mr. Petticrow, Miranda is on the *Golden Fleece*. They must stop firing. Joshua! They'll both be killed."

"Good God," he exclaimed, "I plumb forgot the Lady Miranda in the excitement. No, but wait now." He peered through the gloom. "Well, I'll be . . . Look there, m'lady, on the beach."

Turning to look where he pointed, Adriana saw that the movement below had turned into a flurry. Torches and lanterns blazed alight. Boats were hauled out of places that seemed inadequate to conceal them and launched full-loaded with men into the rolling surf. In no time at all, while her heart thudded and Mr. Petticrow, beside her, cheered till he was hoarse, the *Golden Fleece* was surrounded by the torchlit flotilla. Men swarmed up the tub lines to her decks. The guns fell silent.

15

"Who are the men in the boats?" Adriana asked when she could breathe with any semblance of normality again.

"Local Gentlemen," Petticrow told her. "It was his lordship's notion that they'd be willing, for once, to give us a hand. Word was out there was a run coming in and the locals were warned off by the Sandgaters. Made them angry, so they agreed when Chalford said it was better to put paid to the Sandgaters by taking sides with his majesty than to mix it up anymore. When it's over and done, the locals'll swear till they're blue that they're naught but respectable, law-abiding men, but if what goods were landed be still on the beach then, I'll be surprised."

"Well, I won't," said Adriana. "You saw how many men there were carrying those goods, sir. Mr. Braverstoke told us they don't use horses, only men, so they need a large number. And even if the kegs weren't all ashore yet, there were a good many, and there must have been ten boats, all loaded with men. How many more could have been left to carry goods? They won't have left the Sandgaters unguarded, after all. Not if putting them out of business was their primary reason for being here tonight."

Petticrow gave a grunt that might have indicated agreement, then said, "Well, be that as it may, m'lady, the Lady Miranda will be safe now, and I'd best be getting you back up to the castle. Best you be safe within doors before his lordship's put the *Sea Dragon* to anchor. What he'll have to say about you young ladies being out and about tonight don't bear thinking of, but he'd say a deal to me, I shouldn't wonder, if I was to send you up by yourself. Like as not he'll be leaving her here in the harbor, too, since it don't seem like the wind's meaning to blow up more than what it is right now, so we don't have much time."

"The breeze blowing up was what gave me the first hint that Mr. Braverstoke was part of it," she said, allowing him to assist her to her feet and talking as much to take her mind off what lay ahead of her as for any other reason. "I heard the sound you had described, like fingernails on a slate. The breeze must have caught the rigging on that stern mast. At first, I couldn't think why the sound seemed important, but then that panel fell, and the lantern light flashed on the gilded medallion, and Mr. Braverstoke insisted it couldn't be his boat. If only he had got angry and cursed the men for taking her, I'd never have suspected him. I'd merely have thought it was like—''

Breaking off, shocked by what she had been about to divulge, she could have sworn she heard Mr. Petticrow chuckle, but he said no more than, "Best we shake a leg, m'lady. I ought to be down on that beach. Only came up here because, after I'd seen the pair of you join up with Braverstoke, I heard Lady Miranda set up a screech. We suspected him—first because he spent so much time cruising the French coast, then more when we couldn't find where he got his money—but we had no real proof against the man. I figured when you got away from him, you'd be safer running into me than into any of his lot. Now, hurry, I've got to get back."

He was not to return as quickly as he'd hoped, however, for when Adriana pushed open the tall door leading into the entry hall, there was a stifled shriek and then Lady Hetta's voice came, shaking but in brave, patriotic British accents. "*Arretez-vous, vous mechants français, ou je tire . . . je tue . . .* Ah, bah! Halt where you stand or I'll shoot out your liver and lights!"

Petticrow had stood aside to let Adriana precede him, but at these elegant words, he grabbed her elbow and yanked her back, saying as he stepped in front of her through the open door, "Good God, Hetta, where on earth did you learn your French? They'd never understand a word of it. Now for the love of God, put that thing down before you shoot yourself or one of us."

"Oh, Mr. Petticrow," Lady Hetta exclaimed, rushing forward in her dressing gown and cap, waving a wildly flickering candle in one hand and a horse pistol in the other, "the French have landed. They are on the beach, and ships in the harbor are firing cannon. I told everyone, but no one would pay heed until the cannons fired. Now all the maids have run to the cellars, and I'm sure no one can blame them, and Adelaide will only say I must be mistaken and whoever it is must hush up their noise."

"Give me that pistol," said Mr. Petticrow firmly.

"Aunt Hetta," said Adriana, "indeed, ma'am, it is only free traders again and not the French at all. The revenue cutter fired a couple of shots at Mr. Braverstoke's yacht. And thanks to Mr. Petticrow and the local landsmen they have laid the Sandgate gang by the heels, and Mr. Braverstoke as well."

Lady Adelaide's voice sounded just then from the south end of the hall. "I said those Braverstokes were a presumptuous pair. Now perhaps the rest of you will agree. Mr. Petticrow, why do you have your arm around my sister?"

Mr. Petticrow leapt back as though he had been shot, then bowed and muttered something Adriana could not hear, but Lady Hetta turned sharply at the sound of her sister's voice. "Oh, Adelaide, it is just as you said, and not Frenchmen at all, but they have caught that dreadful gang of smugglers, so we may all be comfortable again."

"Then you may return to your bed in perfect safety," said her sister, still eyeing Mr. Petticrow askance. "And you, sir, have no doubt got business below on the beach."

"As you say, ma'am," said Mr. Petticrow, bowing hastily and casting an amused glance at Adriana. "You'll be safe now, m'lady, I believe."

"Yes, thank you, sir." She was watching Lady Adelaide, uncertain of what to say to explain her appearance on the scene with the riding officer.

Lady Hetta spared her the necessity of speaking by saying rather sharply when Petticrow had shut the door behind himself, "There was no need to be so abrupt with the poor man, Adelaide, indeed there was not. He merely came out of kindness to see that we had not been unduly alarmed by the disturbance below."

"I daresay," replied Lady Adelaide, unimpressed. "Light some of those candles, Hetta. I cannot think why we stand here in the dark. Why are there no menservants about? One would think they would know they are needed. Certainly, no one could have missed hearing that cannon fire."

Adriana said carefully, "I believe they are occupied, ma'am, and Lady Hetta says all the maidservants are in hiding."

"So I was also told. I have sent my woman to rout them out, however, and to order us some hot milk to settle our nerves. Not knowing you would be up and about, too, Adriana, I asked to have it served in our sitting room, but I will have them bring it to the great hall if you would care to share it with us."

"Thank you," Adriana said, grateful to have been asked no difficult questions. "Joshua had a part in the action tonight and he has not yet returned. I ought to wait for him."

"Yes, I think that would be wise," returned Lady Adelaide, giving her a straight look.

Deciding that her ladyship had deduced a great deal more than was consistent with her own peace of mind, Adriana turned abruptly and walked into the great hall.

Lady Hetta, at her heels, moved to light candles in this chamber, too, with her taper, then turning, she said briskly, "I've scarcely had time to think, Adriana dear, but why were you with Mr. Petticrow? Indeed, why were you out at all? Surely, Joshua did not take you with him."

"No, ma'am," Adriana replied, wondering what on

earth to say to her. She had no wish to speak of the incident at all, certainly not until she knew that Joshua and Miranda were both safe. Rescue came from an unexpected quarter.

"You are dripping wax all over the carpet, Hetta," said Lady Adelaide, entering behind them. "Do put that candle into a proper holder or put it out. Then sit down and straighten your cap. You look like something dragged out of a bramble bush."

"Oh, dear, do I?" Lady Hetta quickly snuffed her candle and stepped up to one of the side tables, setting the candle down before peering anxiously at her reflection in the gilt-framed glass set above the table. "Good gracious, what a sight!"

Adriana, seeing that her attention was safely diverted for the moment, cast a glance at Lady Adelaide, who was regarding her steadily. "I suppose, ma'am," she began cautiously, "that you must also wish to know—"

"Don't suppose anything of the sort," said her ladyship decisively. " 'Tis none of my affair or Hetta's. What is my affair is the disgraceful way this castle was left unattended, and you may be sure that I shall have something to say to Joshua on that head. Regardless of his need, he might have left us one manservant to attend to matters here."

Lady Hetta repaired her appearance before their hot milk arrived, but Lady Adelaide managed to keep her from asking Adriana uncomfortable questions merely by requesting her not to chatter the first time she opened her mouth, and then, after their milk had been served, by ordering her briskly to drink up before it grew cold. She herself kept up a running monologue, commenting on the extraordinary noise of the cannon, on the intrusive ways of the Braverstokes and the Sandgate gang, and then once again deploring the lack of guards in the castle.

When she had run the gamut, she began all over again, so Adriana felt little necessity to listen and was soon lost in her own thoughts. Having come to know Lady Adelaide better by now, Adriana was certain she was attempting to keep her from worrying about Joshua's safety, and she was grateful for the kindness, but in truth, it was not his safety so much as the probable state of his temper that concerned her.

She knew it was absurd to hope he would not discover that she and Miranda had been on the beach, and this time she could not pretend to herself that she had obeyed any part of his orders to her. This time she had disobeyed him outright. He would not care for the fact that she had felt obliged to go with Miranda, nor would he be impressed if she admitted that she had not known any way to keep her from going alone if she did not go. No doubt he would simply say, with reason, that if she had discussed the problem with him, he would have stopped Miranda. That she could not betray her sister to him any more than she would ever have betrayed her to Alston or their father was not something she felt she could adequately explain to him under the circumstances.

Shivers shot up her spine when she remembered his chilling anger in Brighton and his later promise that the consequences would be much worse than that if she angered him again. She shifted uncomfortably where she sat, and Lady Adelaide broke off what she was saying just then to demand to know if she was cold.

"No, ma'am."

"That maidservant ought to have stirred up the fire in here while she was about it. Ring the bell, Hetta."

As Lady Hetta got to her feet, however, the unmistakable sound of the entrance doors opening and shutting again came through the open doorway of the great hall. There were voices, too, male and female, and then the sound of rapidly approaching footsteps. Chalford and Miranda appeared in the doorway.

When they paused upon the threshold at the sight of the three persons within, Adriana leapt to her feet, aware of a fleeting look of profound relief in her husband's eyes, replaced in a blink by burning fury. At the same time, but as a dim clamor in her mind, she heard her sister's excited cries.

"Adriana! My God, I thought you must be dead. Oh, my dear, are you really quite safe?"

As Miranda ran into her arms, Adriana's gaze clashed with Joshua's over her shoulder. Though it was all she could do to speak, she said, "I am safe, goose. No one laid a hand on me."

"An oversight that may soon be rectified, believe me," Joshua muttered furiously. Wrenching his gaze from hers with an obvious effort, he said to his aunts, "You must forgive me if I appear less than delighted to see you at the moment, but I am persuaded that at this late hour you would be more comfortable in your beds. I will be grateful, Aunt Adelaide, if you will see Miranda tucked into hers before you retire."

"Of course, Joshua," Adelaide said, getting to her feet with her customary dignity. "Come along, Miranda dear. And, Hetta, don't dawdle. You ought to have been asleep hours ago."

"Well, but I was," protested Lady Hetta as she followed reluctantly in her sister's wake.

Miranda, after one scared look at Joshua and a warning grimace directed at her sister, went with them, leaving Adriana alone with her husband.

Kicking the door shut behind him with unnecessary force, he moved toward her, his mouth a thin slit in his taut face, his eyes shooting fire. His intent was clear. He was going to murder her.

She licked her lips, facing him, breathing rapidly. Had she not seen that brief flash of relief in his eyes, she might have been even more frightened, but he could not be glad to see her one moment only to strangle her the next. At least, she thought, looking into those blazing eyes, she hoped he could not.

"Joshua, I—"

His big hands clamped bruisingly upon her shoulders and he shook her, hard. "Damn you," he said, the words coming with difficulty as though his throat were too tight to release them easily. "Your misbegotten sister told me Braverstoke's men had killed you, that he had threatened to kill her and had ordered them to kill you before he dragged her into the boat. She flung herself, sobbing, into my arms when we got her off that damned yacht, and that's the first thing she said to me. My God, you little idiot, you deserve to be flayed for your insanity."

"Mr. Petticrow helped me get away," Adriana said when he had stopped shaking her and she could catch her breath. "Did you not see him on the beach?"

"Of course I saw him. Do you think I would be here if I had not? I'd be down on that beach throttling one man at a time until I found one who could tell me where your body was."

"They would have had difficulty telling you anything while you were throttling them, sir," she said, less frightened now than she had been before.

"Damn it, don't tempt me," he growled, shaking her again. "I haven't been this angry since I was a boy, and I cannot be held accountable for the consequences if you push me too hard. Don't you understand that I thought I'd lost you, that I didn't believe Petticrow until I'd seen you alive for myself?"

"Would it have mattered so much, Joshua?" she asked softly.

"Mattered? My God, Adriana, don't you know how much it would matter?" He stared at her, his hands tightening on her shoulders, and to her shock she saw tears in his eyes.

"I didn't know," she whispered, adding in a firmer tone, "I told you before, I never can tell what you are thinking. You said when I feared the thunder that I must tell you when I am frightened, and another time you told me it was right for me to tell you of my anger, but you never told me anything about your feelings. Truly, Joshua, I never knew the meaning of 'even-tempered' before I met you. I thought for a long time that you wanted only a mistress for Thunderhill and a mother for your children. I know now I was wrong, but I thought only this pile of rock had the power to stir you to passion. I thought I could never compete with the castle in your heart."

"I love this place," he said quietly. "I thought for a time that you hated it. If I seem overattached to it, blame my sense of duty and the fact that I learned at a tender age to fear what would happen if I left. But you can't say you've never seen my passion," he added more gently. "There have been many times—"

"I don't mean that sort," she said, blushing. "I mean the sort of emotion I am accustomed to seeing in the people around me. My mother was an emotional person, and so, too, are my brother, my father, and even Miranda. They laugh when they are happy and they shout when they are angry. The only person here who is anything like them is your darling Aunt Hetta, and Lady Adelaide continually tells her that such behavior is unbecoming. I suppose that is why you are so restrained."

"No," he said, "don't blame Aunt Adelaide. If I seem restrained to you, it is only that I had to grow up quickly and put away childish things, and I suppose I equated displays of temper with childishness. That isn't surprising, you know. Schoolboys are not encouraged to display emotions of any sort. One keeps a stiff upper lip, and all that."

"Of course one does. Alston is the same. You have only to look at how he behaves publicly. But he is altogether different in the privacy of his home. I expected you to be like that."

"I am four years younger than my sister, Lydia," he said, "and only two years older than Ned. I became rather suddenly not only a marquess but the head of my family, the person who was supposed to take care of everyone else. My mother had been gone for some time before that, and after her death, there was no one to whom I felt I could properly display emotion. My father certainly never encouraged me to do so. His attitude toward me was much like Aunt Adelaide's is toward Aunt Hetta. He loved me but put duty first. I was raised to be Marquess of Chalford, and since I controlled so many others, I felt it necessary to remain in control of myself, first of all." He paused, regarding her solemnly.

"Until you came into my life, I managed very well."

"Well," she said, returning his look with a steady one of her own, "I did *try* for a long time to make you angry, but after my 'success' in Brighton, I certainly didn't intend to do it again. I won't try to excuse my behavior tonight, Joshua—"

"You couldn't do so." He dropped his hands and looked sternly into her eyes. "We have strayed from the point, have we not? I don't know what to do with you, Adriana, but by heaven you do deserve something for this night's work, and that's a fact. Not only did you put yourself at risk, but you risked Miranda's life as well. What you can have been thinking of in agreeing to such a caper-witted expedition, and under the aegis of such a man as Braverstoke, I cannot imagine. . . ."

He went on, maintaining that stern but even tone, albeit with obvious effort for once, and expressed himself with great clarity, describing the folly of her actions that evening, then going on, leaving no previously unspecified fault of hers unmentioned, no misbehavior uncondemned. He made each point plainly, firmly, and without leaving the slightest room for doubt as to his opinion of her behavior in every case.

Adriana made no attempt to defend herself. Indeed, after that first moment, when his gaze held hers, she lowered her eyes to the middle button of his leather waistcoat and did not look up again until he had finished. By then, because she had heard every word and because some were painful to hear, her eyes were swimming, but she blinked back the tears, looked him straight in the eye, and said, "Joshua, do you love me?"

"What?"

"Do you really love me?" When he glared at her as much in exasperation as from any other emotion, she said, "I asked because although I have liked you amazingly well ever since I met you, I did not know I loved you until I thought that dreadful Mr. Braverstoke was going to blow the *Sea Dragon* out of the water tonight with you aboard. Then, even though I knew

Miranda was on the *Golden Fleece* and was concerned
about her because the *Sea Dragon* and the revenue
cutter were returning fire, I was absolutely terrified
about what might happen to you. I knew then. I thought
maybe it was the same with you, that you didn't know
until you thought the smugglers had murdered me, and
then, when you found out they hadn't, you remembered
what a bad wife I have been and you weren't so certain
anymore."

"I ought to put you straight across my knee."

"Very likely," she agreed, watching him warily
through her tears and trying to ignore the sudden
singing in her heart. She hoped she could depend upon
that even temper of his long enough to make him say
what she wanted to hear. "Could you answer my
question first, please?"

"I don't suppose you would believe me if I told you
I've been mad about you since I first laid eyes upon you
at Almack's."

"Well, no," she said, beginning to twinkle, "because
the first time you laid eyes upon me was at Lady
Sefton's rout just after the opening sessions."

"Ah, but it was at Almack's—" He broke off,
glaring at her again. "Is this just a ploy, Adriana, to
divert my thoughts? I warn you we have not finished
with the business at hand."

"No, sir," she said meekly, looking down at her
fingertips. "I doubt such a ploy would be successful,
because of course you're simply stiff with that dutiful
nature of yours and will very likely feel obliged to
punish me no matter how hard I might try to avoid it."
She looked up at him from beneath her lashes. "For my
own good, you know."

"And possibly," he added on a sardonic note,
"because I warned you about what would happen if you
fired my temper again. You, my girl, seem to look upon
a scolding as no more than a consequence to be endured
after you have done as you damn please and *before* you
do so again. I believe stronger punishment is merited
tonight. Shall we attend to the matter here, or would

you prefer that we adjourn to your bedchamber first?''

Dismayed, eyes widening to their full extent, she raised her hands in an involuntary gesture of defense. "You wouldn't!"

He grimaced. "I thought you were up to your usual tricks, hoping to disarm me with this sudden meekness of yours." He regarded her more sternly than ever. "Do you realize now that such tactics will no longer avail you with me?"

She nodded, still watching him uncertainly.

"Very well, then. Come here."

He held out his arms, and she walked straight into them, expelling a long sigh of relief when they closed around her.

"I will try very hard to be the sort of wife you want me to be, Joshua," she said a moment later.

"Don't make me any ridiculous promises," he said, amused. "We will both try harder, but you *are* the sort of wife I want, sweetheart. I wouldn't change a hair on your beautiful head."

"Not one?"

"Well, there is one small thing you might try to change, if you wish to please me."

"What?"

"I find that, try as I might, I cannot reconcile myself to your need to be constantly surrounded by doting admirers."

"But I like having my friends about me," she replied.

"Oh, I've no objection to your friends, sweetheart, just the doting dolts who mutter in your shell-like ear about your flowerlike complexion and fawn over your every word—in short, 'tis the Mr. Dawlishes I find I cannot tolerate. Do you think you could possibly hold them at arm's length in future?"

"Oh, well"—Adriana pretended to think the matter over carefully—"I suppose I could make do with your compliments, sir, if you could exert yourself occasionally to think of one or two."

"It shall be done."

"But, Joshua," she reminded him gently, "you have

not yet even been able to bring yourself to say that you love me.''

The door opened behind them, startling them both. "Pardon me for disturbing you, my dears, but I saw the light under the door, and though I have tried to be patient, I was afraid I'd fall asleep on my feet if I did not take courage and interrupt you.'' Lady Hetta stood upon the threshold, blinking at them, her hand clutching the folds of her gray dressing gown across her meager breasts. "I simply could not go off to bed without knowing what will happen next.''

Recovering quickly, Joshua said, "You must be freezing, Aunt Hetta. Come stand by the fire.'' He strode to snatch the poker from its place on the hearth and stirred the coals to flames again, saying, "I collect you wish to know what happened on the beach and what will happen to Lord Braverstoke's son. The gang members were nearly all captured, I'm pleased to say, and Randall Braverstoke himself is aboard the cutter, on his way to London. They'll not risk sending him overland for fear of a rescue attempt. He was the master smuggler, I'm afraid—in it for the money, of course, for he'll get naught from his father.''

"Well, but Mr. Petticrow—''

"Oh, he is in good trim—a hero, in fact. It was he who alerted the authorities, you know, once he began to suspect Braverstoke and once the rumors reached him that a particularly large run was going to be made. When the dragoons were unable to get here soon enough, he talked the local men into helping him, and they carried the day, so no one will even ask questions when it is discovered that the number of kegs confiscated by the authorities is rather low for the size of the run.''

"He told me you convinced the local men to help,'' Adriana said gently, smiling at him.

"Oh, I suppose I had a hand in it.''

"You did it all, for Jeremiah told me it was their loyalty to you that turned the trick, but that is not what I meant,'' Lady Hetta said, flushing to her eyebrows.

"Please, Joshua, Adelaide said you'd never agree to such a thing in a million years, that I should be throwing myself away, and indeed, she said it all when she was thinking Lord Braverstoke would make me an offer. But I am five-and-forty years old, and I have never cared in the least for anyone . . . Oh, well, perhaps for that young man Papa was so set against, but he was a younger son with not a penny to his name, and Mr. Petticrow at least was not born without a shirt. His father left him fairly well to pass, and he does make something at his job, of course, though he says he will give up being a riding officer if you don't like it. But if *I* do not care, I cannot think why Adelaide, who has been married and widowed, and . . . and everything, should have a word to say about it."

Joshua gave a choke of laughter. "Aunt Hetta, are you saying you wish to marry *Mr. Petticrow*?"

She nodded. "Yes, please, if you do not object."

"Lord, no, why should I? I think it's a famous notion."

"But Adelaide—"

"Tell her it is none of her affair," he recommended.

Lady Hetta's jaw dropped. "Tell her . . ."

Seeing that she couldn't even finish the sentence, Adriana intervened. "Ignore him, ma'am, he is jesting with you. He must know you would never say anything so uncivil to Lady Adelaide. Moreover, I conjecture that she will be so relieved to learn that you have not conceived a tendresse for Lord Braverstoke that she may even be pleased—well, not that, maybe, but resigned to it, at least. Do you love Mr. Petticrow?"

Lady Hetta nodded her head fervently. "Yes, and it is the oddest thing, but he says he loves me, too."

"Then don't you worry about anything else," said Adriana firmly, casting her husband a militant look. "A man who can actually put that feeling into words deserves to be rewarded. You leave Lady Adelaide to Joshua. He will see that she welcomes your Mr. Petticrow with open arms. Will you not, sir?"

Joshua grinned at her. "I think a suitable punishment

for an erring wife would be to make you deal with Aunt Adelaide, my pet.''

"Not on your life, sir."

"Not if I tell the world I love you?" When she hesitated, he said, "Aunt Hetta, I appeal to you. Did my wife not just say that a man who can put love into words deserves to be rewarded?''

Lady Hetta looked bewildered and a little concerned. "She did say that, but truly, Joshua, I think Adelaide will pay more heed to you than to Adriana."

Joshua chuckled. "Very well, ma'am, it shall be as you wish, but then I must think of another punishment for my naughty wife, and another reward for me as well.''

"You will think of something, my lord," Adriana said in a provocative tone, lowering her eyes.

When Joshua chuckled, Lady Hetta regarded them both fondly. "It will be dawn soon," she said. "We ought to get some sleep."

"Again your wish is my command," said Joshua, grinning at his wife, then adding wickedly, "Though I can't promise to sleep, Aunt Hetta, I'm certainly ready for bed."